THE
ICARUS PROJECT

The Icarus Project

LAURA QUIMBY

Amulet Books · New York

Library of Congress Cataloging-in-Publication Data

Quimby, Laura.
The Icarus project / by Laura Quimby.
p. cm.
Summary: Accompanying her father on a mammoth excavation in the Arctic, thirteen-year-old Maya discovers something hidden in the ice that will change her life forever.
ISBN 978-1-4197-0402-4
[1. Scientific expeditions—Fiction. 2. Adventure and adventurers—Fiction. 3. Arctic regions—Fiction.] I. Title.
PZ7.Q3193Ic 2012
[Fic]—dc23
2012015624

Printed and bound in U.S.A.
10 9 8 7 6 5 4 3 2 1

Amulet Books are available at special discounts when purchased in quantity for premiums and promotions as well as fundraising or educational use. Special editions can also be created to specification. For details, contact specialsales@abramsbooks.com or the address below.

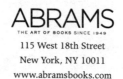

THE ART OF BOOKS SINCE 1949
115 West 18th Street
New York, NY 10011
www.abramsbooks.com

1

The Myth of My Mom

The computer screen glowed in my dark bedroom like a moon. Mom was late logging on to videoconference with me. My mom was totally into ancient civilizations: Mayans, Incans, Egyptians, Greeks, Romans. She even liked Vikings. Her latest expedition had taken her to the jungles of South America. She had told me that in the jungle nothing dries, that everything stays wet. She said even the moonlight felt damp on her skin, as if she had been bathing in milk.

I counted out six gel pens and formed a rainbow of color on my desk. My notebook was opened to a crisp white page marked with pale blue lines. I uncapped the purple pen and held it loosely in my hand. The inky tip bled onto the paper, leaving tiny purple stains. Purple was a serious color. It was the color of royalty, the anchor of the rainbow that held the other colors up in the sky. Steadfast and reliable, purple didn't fool around.

Dad once told me that NASA had spent years trying to make a pen with ink that flowed in zero gravity. The Russians took two seconds to figure out the problem.

They called it the pencil. I'm not sure if that story was really true, but I thought it was funny. I also realized that if I were on an expedition in a steamy jungle where the ink never dried, all my notes on every wing beat or tiger prowl or bird squawk would end up as a smeared mess. So I had loaded up on colored pencils.

In defense of NASA, pencil sharpeners are nonexistent when you are knee-deep in the starry sky. What if one day I dropped the sharpener in the undergrowth of the Amazon floor, or it floated away in the black pit of outer space? It would be pretty much impossible to find a pencil sharpener in the deserts of Luxor. So I practiced sharpening my colored pencils with a Swiss Army knife that I found buried in the junk drawer next to the phone in the kitchen. But I'd never used the knife before, so I cut my thumb and left an incriminating trail of blood drops all over the pile of Chinese take-out menus crammed inside of the drawer. Dad confiscated the knife.

I had Dad to thank for the jumbo pack of colored pens that were now laid out before me on my desk.

I liked to record my observations in vibrant color. All scientists need a thing—a *specialty*—they can talk about like an expert. Mom's thing was dead people, and, no, not creepy zombie dead people but ancient dead civilizations and their dried-up bones. She was an anthropologist. Since I couldn't excavate my bedroom floor, *my* specialty was colors, at least for now. I liked linking colors to emotions and situations. Purple, I realized, was also the color of patience. Sitting at my desk, I imagined breathing out a calm plume of purple air.

Since I was still developing my color theories, I was in the observation stage—collecting and sifting through the facts that would form my hypothesis. The beginning of anything was always bright and shiny, like a brand-new copper penny. Copper, the color of hope.

The computer screen flickered. Butterflies flapped in my stomach, brushing their fiery wings inside my body. I practically felt them crawling up my throat. Suddenly, Mom's face popped up on the screen. Her nose was peeling from the relentless South American sun. Her hair was a long tangle of chestnut waves that caressed her bare shoulders. She was wearing a filthy, sweat-stained tank top.

"Mom!"

"Maya! It's so good to see you."

My heart raced. I inched closer to the screen and rested my hand on the monitor. This was our window. Mom once read me a bedtime story all the way from Brazil. She called it our midnight read. Past explorers never experienced the instant thrill of an Internet connection. Their families back home had to wait months to receive letters scribbled in pencil. Graphite was the color of loneliness.

"You look great. How's the dig going?"

I could hear strange insects screeching from the darkness over Mom's shoulders.

"Soooo much better than I expected. But how are you? How's school?" Her smile widened, the whites of her eyes shining in the darkness.

"Good . . . I guess." I tapped my pen on the page.

"Studying hard?" She arched an eyebrow. "Especially science? My assistants must love all the sciences."

"Yes, Mom. We're studying the ecosystem of the bay, and I did my report on mollusks. Dad and I dug for clams." I sighed. "Can I hear about the expedition now?"

"I suppose digging is a family trait," she said with a giggle.

As a respected anthropologist, Mom saved giddiness for special occasions—usually when a shard of bone or bit of broken clay pot had been extracted from the dirt. *Exhumation* was the scientific term, a splinter pulled out of the past. "Tell me," I begged. "You found something, didn't you?" I quickly wrote *Mom found something in the rain forest* across my notebook page.

"I can never fool you."

"Are you going to tell me or what? I've heard that keeping a kid in suspense stunts her growth."

She stood, and now only her tanned arms and muddy cargo pants were visible. "One second," she said. And then she stepped out of the camera's view.

All I could see from the glow of the solar-powered light was a wooden platform and ropes tied to the tree trunks. But a bit of the jungle peeked through, and my heart leaped when I realized that she was in a tree house. The dark night pressed into the lens. I imagined at any second a jaguar would leap from the treetops. Dozens of animal eyes were watching my mother from their perches in the canopy.

I scribbled *jungle, tree house, vines,* and *nighttime.*

This was her bedroom. The ropy hammock was her bed. My face was pressed so close to the computer screen, my eyes hurt, and I was getting fingerprints all over the monitor. It felt like our window was closing up. Or that it was too small for me to climb through. I wanted Mom to hurry back to show me her special find. It could be our secret.

She was there to research the indigenous people of the rain forest. Really, I knew she was looking for links: evidence that proved a certain behavior. A rock was just a rock until some scientist found a rock that had an edge chipped away and formed what looked like a knife—the evidence of a cutting tool . . . like a prehistoric Swiss Army knife dug out of a junk drawer. Links are big in the sciences of the past. They prove stuff. *See, I'm right,* they say. Or *Whoa, I'm wrong.*

Mom's face peered back through our window. At first, all I saw was the red earthy color of dirt and some kind of bundle. It wasn't a piece of broken pottery or a stony knife. In her arms, she cradled a tattered cloth that might have been a dress once, a thousand years ago. She loosened the swaddled fabric and held her hands out, palms up, cupping the *thing* toward the camera. It looked like she was holding a dehydrated mango that had a puckered nose and sunken cheeks. But from the way she cradled that ugly, shriveled *thing* I realized it was precious. The butterflies took flight again, flying up into the sky of my stomach. I swallowed and breathed hard through my nose.

"What is it?" But I had a bad feeling that I already knew.

"You tell me. What do you see?" Her eyes glowed.

Mom was taking necessary scientific precautions, holding the *thing* gingerly and looking at it with warm, adoring eyes. My face flushed hot, but I shrugged the feeling away. *Don't be immature.*

"Think it out. You've got to have at least one good guess." The light flickered in the background. Mom curled her legs up in her chair like a cat, waiting for me to move. She tilted the shriveled mango *thing* toward the camera so I could get a better look.

"Is it a baby?" I asked, my mouth dry as dust. The mango looked like a person, a tiny clay-caked body. Maybe Mom had found an ancient tomb with the remains of a dead baby buried in the ground, and now she was holding it up like a present for me to gawk at.

She smiled triumphantly. "No, it's not a *real* baby. It's a doll."

"Oh." The more I looked at the *thing*, the more foolish I felt. It didn't look like a real baby but rather one made of cloth that was all dried up and puckered, the way a wash-cloth shrinks up on the side of the tub. "Um . . . that's great."

"Isn't she beautiful?" Mom rocked her gently back and forth in the cradle of her palms.

"I guess."

"It belonged to a little girl hundreds of years ago, just like you."

Stupid, ugly, shriveled doll. I smiled, showing every tooth in my mouth. "Cool."

She laughed, reading my glued-on expression. "OK. I know you're too big for dolls. I'm sorry." She smiled right through the window at me.

Mom had the best laugh and smile in the world. She looked even more beautiful in the jungle with her tangled hair and dirty shirt. She was like a goddess, a mythical woman both good and not so good—because goddesses weren't perfect. That was one of their trademarks. They were fearless and tough and always stood up for them-selves. But they also had one major flaw, like jealousy or arrogance or selfishness. That was their nature. It wasn't her fault she was in demand and traveled a lot. That's how goddesses were. I smiled for real now.

"The eye is made of a bead," Mom said.

Her finger hovered over a tiny black dot on the scrunched-up face. The ugly *thing* only had one eye, yet Mom loved it. That one stupid eye made it all the more valuable. A tiny detail of *seeing* sewed onto the doll's face.

It was a link. The bead was kind of cool, but I was so far away that I could barely see it through the glass window of the computer between us. I touched the screen. I traced my finger over the ugly face and wrinkled nose. I tapped the beady eye. Dumb doll.

"I miss you," I said suddenly.

But I didn't want her to come home. Instead, I wanted to crawl through our window and join her in the tree house. Sleep in a hammock. Dig in the dirt. Find a precious doll to cradle in our palms.

"I miss you too, baby. How's school? Are you studying hard?" she asked again.

"Yes. Everything's fine." If I studied any harder, my head would explode.

"Good girl. I can always count on you when I'm away. I was just telling Sam how mature you are. I'm a lucky mom to have you."

A layer of guilt settled over me. This was her moment. "I'm glad you found the doll."

She jerked her head, and the sound of cheering filtered into my room, probably from the rest of the campsite. She looked back at me, a guilty shrug forming in her shoulders. "I should go. Always something."

"I have to go, too. Dad's making dinner," I said.

"Oh, good. That's nice. Your dad's a great cook. I always know you'll be well fed," she said. "Work hard. I'm proud of you."

Proud of what? I wondered. I hadn't done anything important, like find a precious artifact.

"You too. Congratulations."

She beamed, and the screen went dark.

I was happy for Mom and her discovery. That was what anthropologists lived for—the puzzle pieces of old broken things—and she had one in her own hands. Some day that would be me, on an expedition, discovering a link—but to where or what I could only dream.

2

The Myth of My Dad

There was a myth going around that dads couldn't cook. I could verify the blatant wrongness of this terrible stereotype. Dad was a genius with meat loaf, cheeseburgers, and ribs. Meat was a big theme with dads and dinner, and mine was no exception. But that was OK because I wasn't about to go vegetarian anytime soon—I was more T. rex than brontosaurus.

I raced into the kitchen, my socks sliding across the linoleum. Tonight Dad had made all my favorites. Spaghetti with meat sauce, Caesar salad, and garlic knots crowded the table. I grabbed a roll and pulled it apart. Somehow warm bread made everything even better.

"Load up your plate. I thought we could eat outside."

A great thing about Dad and dinner was that he didn't make me sit at the table. He was cool that way. He was wearing a sauce-splattered T-shirt that read "I Dig Mammoths!" His jeans were worn, and so were his tennis shoes. He liked to call himself a "creature of comfort." My parents had been divorced since I was seven. Now I was thirteen and well adapted to Dad's cuisine.

As I grabbed my plate, he asked, "How's the gypsy doing?" He thought Mom had a wandering spirit.

"Good," I answered. "She's found an old doll."

"Cool." Dad's mellow voice filled the kitchen. Supportive comments, even about Mom, came naturally to him.

I mentally noted that gypsies were the color of swirling paisley.

After getting my food, I followed Dad out to the backyard. It was early April and perfect sweatshirt weather. He flipped the back-porch light on, and we made our way to the tent. Some people might think it strange that we had a tent set up in our backyard. But why not? Our neighbor had a rickety old shed that leaned to the side at a forty-five-degree angle and had a giant padlock on the door, protecting its precious contents. I could kick the thing down with one foot. A tent was much nicer than a near-death shed, plus we could hang out in it. No one wanted to hang out in a shed.

Our tent wasn't your typical nylon camping-in-the-woods tent. It was made of sturdy canvas—the kind of tent used at excavation sites. Dad got it from his university back when he was in grad school. It had seen better days and had some holes gnawed in the sides, but it was still cool. It looked like it could have been lifted right off the sands of Egypt.

I've always wanted to go to the desert and unearth a mummy or a golden tomb of a newly discovered girl queen. I would get a big grant from a university and stake my claim right next to the great statue of the cat-bodied Egyptian god the Sphinx and kiss it on its broken nose while I dug beneath its paws.

Dad and I sat in camp chairs and ate our dinner at a card table. The tent was filled with Dad's old college stuff like camping supplies, crates of books, shovels, and tools. Those were his glory days, he always said. He was a paleontologist, which meant he studied fossils—not *just* dried-up bones and imprints in stone but the animal's actual bodies captured and preserved in the earth and ice. He was really into bones, especially the bones of one particular favorite animal of his—the woolly mammoth. I always thought of the mammoth as a giant hairy elephant with super-long curled tusks. Mammoths were like prehistoric snowplows making their way across the icy tundra of the Arctic. The majority of mammoth bones have been discovered in Siberia, which is probably one of the loneliest places in the world. The last place I ever wanted to go on an excavation was in the frozen world of the Arctic.

The Arctic was the kind of place that looked pretty in pictures. The snow peaks towered over the landscape like freshly whipped cream, and the ice forges glittered in the reflecting sun against a pure blue sky. I was sure it was fun to play for a while in the snow, building snowmen and making snow angels and igloos. But it was a bad sign when the indigenous mammals wore thick layers of blubber. Who would want to spend time in a place where the temperature was walk-in-freezer cold?

Luckily, mammoth bones had also been discovered in North America. A huge cache of bones had been found in the Black Hills of South Dakota, and some were recently found in Colorado, which, from a tourist standpoint, was cushy compared with Siberia. Dad was trying to get funding to do fieldwork on Saint Paul Island in Alaska. He spent many sleepless nights writing up his proposal and doing research. I could handle a trip to Alaska—even in winter it wouldn't be *that* bad.

"Did you hear about the grant?" I asked through a mouthful of spaghetti. I had seen an official-looking letter in the pile of mail by the door and had wanted to rip it open and read it, but instead I had put it on top of the pile and waited.

Dad stared at his plate and twisted his fork around and around, building up a massive ball of spaghetti strands. I swallowed. This was not a good sign. For some reason, Mom had all the luck in our family; grants flowed her way, and she went on expedition after expedition. But not Dad. Science wasn't fair.

"Not this time," he finally said. "The economy's tight."

"That's just another excuse. The economy is always bad."

"What can I say? The grants are fewer and the competition gets fiercer every year." He tore a piece of bread in half. "We have to adapt."

I groaned. Why couldn't he fight back, get angry? "But you worked so hard."

"I'll apply again next year. There's always another chance."

"You'll get one soon," I said, but it felt like a lie. What was I supposed to say? Pep talks were tough.

After dinner Dad made me wait in the tent while he brought out a surprise. Even though he was a whiz with turning ground meat into a delicacy, he was not as good in the baking department. I peeked out of the canvas flap and saw the sparkler on top of a huge brown mound. I held the tent open while he carried in a cake.

"Wow! It's beautiful." The sparkler glowed, and a warmth spread over me. Dad always came through. I leaned my head on his shoulder, then gave him a quick kiss on the cheek.

"I know you miss your mom, so I wanted to make a surprise," he said. "Wait till you see what's inside."

"Inside?"

Once for Thanksgiving, a teacher at my school baked a dime in a pumpkin pie and whoever found it got good luck. I got it—and swallowed the dime whole. It was never seen again. I really hoped there wasn't any loose change baked inside my surprise cake.

"You'll see," he said, a mischievous grin spread across his face. "Now make a wish and blow out the sparkler."

I closed my eyes, but it only took me a second to make

my wish . . . I wanted to go on an expedition—a real one, far, far away. I focused really hard on my wish, willing it to happen. I visualized hot sands and great stone pyramids. I imagined myself floating down the Nile in a slow boat, the way Cleopatra drifted along on not a boat but a sedan carried on the sturdy backs of men. I wished for an adventure where I could dig up something important, something really rare that none of the scientific experts saw coming. I opened my eyes, pulled the sparkler out of the cake, and waved it across the darkening tent as looming shadows stalked the canvas, until at last it sputtered out in my hand.

Dad cut the cake and then proudly pointed to the inside.

The cake was made up of a half-dozen layers, each in a different shade of brown, from light beige to putty, then tan, on to a mocha layer, then plain chocolate, and finally to a dark devil's food chocolate. "I wanted it to look like the layers of rock," he said. "And, trust me, it wasn't easy. I have a newfound respect for Betty Crocker."

I laughed. "It's so cool!" I dipped a finger into the icing and licked it off. "Very chocolaty." This was the kind of cake one might expect from a science-nerd dad—both delicious and educational. "It's the best cake ever."

"You might want to wait until you take a bite to decide that." He cut off a huge slice. The tower of chocolate toppled over onto my plate. It looked a little shiny and wet. I dug my fork in and took a big bite.

"It's a little raw in the middle. Oh, is it one of those molten cakes?" I asked.

Dad tilted his head like he was considering the possibility. "Yes!" he answered a little too eagerly. "It's molten, like a volcano." He wiggled his eyebrows at me. He was totally making that up.

I swallowed a mouthful of the undercooked batter. "It's really good." And it actually was.

After I had finished eating and had helped do the dishes, I headed to my room and changed into my pajamas. As I was climbing into bed, I saw my reflection in the now-black computer screen. I'm very different from my parents, at least in appearance. Mom's hair was glossy brown, and Dad's was dark blond, like an old golden retriever's. Due to some freak of nature or some warped gene, my hair was . . . pure white.

Not blond, not honey, but snowdrift white.

It was cute when I was a baby. Everyone thought my hair would darken as I got older, but no. My hair was born old—the color of powder, the color of milk. Now everyone thought it was weird, definitely stare-worthy. The other kids said I was part albino or part mutant spawn.

Once I overheard one of my parents' friends say that it was no wonder my hair was white—Mom and Dad loved the past so much they had made an old baby.

Dad said that one day I would be a famous scientist like Jane Goodall and everyone would recognize me on sight, because my white hair would be my trademark and make me look both glamorous and wise at the same time. Which, he said, was a really hard thing to do. He said it was just like the way movie actress Katharine Hepburn was really tall and always wore pants back in the days when most actresses were petite and always wore dresses, but she could pull it off because she owned the thing that made her different. She didn't slouch.

So I handled it. I grew my hair out really long and wove it in two long braids. I cut my hair into blunt, serious bangs. But I also wore hats a lot—especially in winter, when it wasn't strange to wear a hat, because stares could be tiring.

I snuggled down under the covers and turned off the light. My best friend, Zoey, and I had stuck star stickers to the ceiling in an ill-fated attempt at creating a galaxy, but even though they didn't look like a real sky, they made the room feel less lonely, which was strange because the real stars were light-years away, and Mom was only on another continent. She was probably swaying in her ropy hammock at this very moment, staring up at the stars, and hers weren't made of plastic.

3

Zoey

I saw Zoey's head bobbing over the tops of a troop of field-trip kids linked arm in arm, all of whom were wearing yellow shirts. Zoey and I had decided to hit the Air and Space Museum first because there was a new exhibit in the planetarium that she wanted to see. Not that we hadn't seen a million star shows, but they never got old.

Zoey and I had been best friends for about three years. Her parents were space freaks, and her dad worked for NASA and her mom at the museum. That's how we met. We were Smithsonian kids.

The Smithsonian in Washington, D.C., isn't one museum. It's a group of museums all lined up in a giant rectangle, and the whole area is called the National Mall, with the sharp pointy pencil of the Washington Monument in the middle and the Lincoln Memorial at one end, with lots of trampled grass in between. Zoey's mom and my dad both had office space at two of the coolest museums. The fact that Zoey and I had embraced the coolness of museums just helped cement our friendship.

Zoey had a brown mocha mustache on her upper lip. I wasn't allowed to drink mochas, because they had coffee in them and my parents said that coffee would stunt my growth. Zoey's mom was German and didn't buy into the coffee growth-stunting myth. She let Zoey drink coffee if she wanted, except that Zoey said coffee tasted like boiled bark, so she opted for mochas, which were coffee mixed with chocolate, and she always gave me a sip. Plus, Zoey was a head taller than I was, so growth stunting wasn't a concern.

Zoey zipped around the group of kids and came over and linked her arm in mine. We darted to the line for the star show. The security guard, George, gave us a nod. We were regarded as regulars, having come in many days in a row when the Pluto travesty hit a few years back. Zoey was a diehard Pluto fan and still couldn't bring herself to accept the terrible fate that had befallen her beloved planet when some superior-brain-celled scientists decided to flick Pluto right out of our solar system, declaring, blasphemously, that it wasn't really a planet anymore.

She would much rather have traded in Mercury. "Let the sun eat it for breakfast," she said. "Just keep Pluto." When I had asked her why, she said it was because Pluto needed us. It was way out there, alone in the freezing darkness of space, and it needed all the friends it could get.

It was during the Pluto travesty (as it will be forever known) that Zoey and I bonded as best friends. Then one day George called us *the ghost girls*, and I cringed, thinking he was making fun of my long white hair—*white as a ghost*. And George must have realized it, too, by the look of utter terror on his face. Zoey took it in stride, though. She asked him what made us ghost girls, and George said it was because we always *haunted* the museum, which was true.

One night I had a sleepover at Zoey's house, and I drew a picture of Pluto with my gel pens on her shoulder blade like a tiny tattoo. Zoey's mom had a case of hair dye stashed in the garage from when it had been on sale at Sam's Club. We borrowed a box and Zoey dyed my hair. The name on the package was Cinnabar, and in the picture on the front the model had gorgeous reddish-brown hair. Little did we know that red dye on my white hair would turn it vibrant pink. Don't get me wrong, I like pink. Pink has a bad rap as far as colors go, ever since it was usurped by princesses. Pink by itself was pretty enough, but a head full of pink stood out, and I had been going for subtle. An explosion of hot-pink hair wasn't subtle. Plus, my parents freaked. Luckily, the color was only *semi*permanent. My scalp still tingled at the memory of the dozens of shampooings Mom had subjected me to.

✦ ✦ ✦

The planetarium was filling up fast. Zoey and I leaned back and stared at the artificial black sky. Zoey knew I missed my mom, and she didn't have to say a word. Instead, we let the silence fall over us while people shuffled in to watch the show. Finally, she said, "Only humans would make a fake sky so that they could watch the stars drift by over and over. I bet the aliens in outer space are laughing their little green butts off at us."

"OK—green is now the color of alien butts," I said.

"If you add that to your color theory," she replied, twisting a strand of her long curly hair around one of her fingers, "I expect a footnote to reference this date and time when you publish."

Parents who are academics are obsessed with publishing. Getting papers published is really important, because it puts scientific ideas into scholarly journals, where colleagues can review and comment on them. This builds credibility. (At least that's what my parents told me.) Being published makes it much easier to get grant money for research and fieldwork.

That reminded me of my dad and his failed grant application. Zoey must have received some brainwaves, because she looked over at me and asked, "Hey, did your dad ever hear back about his proposal?"

My stomach knotted. A big pink knot, I decided. Pink was the color of stomach knots.

I sighed, a long drawn-out Pluto sigh. "Yeah. He heard and it sucks. Denied once again. It's not fair."

"Man, you would think with the discovery of that baby mammoth a few years back that mammoth research would be a hot topic."

"'Money is tight.' That's always the excuse. Never enough money." I rolled my eyes.

"I hate money."

"Me too. Money doesn't deserve a color. It's the color of trouble."

The lights in the auditorium flickered, and a wave of hushed silence spread over the crowd. Blackness engulfed us as we looked up. Black was the absence of color. It was the color of freezing outer space. And of closed eyes. Where colors went to die.

After watching the show, Zoey and I headed over to the Natural History Museum. Tilda was the administrative assistant who worked for Dad and all the other professors who shared office space in the corner of the building. She waved us forward with long, glittery red fingernails.

"Something's up," she whispered with minty breath.

A bowl of individually wrapped Life Savers rested on her desk. Zoey and I both dug our hands in at the same time.

"What?" I asked.

"A call came in early this morning. There's been a major find . . . and your dad's been on the phone all day." Tilda beamed.

"What kind of find?" Zoey asked. "Animal, vegetable, or alien?"

"Fossil evidence." Tilda drummed her fingernails on the desk blotter. Someone had drawn a childish sketch of a mammoth with long curly tusks on the calendar.

"Mammoth evidence!" I blurted. Excitement flooded through me. I couldn't believe this was happening. "Wow! That is so awesome."

Tilda nodded, her lips curling into a satisfied smile.

"Where did they find it?" I asked.

"Well, we don't know all the details. At least I don't. But the call came from the Canadian Arctic."

"The Arctic . . ." Zoey crunched down on her Life Saver.

"This sounds big," I said.

"Very." Tilda jabbed the button on the phone for Dad's office line with her sparkly red fingernail. Red was a vibrant color, exciting and full of energy. "Jason, your daughter and her friend are here. May I send them in?"

She nodded her head toward Dad's office while scribbling whatever he was saying down on a pad of paper.

The office was the size of a rich person's closet, so it was small as offices went but gigantic for a closet. Dad said that academics didn't need a lot of space—it was the ideas that were big. I pushed on the door, which didn't open all the way because of the stack of books behind it.

Dad hung up the phone and waved us in. Zoey and I squeezed into the cluttered space. Though the office was small, the ceilings were high, and all the stuff was stacked upward. The shelves were filled with books, and replicas of bones seemed to go up and up into the fluorescent sky.

Dad's face lit up when he saw us. His ear was bright red

from having been pressed to the phone. "Did Tilda tell you about the mammoth?"

"Not much. Just that there was a big find." I wanted to hear the news from him.

"A major find in Canada. Do you know how lucky we are? The site is close. Really close." Words spooled from his mouth. "Plus, an ecotourism company discovered it— Clark Expeditions." He read off his notepad.

"What did they find?" I asked.

"Mammoth bones." He lowered his voice even though it was just the three of us shoehorned into the office. "And maybe . . . *more*."

"More what?" I asked in the same hushed, quiet voice.

"Organic material." He used a loud stage whisper for dramatic effect.

When Dad talked about organic material, he meant the good stuff, the meaty stuff—like animal flesh, which wasn't gross if you thought about it scientifically.

"Like a mammoth *body*? Do they think they found a frozen one?"

He beamed.

If there was a real frozen mammoth buried in the ice up in Canada, this was huge. Mammoth bones were not rare. In fact, though always an important find, the bones were nothing new. There was an entire creepy mammoth graveyard filled with hundreds of bones in Siberia. Russia had cornered the market as far as mammoth finds went. But a body was entirely different. No wonder Dad was so excited.

"Is it a baby? Like the ones found before?" Three baby mammoths had been retrieved from the Siberian steppe, in various stages of preservation.

"Not sure. Let's not get overly excited," he cautioned. "We're not sure what exactly was found—it could be nothing."

"But it's serious." I looked at Zoey, and she gave me the thumbs-up sign.

"Yes. We're taking this very seriously. A team will be assembled and sent to investigate the find."

"Wow. That's colossal." Zoey's smile showed off her shiny braces. "So are you going to Canada or what?" Zoey always got to the point.

"What's this mean, Dad?" I was starting to get a little nervous, the thrill of discovery ebbing away. "Are we going? Wait, who gets to go? I get to go, too. Right?"

Dad's mouth hung open. He sighed, clearly not knowing what to say. "We'll talk when I get home. I don't know."

"What do you mean you don't know?" Panic washed over me. "You can't leave me at home," I snapped, and dropped my backpack on the floor.

"Don't get excited. We'll discuss it later tonight when I have more details."

Which really meant *Don't embarrass me in public with a hysterical outburst.* Sensing trouble, Zoey ducked out of the office.

I suddenly felt hot and claustrophobic. I couldn't let another one of my parents jet off on an expedition without me.

Dad stood and gave me a quick hug and pat on the back.

But I wasn't going to let it go. "Come on, Dad. Please." *Please* was the last refuge of the desperate, but begging was not beneath me. I *had* to go with him.

At that moment, the phone rang, and he snatched it up. He turned his back to me and spoke hurriedly into the receiver. With a glance over his shoulder, he said, "I have to take this call. It's Randal Clark. Can you get a ride home with Zoey's mom? Thanks. You're a trouper, Maya."

Then he pushed me. Not hard, but enough.

Dad had never pushed me before. He pushed me right out of the office and shut the door. I stood in the hallway and stared at the carpet. It was the color of ground-up corn. The color of broken chips left at the bottom of the bag after all the good chips had been eaten. I felt chewed up. Left over. That ugly carpet was me, stepped on and ignored. Was Dad going to suddenly up and leave because some cool mammoth was found in the Arctic?

I was getting ditched for another discovery.

"That was weird," Zoey said.

"Not like Dad at all."

"He'll come around."

"I don't know."

"Want to have dinner at my house? You could use some pizza therapy right now."

I didn't know what to think, but at least Zoey was there with me. We headed out of the office. Tilda's head was down and she was writing furiously on a piece of paper, her glittery red nails sparkling in the halo of light from the desk lamp.

Words I never thought I would utter sprang from my mouth. "I'm *going* to Canada," I declared. "I'm going to the Arctic."

4

The Hairy Elephant
in the Room

I purposely stayed late at Zoey's house. I went on her computer after dinner, my fingers flying across the keys as I searched for information online about the mysterious benefactor who had called my dad. I clicked on a link that took me to a recent article about Randal Clark. A photo of a dashing businessman with his hair windblown and his eyes sparkling came up on the screen.

I scanned the column. "It says Randal was a daredevil in his youth with the heart of an explorer."

"It looks like Mr. Clark comes from old money, like from back in the days when railroads were being built," Zoey said, pulling a bag of gummy bears out of her top desk drawer.

"He's driven, that's for sure." The article said that Randal had taken his family fortune and turned it into a bigger fortune. He could have hung out all day and counted his money if he wanted to, but he worked really hard instead.

Green gummy-bear parts were stuck in Zoey's braces. "It says Clark Expeditions is part scientific exploration and part ecotourism. It sounds cool. Your dad is lucky."

"We're both lucky," I said. "Because I'm going with him."

Zoey leaned back into a pile of clothes, stretching her arms out and flapping them up and down like she was trying to make a snow angel. "You'd better text me. I want to be the first to hear about the mammoth when you find it."

I plopped down on the bed, and from my backpack I pulled out one of Mom's old cameras. I tended to get the hand-me-down electronics. "I've got my camera with the video recorder, so I'll take some video messages for you and post them."

"Great. And I want to see a live polar bear and a dead mammoth up close and personal. Oh, and don't forget the tusks. Get a shot of the tusks." She picked a gummy bear out of her teeth and proceeded to eat it.

"I'll make a mental note. 'Zoey wants to see some tusks.'"

Zoey's mom had come in about three times, prompting me to get ready to go home. Finally, she stood in the doorway in all her Germanness, with her hands on her hips and a look that needed no explanation. The car was in the driveway with the engine running. No more avoiding it.

Even though I wanted to hear about what happened after I left Dad's office, I was still mad at him for *the push*. Once I was through the front door, I headed straight for my bedroom.

"Maya, is that you?" Dad called from the family room.

He must have literally jumped up from the sofa and run to intercept me, because I didn't even make it to the hall before he was standing right in front of me. I stared at the floor, the wall, and the gigantic dust bunny that was collecting in a corner. I examined every inch of the hallway, looking everywhere but at Dad. Silent as a mollusk, lips pursed shut in defiance. Let Dad do all the talking. Let him try to talk his way out of leaving me behind.

"Did you have fun at Zoey's house? I was about to send out the cavalry."

I glanced up momentarily. He had a big goofy smile on his face. He probably didn't even remember *the push*.

I shrugged. Technically, a shrug could be considered a silent response. It was body language.

"Something wrong?" he asked.

I did a mental eye roll. A physical eye roll was beneath me.

"Come into the family room. We need to talk."

I followed him and plopped down on the sofa. I hugged a throw pillow and pulled at the fringe. I had no plans to talk, but if he wanted to chat, that was fine by me. Dad sat on the arm of a worn leather chair.

"About today at the office. I know you were a little shocked with all the excitement." He took his glasses off and cleaned them with his T-shirt. "I'm sure you're bursting with questions. I know I was."

I punched at the pillow's soft insides. Maybe I was bursting with questions, just a little. But he wasn't getting the mad part. I wasn't in shock. I was angry. I was red, and not hungry red or sparkly red. I was old-fashioned angry red.

"It's just that nothing like this has ever happened to me before. You know how hard it's been."

I looked up at him. I remembered the envelope with the latest rejection letter, the one I had been sure was filled with good news. But it hadn't been. He was right—I did know how hard it had been. The anger started to drain away.

"No one ever thinks of me when they need a mammoth expert. Oh, sure I get called to give speeches and give tours, but the real stuff, the fieldwork, always goes to some other guy with more experience or more degrees. Not me—I never get the real work that matters."

I felt terrible. He had worked for this for years—no, decades—ever since he was in college. And finally he was so close to having his dreams come true, and all I was thinking about was myself.

I made myself smile. "Well, what happened? What's different this time?" I asked.

His face brightened. "Randal Clark needs someone fast. He was out with a group of ecotourists and stumbled upon some mammoth tusks up in the Canadian Arctic. Mr. Clark owns the operation and runs the business. He decided to check out the discovery with his nephew, who is an amateur filmmaker."

"That sounds cool."

"They took video of the tusks, and while they were trying to dig them up, something stuck, and it looks like there may be something buried in the permafrost."

"Can't they just dig it up and see what it is?"

"Thankfully, they didn't. Mr. Clark didn't want to ruin the find in case it's worth a lot of money. Which is actually smart of him, even though he's only thinking of his bottom line. If it *is* mammoth remains and they dig it up, the carcass could thaw and be attacked and eaten by animals, or poachers could steal the ivory."

"It has tusks?"

"Yes!" Dad jumped to his feet. "Can you believe it? That's why they called us! The tusks breached the ice."

"This is big. And they want you to come to the Arctic to check it out."

"Basically, yes. Mr. Clark is willing to fund the whole expedition. And it won't even cost him that much since he already has camps established. Apparently, the guy is a real Arctic buff and lives year-round in the compound."

"That's great! When do we leave?" The Arctic wasn't my top choice for my first real expedition. But luck was a funny thing, and this mammoth had just fallen in our laps. I would brave the snow and ice for science's sake.

"About that . . ." Now it was Dad's turn to stare at the floor. He eased down on the sofa next to me and put his hand on my shoulder. "You'll have to skip this one. I was thinking you could stay at Zoey's house. I was hoping to speak with her parents tomorrow after we talked. Won't that be fun, a whole month just the two of you?"

"A month! And you're just going to leave me here?" My emotions flared. I was sick of being left behind.

"I'm not *leaving* you. The time will go by in a flash." He squeezed my shoulder, but I shrugged him off.

"Mom leaves all the time and I have to deal with it. I have to be mature and do my homework and pretend that it's fine. But it's not fair."

"I know it's not fair. But you'll hardly know that I'm gone. This is a big opportunity that I can't pass up."

"I know it's your big chance. That's why I'm going with you. It's *our* big chance."

Dad shook his head. "You have school. And should stay home."

I had to think fast. "The expedition will be educational. What kid gets to go to the Arctic to watch real fieldwork in action?" I crossed my arms over my chest and raised an eyebrow. "Plus, spring break is coming up."

"No, Maya. It's too dangerous," he said.

The danger card was the last play of a parent on the edge of caving in. I knew I was close. "I can handle it," I said. "I'm not afraid. And you'll be there."

"The Arctic can be treacherous, and I won't be able to watch you all the time."

"Watch me!" I scoffed. "I'm old enough to *babysit*

myself. Thirteen is not a kid. And you said that the mammoth was found by *tourists*, so how dangerous can it be if people are traveling there for vacation?"

Dad paused. "That's a good point."

"You said the billionaire had a compound and lived in the Arctic year-round, so I could stay there. And I promise to keep out of the way. Please, Dad."

He started to waver. "OK . . . Let me make some calls. It's not entirely up to me."

"Yes!"

"No, that's not a yes." He pointed at me as he stood. "It's a possible, a maybe. I don't know if your principal will allow you to miss school. We'll just have to see."

"*Please* don't make me stay at home. I really want to go."

"I'll try."

There was no way I would hear tonight. It was late. I ran to my room and jumped on the computer. Maybe I could convince Dad that I was serious about going by doing some mammoth homework, even though I already knew more about mammoths than any other thirteen-year-old on the planet. Dad had been telling me bedtime stories about the hairy beasts since I was a kid. Mammoths had dark gray skin with reddish-black woolly hair and stood ten to twelve feet high.

I read through a few websites, picking up more details. As I was scrolling through a web page on the National Geographic site, Dad knocked on the door. "Can I come in?"

"Sure," I said.

He sat on the side of my bed. "I don't want you to think that I am punishing you or that I don't want you to come with me. We're pals, and there is no one I would rather have by my side at the dig site than you. It's just that I don't want anything to happen to you. Your safety means everything to me."

"You mean like baby Lyuba?" I asked. I sat down next to Dad. Baby Lyuba was an important mammoth discovered on the permafrost of the Siberian steppe. She had been caught in a mudflow and had suffocated. Sediment had been found in her tiny lungs. I was trying to impress Dad with my mammoth knowledge, which was really not mammoth at all, but puny in comparison.

"What do you know about Lyuba?" he asked.

"That the scientists don't think her mother left her, but that she was too small and got stuck in the mud during migration. She drowned or suffocated in the mud."

He stared at his hands. "I couldn't forgive myself if anything bad happened to you. This is real. It's not a movie or a TV show. I will have high expectations put on me, and I won't be able to spend a lot of time with you."

"I know. But I'll be good. I promise. I won't get in the way. Plus, Mom is always saying how responsible and mature I am."

"Well, she's right about that. Let me see what your principal says tomorrow, and we'll decide from there. If she approves the trip, then we'll talk. Deal?"

I jumped up and threw my arms around Dad in a bear hug. "Deal!"

+ + +

Dad drove me to school, and we walked to the principal's office together. It turned out that the expedition was starting immediately, so if I was going to go with him, we needed to get permission right away. I sat on a dingy orange chair in the waiting room outside the office and stared out the window. Pale green daffodil stems poked through the soggy spring dirt. Pale green was the color of potential, of "maybe."

Dad was taking forever. I hoped he was convincing. Finally, he emerged from the office and headed right out the front door. I followed quick on his heels.

"What did Mrs. Pettyfield say?" I asked, my pulse racing as we headed across the parking lot toward the car.

He stared at his shoes, fumbled with his keys. Dad was a terrible liar. I knew by the way he was trying to suppress a smile that I was going.

"Yes!" I yelled. "How did you convince her?"

We climbed into the car.

"Well, the fact that you have a week off for spring break helped. But the clincher was that Mrs. Pettyfield owes me big-time after that night-at-the-museum fiasco from three years back." Dad put on his seat belt and wrinkled his nose.

"I had forgotten about that." I cringed at the memory.

"How could you forget?" He shuddered.

A few years back he had done a favor for the principal by setting up a night-at-the-museum slumber party at the Natural History Museum for the entire fourth grade. We had a tour of the museum, followed by watching short films and playing dinosaur games, and everything was going great, except that one of the parent chaperones had brought along her famous pork pockets as snacks. Everyone who had a pork pocket got food poisoning. It wasn't pretty, and it smelled even worse.

"They should've known better. That pork looked a little gray. And besides, who eats pork that late at night?"

"Twenty of the kids and three of the chaperones, that's who. It was a nightmare. The janitor resigned the very next day." He shook his head to clear it, then looked at me seriously. "Now, there are conditions in allowing you to go on this trip. You have to stay caught up on all your schoolwork, and you have to write your own field report and do an oral presentation when you get back, sharing everything you learned on the expedition with the other students."

"I can do that! I can bring my camera and record videos and e-mail them to my science and history classes." I didn't tell him I was already planning on doing that for Zoey. "It can be a serious expedition, not a vacation. I'll have a field notebook and do reports." My mind raced with plans for the trip.

"Good idea. Once I finalize it with Randal Clark and OK it with your mom, we'll be all set. As long as they don't have a problem with you joining the team, then you can go." He ruffled my hair. "But be warned, it's going to get cold up there."

"I can handle the cold. No problem." I beamed.

It was really going to happen—my first expedition.

5

The Station

I clutched the shoulder strap of my backpack and glued myself to Dad's side. I wasn't exactly afraid to fly, but the nerves and excitement had kicked in. We were flying to Montreal, Canada, and then on to Kuujjuaq, Nunavik, which was in the northern part of Quebec. Once up there, we'd take a helicopter to the base camp.

The first flight was uneventful, smooth as silk. Not the second flight. We were crammed inside a small commuter plane, and my whole body rumbled along with the engine and my teeth rattled in my head. The plane glided over the earth like a silver bird, and I watched the world float beneath my feet, rough as cement.

Wisps of torn white clouds drifted by my window.

White was the color of an open door. We had come to a frozen place of sky and ice. Seeing the pale surface, I realized I was entering a world that was almost colorless. My theories seemed shallow up here, hovering above the real world. Mom had said digging was a family trait, but colors were just surface traits. In the Arctic, if I wanted to find something, I was going to have to dig.

When I stepped onto the runway to catch the helicopter, a stinging coldness slapped me in the face, a wake-up cold. My nose started to run. Dad and I prepared to board the helicopter. The pilot's name was Justice, and he was an Inuit guide who also took care of Randal Clark's sled dogs. He wore mirrored aviator sunglasses, a black jumpsuit, and black lace-up boots.

"How long have you worked for Randal?" Dad asked him as our gear was being loaded into the back of the chopper.

"About four years. Since he came up here and set up shop. He's put a lot into his place. Living the dream." Justice smiled a big white toothy grin. White was now the color of charismatic pilot smiles.

"It's a big investment. Never know if it's going to pay off," Dad said.

"That's right." Justice handed me a piece of peppermint candy. "Ready to head out? You're gonna love it."

Two other passengers made their way over to the helicopter. While passing out headphones, Justice introduced them as Dr. Katsu Takahashi and Dr. Ivan Petrov. More scientists. Randal must be spending a fortune on this expedition.

Dad was going to sit up front with Justice, while I would be squeezed into the backseat between the two strangers. Dr. Petrov was Russian. He told us to call him Ivan. He had a peppery beard and a cracked front tooth, and there was a star-shaped scar next to his eye. I wondered if science was a rough profession in Russia. He slid into the chopper first and immediately buckled his seat belt. He clutched the armrest so hard, his knuckles turned white. And I thought *I* was the nervous one.

Dr. Takahashi was from Japan. He wore thick, round black glasses and nodded politely when our eyes met. After buckling his belt, he pulled off his gloves, took a tiny bottle of antibacterial gel out of his pocket, and squeezed a drop in his palm before he shook my hand. The sharp smell of alcohol tickled my nose.

Dad waved from the front seat. "Nice to meet you, Doctor Takahashi."

"Please call me Katsu. We will be friends and colleagues." His smile was kind, but his eyes dissected me like a surgical knife. He held a silver briefcase on his lap. He fiddled with the combination lock on the side. He saw me watching him. He patted the case. "The instruments of my trade are safe inside." I knew when he said *instruments*, he wasn't referring to an innocent flute or clarinet, but something sharper.

I shifted uncomfortably in the stiff seat, and our nylon coats rubbed together. My backpack weighed heavily on my lap. It was stuffed full of reference books on the Arctic. I had probably brought too many, but I wanted to be prepared. Books were my anchors.

"Maya is a pretty name," Katsu said in a casual tone.

"Did you know that in my language my name means victory? I must live up to it. Victory always."

"Sounds like a motto—victory," Dad said.

"A motto. Yes, I am always victorious. You will see." He gripped the case. "We will have a great expedition."

What a strange thing to say. Dr. *Victory* was going to be an interesting person to watch on the trip.

The helicopter lifted off the ground and my stomach dropped. Just an arm's length away, the scenery pressed in, dizzying. There was nothing else around for miles except for the jagged icy teeth of the rugged landscape. It felt like the sky went on forever. Emptiness washed over me. We were so far away from . . . everything. The helicopter dipped. I gripped my knees and felt my teeth grinding. I hoped Justice would hurry up and get us to the base camp.

"You look a little green," Dad said, glancing back at me.

I gave him a weary smile. Green was now the color of airsickness, I guessed.

"Press your tongue to the roof of your mouth. It helps with equilibrium," Justice said. "Don't worry. You're safe with me."

My peppermint had dissolved, leaving my tongue coated in sticky sweetness. I didn't want to think about my tongue or my mouth or what might come out of my mouth if he didn't land the helicopter soon. Ivan gnawed on his gum and when he caught me looking at him, he pointed at his ears, buried under thick furry earmuffs on top of his headphones and said, "Popping," and kept on smacking his gum.

After about twenty minutes Justice motioned to the ground. Our destination appeared below us: an outcropping of rectangular wooden buildings that were linked together. From the air, they looked like a lost herd of caribou. There was a landing pad built for the helicopter—a big red X—that would be our main way in and out of the station.

Finally, we descended. It felt like the ground rushed up to meet us, even though we were floating downward. I closed my eyes and rested my head against the back of the seat.

"Takes a few days to get used to the environment up here. But you'll acclimate," Justice said as he set the chopper down, soft as a metal feather.

A man wearing a black snowsuit with a silver Clark Expeditions patch on the front waved us into the nearest building. Once we were all inside, he shook everyone's hand and introduced himself as West Higgins, Randal Clark's assistant. West had a full brown beard and a sharp crew cut. His face was rugged, reddened from the cold and wind, and he chewed on his chapped lips.

West led us through the main building, which held some offices and the communication center, a room with a radio, satellite hookup, and computers. West kept calling this room "the comm." On the way from the comm center, we passed by a closed door. West stopped abruptly and crossed his arms over his massive chest. He waited for us all to gather around him before he spoke.

"Randal wants you all to feel at home. His station is your station, and you should come and go as you please. But there is one area that is off-limits." West rapped on the door with his battered knuckles. "And this, my friends, is it. This room is Randal's private room. No one is allowed in, ever. Do I make myself clear?"

"Of course," Dad said, and nudged me.

"Yes, sir," I said, my curiosity piqued.

West continued down the hallway, but I lingered, letting the rest of the group go on ahead. Dad held back and put his arm around me.

"Why do you think Randal has a secret room?" I whispered to him, glancing back at the door.

He shrugged. "I don't think it's a secret. Just a private place for him. I'm sure it's a library with leather chairs and a fireplace. He probably has shelves filled with books."

"Hmm. Then why not say that? Why was West so gruff about the room being off-limits?" I shifted on my snow boots, my backpack growing heavier by the second.

"I don't know. But it's Randal's station. He's entitled to his own space."

"I guess . . ." But if Randal wanted the room to be off-limits, telling people to stay out was one way to make them want to see what was inside. "You're probably right," I said. "But I'm still curious."

The group was about to turn the corner up ahead. Katsu caught my eye and held my stare for a second too long. The silver case was still in his hand, hanging by his side, and I wondered if he had a secret, too.

Dad motioned me forward. "Come on. Let's catch up before they leave without us. I don't want to miss anything."

When we exited the main building and headed for the next, West reached down and grabbed a blue cord. "Rope line," he said over his shoulder. "Best get used to holding on to them, even when it's not windy. It's a good habit."

He looked at me. "You don't want to blow away in a storm. The snow and wind come on fast and can blind you and blow you around like a petal on the wind."

I pictured a bunch of pink petals blowing across the icy landscape. West didn't look like the kind of guy who got pushed around a lot by anything, including the wind, so I decided to listen to him.

"Even going a short distance?" I asked as I grabbed the line. The blue lines fanned out from each building, connecting them in a spidery blue web.

"Especially. The cold is a monster. It will swallow you up in a second."

Next, he showed us a state-of-the-art medical facility and the laboratories where my dad and the other scientists would be doing most of their work. As we toured the science lab, it became obvious that the station was totally decked out with tons of fancy equipment and supplies. Randal Clark had spared no expense. Dad's eyes practically glazed over in awe. I had never seen him so excited. I just hoped he didn't start drooling. This place was like summer camp for science nerds.

Dad and I followed West single file to the next building, where the bunk area was located. We stopped to "stow our gear," as West said. He carried himself with a stiff-backed military bearing that I found comforting. He dropped my bag outside a room and pointed a gnarled finger to the empty bunk bed. "You'll be bunking in here with Dr. Karen Gardner. She arrived yesterday with her son, Kyle."

He turned to Dad and the other two scientists. "The rest of you are down the hall. Men at one end and women at the other."

So Dad and I had separate rooms. "I'll be back in a few minutes to check on you," he said, and followed West down the corridor.

My room had a bunk bed pushed against one wall and a single bed against the other. The doctor had already unpacked her things, and it looked like she had been working at the small desk in the corner. Notebooks covered its surface. I tossed my backpack on the bed of the bottom bunk and my suitcase on the floor. A bag of knitting needles and balls of yarn sat next to Karen's bed. I knelt down and fingered a woolly thread.

The room was warm. My scalp was beginning to sweat, so I pulled off my hat, setting my braids free and my bangs shooting upward in an awkward hat-head style.

Next thing I knew, a boy about my age walked into the room. He had dark wavy hair that peeked out from under a baseball cap that he wore backward. A brightly colored knitted scarf was wrapped around his neck about three times and still trailed down past his knees.

"Hey, I'm Kyle," he said casually, shoving his hands in his pockets. He had a stuffed polar bear buried under one arm. I was surprised he didn't say anything about my hair right away. "Have you seen my mom?"

"Your mom?" I said.

"Yeah, you're sharing this room with her." Kyle plopped down on her bed.

"Oh, right." Dad hadn't mentioned there was going to be another kid here. "No. I haven't seen her. We just flew in. I'm Maya. Here with my dad." I loosened my scarf. The room was a million degrees.

"Is your dad the paleontologist guy? 'Cause I'm in his room." He tossed the bear from one hand to the other. His blue-eyed gaze stayed on me.

"That's him," I answered, and then I said the first thing that came to mind. "My dad snores, so better you than me."

Kyle grinned and turned his attention to his mom's bed. He pulled down the covers and hid the bear under the bedspread and the pillow.

"Nice bear," I said, running out of topics of conversation in record time.

"My mom and I have a standard joke. We travel a lot, and she likes to have a mascot for each trip." Kyle focused on perfectly concealing the stuffed animal. "Then we try and hide the mascot in each other's stuff without the other one knowing. She snuck it in my suitcase and got me this time." He rolled his eyes. "She's into that kind of thing."

"That's cool. What's his name?" I asked while pretending to organize my backpack and shoving my suitcase under the bed.

"I call him Bear. He's a simple guy." Kyle smoothed out the spread and stretched back on the foot of the bed with his hands behind his head. "Not very original. Don't let on that the bear's there, OK?"

"I won't." I smiled. "She'll be surprised when she goes to sleep tonight."

"So is this your first trip?" He stared at my backpack, which was practically bursting at the seams with books.

I cringed. "Does it show?" A half-dozen spiral notebooks spilled out of my pack. I had brought too much stuff. Overprepared, as usual.

"A little. I'm not a book guy myself. More of a seat-of-my-pants type."

"It's for school. To stay caught up while I'm here."

"I'm in the school of life," he countered. "I call it adventure ed." He adjusted his baseball cap.

"Sounds more like a vacation."

"It makes school fun. Plus, I travel all the time. You'll like it here, out in the field." He shrugged. It was obvious that he was trying not to stare at me, but he finally gave up. "Nice hair," he said. "I've never seen anyone with white hair before. I mean, old ladies, sure, but no one young."

I caught a glimpse of myself in the mirror and saw my freaky-looking bangs sticking up in all directions. My stomach plummeted. The bright whiteness alone would cause stares, to say nothing of the wild angles. I grabbed my hat off the bed and resisted the urge to pull it back on. "Well, before you ask, yes, it's real. And, no, I am not an albino or fairy spawn. And, no, I am not aging backward like Brad Pitt in that movie. It's just white. Really white. But I'm human. Really, nothing special or strange about me."

Human? Did I just say that I was human? *Who says that?*

He smiled. "Are you sure you aren't a fairy? 'Cause that would be cool."

"I wish." I blushed, relieved that he didn't think my hair was too weird.

"And at least now I know you're human."

That was a dumb thing to say. *I'm human.* Duh. Way to break the ice.

Luckily, West came into the room at that moment and saved me from additional embarrassment. "Good, you two have met. You can unpack later. Randal wants to meet with everyone in the mess hall for introductions before dinner." Quickly, I shoved my hat back on and tucked my braids up.

West led us down the hall to join the others. Dad raised his eyebrows at me when he saw the boy, but I just shrugged.

"We're roomies," Kyle said, reaching out his hand to Dad. "I'm Kyle."

"Please call me Jason," Dad said, and then he winked at me.

Katsu and Ivan shared the room across the hall from Dad and Kyle. We waited for them to finish organizing their stuff, and then we all fell in line behind West.

He took us past a recreation room that was decked out with a wide-screen television and video games. A pool table and a Ping-Pong table were surrounded by comfy-looking couches. I had a feeling I'd be spending a lot of time there. "Looks like you won't be bored," Dad said, elbowing me. He had a goofy smile on his face. It was clear the station blew his expectations out of the water.

The mess hall was buzzing with activity. The welcome dinner had been prepared, and the smell of cooked food made my stomach growl. A long buffet table was loaded down with grilled fish, piles of roasted potatoes and vegetables, bowls filled with wild rice, and an entire tray of chocolate cupcakes. I wanted to run to the table and dive in, but I had to wait. Chair legs scraped the floor as people stood when we entered the room.

Randal strode forward. He looked exactly like his photo online, just as suave and dashing as a billionaire adventurer should be. He was tall, with broad, squared shoulders, and his hair and beard were flecked with gray, which made him look even more distinguished. He had sparkling green eyes and a disarming smile. He spread out his arms and welcomed us in a voice that boomed over the low chatter.

"I want to take a moment to welcome everyone here to my kingdom." A hushed silence spread over the room. "This station is the little place I call home. And for the next month, the station is your home, too. I want you all to feel like family." Warmth and sincerity oozed from him.

Everyone clapped. His enthusiasm spread through the room like electricity. Even I was thrilled to be a part of the expedition. I almost blushed. Dad shook Randal's hand, and then we found seats at the table.

"Introductions are in order. You've all met Justice, my pilot and dog trainer, and West, my right-hand man. We also have our medical doctor, Doctor Kernel." Randal motioned to a woman with blond hair pulled up high on her head in a tight bun. She nodded and smiled.

"This is my nephew, Jake, our resident film student. He will be following everyone around with his camera, filming the expedition for a documentary he's making. He may be only eighteen years old, but he is very accomplished."

Jake was tall and skinny and wore a heavy fisherman's sweater and had a black scarf wrapped around his neck. He was down on one knee, filming his uncle making the introductions. The camera made me pause. I hated getting my picture taken and quickly decided that I would do my best to steer clear of Jake and his camera.

"Doctors Ivan Petrov and Katsu Takahashi." Randal gestured to the Russian and Japanese scientists who had flown in with us.

Katsu waved his hand as if he were on a float in the Macy's Thanksgiving Day Parade and smiled broadly. Ivan simply nodded and grunted. I got the feeling that Ivan didn't like attention, either.

Next, Randal introduced Dr. Karen Gardner and Kyle. Karen was an anthropologist. She was petite and had a wild mane of curly auburn hair that poked out of a colorful beret that looked like she had knitted herself.

"Now, please welcome Doctor Jason Parson and his daughter, Maya. Doctor Parson is our resident mammoth expert and will be leading the exploration tomorrow with Doctors Gardner and Petrov."

Dad waved to everyone, but I noticed his eyes widen. He hadn't mentioned to me that he was heading up the project, and from his expression, I don't think he knew, either. Strange that he hadn't been told. Heading the expedition seemed to be an important detail, one that should not have been left out until we had arrived. But I knew Dad could handle it.

With the introductions finished, we all headed over to the buffet table to get some of the delicious-looking food. Dad and I sat with Karen and Kyle. Karen was a fast-talking dynamo. She chatted about her studies throughout dinner. Film student Jake sat with us for only a few moments while he wolfed down some food. He put the camera down just long enough to eat his dinner, and even then he held it in his lap the whole time.

Dad turned to Kyle. "So we'll be sharing a room," he said. "Are you in school?"

"School's overrated," Kyle said, shoveling food into his mouth. "Experience is what matters."

"Homeschooled," Karen answered. "We travel a lot."

"And he's allergic to books," I said. Kyle had the too-cool-for-school vibe down, but I suspected he was smart, too, what with all the traveling he did with his mom. Seeing the world had its perks. He had probably been to exotic locations and had tons of adventurous stories. Then I saw that the two fingers on Kyle's left hand were missing, the pinky and ring finger. He noticed me looking and said, "Shark attack."

I laughed, even though it's not funny to be attacked by

a shark, because I realized he was kidding. He slipped his hand under the table when Jake looked over, suddenly interested in what we were talking about.

After we had eaten, Randal stood to again address the group. Jake hurried over to a computer console and started pushing buttons. He put on a headset and motioned to his uncle when he was ready, at which point Randal began to speak. His deep voice resonated throughout the room. "I want to let you all know how exciting it is to have such a distinguished team assembled for this important expedition, and I am sorry that there has been so much secrecy around the find."

A buzzing sound focused our attention as a wide screen slowly descended from the ceiling. The lights dimmed. "Adult mammoth tusks have been found protruding from the ice," Randal said, "and I believe that they are still attached to the beast."

Excited chatter filled the room. An image flashed up on the screen. Two huge mammoth tusks curved upward from the side of an icy wall. Karen gasped. Everyone clapped. I couldn't look away. I grabbed Dad's hand under the table. This was what he had waited his whole life to be a part of—a real mammoth discovery! He squeezed my hand, but his eyes never left the image of the giant tusks.

Next a series of pictures flashed slowly across the screen. I had to admit that Jake was pretty good. The images of the tusks and the dig site were awesome.

Dad's attention was riveted to the screen. "Who found the mammoth?" he asked.

I saw Randal's gaze dart over to Jake for a quick second before he answered. "A local Inuit, who would like to remain anonymous. Superstitious, doesn't want any attention drawn to him or his family."

"Oh, I see," Dad said.

Randal cleared his throat. "A secure dig site has been established at the mammoth and is protected against poachers and wild animals. The carcass is safe and sound."

Both Dad and Karen nodded.

The thought of animals eating a dead carcass that had been frozen in the ice for tens of thousands of years made my stomach roll over.

"I don't see a carcass," I whispered to Dad. "How will wild animals get to it if it's buried in the ice?" I asked.

"Shh, Maya. Let the man speak. Randal knows what he's doing."

In all the pictures that Jake projected, not one of them showed the actual mammoth. The tusks looked cool, but I wanted to see the woolly creature inside the ice, and so far all we had gotten were dramatic aerial shots of the excavation site and those giant curling tusks.

"Maintaining the integrity of the site has been of the utmost importance," Randal said.

Then he told us that we would be going to the site tomorrow "to inspect the find and assess the process moving forward." He concluded by saying, "Our goal is to remove the creature for study."

Dad was taking notes in a small field notebook. His brow was knitted and his lips were pursed. I had a feeling something was wrong, but I didn't want to ask in front of everyone. I nudged his arm. He sighed, deep in thought.

"How about we gather in the laboratory to discuss tomorrow's events further?" Randal said. "Perhaps the young ones would like to explore the games in the recreation room. No need for them to listen to all the details, since they will be staying here at the station."

"Not going?" I whispered to Dad. My stomach sank. How was I supposed to experience my first expedition if I was stuck here at the station? I needed to get to where the action was—and playing video games wasn't the kind of action I was hoping for.

"We'll talk about it later," Dad said. "You and Kyle can stay here and man the fort. Now head on over to the game room."

I don't know why I was surprised to learn that Kyle and I were not going. We had to stay behind and *man the fort*. This was the most annoying statement ever and clearly was code for *stay out of the way and fill your time with meaningless tasks like watching movies, playing games, and having fun*. I didn't want to sit around with a guy I didn't know and "have fun." I wanted to go on an adventure. I wanted to be a part of the discovery, feel the excitement.

How was I supposed to prove myself if I couldn't even get to the expedition site? That's what I came for—not to stay behind.

Dad gave me one of his stern don't-argue-with-me looks. Complaining was not an option. Neither was begging, and whining was utterly forbidden. No matter what I said, Dad wasn't going to let me go.

+ + +

"It's not fair," I blurted out. Kyle and I had been banished to the recreation room, which wasn't total torture. There was a dartboard and a pile of board games, but after the tenth game of Ping-Pong—I was winning, 6–4 (though I suspected that Kyle threw a couple of those games to be nice)—I was done playing games. "What's the point of being here if Randal won't let us near the site?" I said, and collapsed down onto the sofa. "We could be helpful. We're like free labor and can be assistants."

"Patience. It's just the first day." Kyle scooped up a pile of darts and sent one sailing toward the board.

"I bet Randal doesn't take us seriously. He doesn't realize how important this is to us," I said, letting my body sink into the sofa cushion.

"Just wait. We'll get our chance out there."

"How can you be so sure?" I asked.

"Because when an expedition starts, everyone goes by the book—follows protocol and stuff. But expeditions take time, and once people are settled in, protocols relax. Then we'll be able to go to the site." Kyle nodded reassuringly.

"I hope you're right."

"I'm always right." He aimed and launched another dart, and this time he hit the bull's-eye.

I sat up with a spark of energy. "Hey, we could do some work in the lab while they're away, to prove that we're willing to work hard. Pay our dues. That kind of thing."

Kyle's eyes went wide. "Hold on." He put his hands up. "I'm staying away from the lab and any kind of work for as long as possible. Who wants to stay cooped up in a lab all day?"

"Well, if we can't go to where the action is, then I do." I wanted to prove to everyone that I was serious about this expedition, and I knew I could do that with work.

"Knock yourself out, bookworm." Kyle pulled the darts out of the board.

"I will," I said. "And what's wrong with liking books?"

"Nothing. I just didn't know a bookworm could survive in the Arctic."

I rolled my eyes, refusing to let him get a rise out of me. "Do you think it's weird? That we know so little about who found the mammoth and how?" I asked.

"Scientists are territorial, especially with finds. That mammoth could be worth a lot of money. Randal's a businessman, so, no, I don't think it's strange at all." A dart sailed into the board.

"But Randal is a billionaire. It's not like money matters to him." I slipped off my boots and curled up on the sofa.

"Maybe he wants to do something important that's remembered and written about. Fossils are sometimes named after the person who finds them. He wants glory."

"Like the Adams mammoth." I had to throw in some of my mammoth knowledge, so Kyle knew I was serious. "He'll call it the Clark mammoth."

"Right," Kyle said.

"Are you into mammoths?" I asked, before realizing that was the nerdiest thing ever. I hoped he said no. Not that Dad was a dork or anything—not that *I* was a dork, either.

"They're pretty cool, I guess. Finding a whole one would be pretty wild." He looked over at me and tilted his head.

"Tell me about your hand," I said before he could ask me a question. "What happened? It wasn't really a shark attack, was it?"

Kyle was silent. He twirled the darts in his good hand. "It's nothing." He looked away. "Just a car accident. I don't want to talk about it." He turned his back on me and tossed a dart at the board. It bounced off and landed on the arm of the sofa.

"Sorry, I didn't mean to pry."

"No problem. I still managed to kick your butt in Ping-Pong."

"I knew you were letting me win," I said.

Karen appeared in the doorway. "Hey, you two. Having fun?" She smiled wearily. Her eyes were glassy. "Time for bed."

"Mom," Kyle said, "it's early."

"Time to go to your room and at least pretend you are sleeping while you read or play a computer game," she said.

"All right." Kyle sighed and started to put the darts away. "For you, Doctor Gardner." He kissed his mom on the cheek.

"Maya, your dad asked that I tell you to settle in also. He's speaking with Randal, lining up the schedule for the dig tomorrow. He said tomorrow you could try and contact your mom on the computer if you wanted."

"Great. See you tomorrow, Kyle."

The month was just beginning, and I hoped Kyle was right—that there would be plenty of time to make discoveries.

6

Digging Up Dirt

When I woke up the next morning, my body felt as stiff as the Tin Man's in *The Wizard of Oz*. Overnight, the cold had seeped in and chilled my bones. I creaked out of bed. I wanted to hurry and wish Dad good luck on his first big day. Luckily, the room I shared with Karen had its own bathroom, and within seconds I was standing under a hot shower.

I had given up on tagging along—I couldn't figure how to stow away on a dogsled. By the time I got to the lab, it was buzzing with activity. Dad was running around, organizing gear and directing West and Justice on what to pack next on the sleds. The dig area was accessible only by dogsleds or snowmobiles. Two huge sleds waited outside, each with a line of dogs yapping next to it. They looked much skinnier than the huskies I had seen on television. Justice loaded up some boxes on the back of one of the sleds. He raised a hand and waved to me, and I waved back.

"What can I do to help?" I asked Dad.

"No need," he said, winking at me. "We're almost ready to go."

"Are you sure? I can get the lab ready for when you get back. Research, prep work—just write me a list," I said, pushing forward through a pile of gear.

"No, thanks. Have some fun. Explore the station," Dad said.

"But I want to help. Are you sure there isn't something I can do?" I asked, but Dad had already walked away, his attention on the task at hand. There was nothing I could do but observe the scientists packing up their gear.

Dad, Karen, and Justice were on one sled, and West, Ivan, and Randal were on the other. Katsu was staying behind, which I found a little odd. Why come all this way and not go to the dig site? I would've gladly taken his spot.

The dig site was about ten miles away from camp, and the group didn't expect to return until late in the afternoon. As the sleds slid away from the station, I found myself crossing my fingers and hoping really hard that Dad would find the mammoth that he had spent his whole life seeking. But if he wasn't going to put me to work, then I was on my own.

+ + +

Kyle had plans to work on the helicopter with one of the mechanics. I watched as he followed a black-clad worker to the hangar where the helicopter was kept. It must be nice to have a helicopter, a hangar, and mechanics of your own.

I cracked open my field notebook and selected a studious blue pen. I wondered if ink could freeze and realized what a great experiment that would make—trying to determine the exact temperature that freezing occurred. In the meantime, I made a mental note not to do any writing outside.

Day One: Explore the station and take pictures for my presentation to the class.

Mom filled her field notebooks with scribbled thoughts, observations, and drawings in the margins. Pressed flowers and leaves would fall out when I flipped the pages. Once, a dead bug fell out, though I wasn't sure if she had meant to keep it or if the poor bug had accidentally crawled in . . . and hadn't crawled out. But ice and snow did not mix well with paper, so I would have to take pictures instead.

I drew a map of the station in my notebook and started snapping photos of each area. The first pictures I took were of my room and Dad's room. Next, I hit the lab and the medical facility. I was starting to feel a little like Jake, snooping around every corner, taking pictures of anything that might be interesting. Maybe my project was a little like a documentary, except so far I only had still-life photos of the station.

When I stepped outside, I reached down and grabbed the blue guideline. Hanging by each door were hooks attached to nylon belts that we were supposed to wear and then clip on to the guide rope, but it wasn't that windy and there was no storm forecasted, so I just held the rope loosely under my gloved hand and walked along. Still, I was glad the line was there.

I wanted to get a shot of the door to Randal's private room as a joke to send back to Zoey. When I turned the corner that led to the room and looked through the viewfinder, I saw Katsu slinking out of the off-limits room. He glanced quickly over his shoulder and then hurried away, pulling the door closed behind him. A big round ring of keys jingled in his hands. He had a key!

I snapped a few shots of him and then ducked back out of sight. The sound of the clicking camera was deafening. I flattened against the wall and forced myself to breathe slowly. What was he doing sneaking around in the off-limits room? Katsu had been with Dad and me when West gave us the tour and told us *never* to enter Randal's private space. Busted!

Hoping that Katsu hadn't seen or heard me, I peered around the corner. I waited a few more seconds until I was sure that he had gone, and then I followed. I stopped in front of the door to Randal's secret room. The sign clearly said "Private." I tested the doorknob—locked, like I knew it would be. So . . . had Katsu stolen the keys, or was he allowed inside? And what big secret was Randal hiding behind that door?

+ + +

Once I had finished taking pictures of the base, I decided to go and see if I could get on one of the computers to e-mail Zoey and Mom. As I approached the comm center, I heard Katsu's voice coming from the room. Clearly, he was using the satellite phone. And talking quite loudly. Eavesdropping was a terrible thing. It was nosy, rude, and unacceptable behavior for good, upstanding girls, but it was also occasionally entertaining and enlightening. I wedged myself close to the crack in the door. Katsu's back was to me. He was sifting through a stack of papers as he spoke.

"Yes, yes . . . Calm down." He pulled a folder from his papers and opened it on the desk in front of him. "Hold on a moment. Let me check my documents." He flipped through some pages until he found the one he wanted. "Yes, it's right here in writing. The contract is very clear." He turned toward the light, and I could see him squinting at the paper. "Don't you trust me?"

He rubbed his temple and held the phone a few inches from his ear. Then he said, "No! What? . . . We need more space. That's too small . . . And make sure there's parking. And no food. The last lab you arranged for us smelled like cabbage." He cradled the phone against his shoulder and cleaned his glasses with a handkerchief.

I muffled a laugh. Who wants a lab that stinks of cabbage? But I was thinking that he must be serious about his research back home if he was already getting a lab set up.

He rubbed his eyes and exhaled an impatient sigh. "Figure it out. And do it quickly . . . From what I've seen today, everything's on track." He paused. "No, he has been at the dig site all day."

So, if the "he" that Katsu was talking about was Randal—who was indeed at the dig site all day—then it sounded like Randal didn't know that Katsu had broken into his private room. But I still wondered what it was that Katsu saw that made him so convinced the project was going well. I inched closer, eager to hear more.

"Of course I'm sure. What do you take me for? . . . We will have the DNA samples, and I will be returning to the lab—unless you are unable to get a decent facility. What about the one we saw last week? . . . Then call an exterminator! Must I do everything myself?"

He was silent for a moment, listening and collecting his papers. Then he laughed loudly in a barking, seal-like way. "There is no one here interested in the serious science. One of the scientists is an anthropologist and the other is a paleontologist. But both are lightweights."

He was talking about Karen and Dad. I scowled. I didn't know about Karen, but Dad was no lightweight. I couldn't wait to tell him what Katsu was up to. I listened more intently than ever.

"Randal's ego is huge. It's all about legacy with these guys. He's a buffoon. He wants to be remembered. He is a rich walrus playing on the ice . . . I can't wait to get home."

Though I was a fan of walruses, normally it wasn't a

compliment to be called one. And neither was it nice to refer to someone as a buffoon. Katsu had seemed so polite before, but now I was seeing another side of him.

"It will all be worth it when I break the genetic code. Results are everything . . . Good, good. Now I must go."

DNA? Genetic code? I pulled out my notebook and started taking notes.

What was Katsu after? If it was money, Randal would be a good target. He had already funded the expedition and brought everyone out here. But Katsu hadn't mentioned money. He wanted results. The question was, what kind of results was he looking for?

I leaned in more closely . . . and accidentally nudged the door with my shoulder. The hinges squeaked, and the door swung wide open. Katsu jerked up and turned around in his chair. I tried to back out of the doorway, but it was too late. He knew I was there.

I stepped into the room. Maybe he hadn't seen me crouched at the door, eavesdropping.

I tried to pretend that I had just arrived. I breathed deeply and slapped my arms together, pretending that I had just walked in out of the cold. "Hello. It's freezing out there," I said a little too loudly. I put a big smile on my face. "Oh, sorry—are you on the phone?"

Katsu eyed me suspiciously but just nodded.

"I was hoping to use the computer to send my friend some pictures of the station. Are you using it?"

"No," he said, and held up the receiver.

"Right. Sorry." I used a mock whisper and inched over to the computer. "I'll be as quiet as a mouse."

I sat at the desk and pulled out my camera. Katsu turned his back to me and whispered into the phone. The high-end computer zinged to life.

Randal had spared no expense on the equipment. I connected my camera and uploaded some images. Then I pulled up the browser and began to write an e-mail to Zoey.

I wanted to research DNA and genetics, but with Katsu hovering and eyeing me suspiciously, I couldn't risk him seeing what I was reading. Instead, I sent an urgent message to Zoey. She would have to do the legwork and dig up some dirt on Katsu's and Ivan's scientific specialties. Zoey loved a good mystery. Plus, it involved DNA and genetic code. Anything sciency got her excited.

Zoey,
Need assistance. Research mammoth DNA and genetic code? Also, look into Dr. Katsu Takahashi and Dr. Ivan Petrov. Something is up. Secret room. Eyes everywhere. Pictures attached.
Later,
Maya
P. S. Adventure boy on premises!

Then I opened a new blank message and wrote an e-mail to Mom.

Katsu kept talking. Now he was speaking in a normal voice and I could hear what he was saying. "It was good to speak with you . . . Yes, I will keep you posted on our progress here at the station," he said. Then he hung up the phone with a loud clunk.

He glared at me the way a crocodile eyes its prey from right below the surface of the water. He eased closer. His face went neutral, calm as a pool. He leaned on the desk. His sweater was made of knobby green wool—the color of a reptile.

"I see you have been taking pictures." Katsu motioned to my camera.

"For a school project and my friend back home. I'm photographing the station." My throat was dry.

"I see. Very studious of you."

"What are you doing today?" I asked. I tried to read his expression, but his face was too carefully blank. Crocodiles are emotionless creatures. "Working on something secret?" I pried, tiptoeing near the water's edge.

Katsu blinked slowly but didn't take the bait. "No, just some boring business. My work begins when the mammoth is brought back."

"What will you do with it?"

Katsu's teeth looked small and sharp when he grinned.

He reached over to collect his papers. "I will study it in great detail. Just like your father."

I may not have known what he was up to, but he was nothing like my father. He watched me from the corner of his eye as he left the room, and I wondered if he realized that I was watching him, too.

My stomach rumbled. All this sneaking around was making me hungry. I decided to head for the mess to see what there was to eat.

When I got there, Kyle was digging through one of the cabinets. He had a grease stain on his sweatshirt and a spot on the tip of his nose that made me smile.

"Hey, I found freeze-dried chili. Want some?" Kyle asked. "No one's here, so I think we're on our own as far as lunch goes."

"Sure," I said. "That sounds great." Actually, it didn't. Zoey and I had done an experiment a few years back where we ate nothing but freeze-dried food for a whole week, trying to acclimate our bodies for space travel. (That was a long story, and it involved Zoey's failed application to space camp.) All the freeze-dried meals came in shiny metallic pouches and *sounded* great from the description. But dried beans and meat weren't tasty, especially after the water was added. I didn't tell Kyle that, however.

Once we had reconstituted the chili and heated it up in the microwave, we poured it into mugs and sat down at the table. I toasted some rolls that I found in a cabinet, but it was hard to focus on the food.

"Is something wrong?" Kyle asked. "You seem sort of jumpy."

I pushed my chili around in my mug. "It's nothing."

"It doesn't sound like nothing."

I really wanted to confide in Kyle, tell him what I had heard and ask him what he thought. But I wasn't sure that was a good idea. What if it was nothing? What if I was overreacting? If I told him and it turned out that Katsu was fine, I didn't want to get Dad in trouble. I decided to change the subject. "I'm just acclimating." I took a bite of my roll.

"I know how it can be. It's tough being away from home, especially your first time on an expedition."

"It's not that. Though I guess I do miss my mom and my best friend," I said. Kyle seemed really nice, and of all the people here, he would understand, but I hesitated. "Have you met lots of other kids on expeditions?" I asked.

"Hardly ever." He swallowed a bite of chili. "I was really glad when I heard that you were coming with your dad."

"Really?" My pulse raced. I had no idea he would be excited for company.

"Sure. My mom works all the time, which is cool, but I get bored. You have to make your own fun in these places." He shrugged and stuffed a roll into his mouth. "It's tough meeting people and making friends—real friends in person, not just on the computer."

"Well, now you have a real-life friend," I said.

"What do you think they will find out there?" Kyle asked.

"*Mammuthus primigenius*," I said with a raised chin. "Or as it is more commonly known, a giant hairy elephant."

He snorted. "Then they'll lug it back and study it. Take pictures, measure it, record every little detail."

"Then the poor mammoth will probably go to a museum. So more scientists will be able to study it up close and personal," I said.

"My mom told me that lots of indigenous people believe that removing bones and creatures from their resting place is bad luck and that to do so brings a curse."

"You mean like the mummy's curse in Egypt? Many of the Egyptian tombs were said to be cursed and anyone who opened them would die a terrible death."

"Do you believe in curses?" Kyle asked.

"Maybe. Lots of archaeologists died after opening King Tut's tomb, so it could happen." It didn't seem very scientific, but I had to keep an open mind.

Kyle's eyes went wide. "Do you think mammoths bring curses? Do you think this site is cursed?" Suddenly, he jumped up and ran out of the room.

After a minute or two, I heard moaning. Then the lights shut off.

Kyle came back into the room with a flashlight held under his chin, casting a creepy glow over his face. His head and arms were loosely wrapped in toilet paper that *kind of* looked like the decaying bandages of a mummy. "You have entered into my tomb. You are under the mummy's curse." He held out his arms and lurched toward me, groaning like the walking dead. "I'm going to eat you."

I dodged his mummy arms as he tried to grab me. "You make a great mummy," I said. "Not very scary, though." But then I sat down and let him wrap a roll of toilet paper around my head and shoulders.

"Join us . . . join the extraordinary league of mummies."

A shiver went down my spine as he continued to wrap me in toilet paper. I decided to play along and stood up, taking the stumbling mummy position with my arms outstretched in front of me. Groaning, I followed Kyle. We stumbled around the room for a while, then headed down the hall to the rec room, where we finally collapsed onto the sofas.

I pulled toilet paper off my face. "I think we'll find a mammoth and everyone will be happy." Wishful thinking, perhaps. Excavation digs could take weeks to uncover real results. But Randal had brought us all out here for a reason, and we were going to find something big. We had to.

Filled with that good feeling, as well as a bunch of freeze-dried beans, I decided to tell Kyle about Katsu sneaking out of Randal's private room.

He listened to my story intently, and when I was done, he said, "Sounds like we have only one option."

"And what's that?" I asked.

"We get inside that private room and see what Katsu found that was so convincing."

I hesitated, knowing that once I agreed, I couldn't turn back.

Kyle wiggled his eyebrows at me.

"I'll do it, but we really shouldn't try to break in." But I couldn't keep from smiling. "Who knows? The private room might be cursed like a king's tomb," I said, and we both laughed.

I was relieved. I didn't have to investigate this alone.

7

The Private Room

Kyle and I were on a mission. Break into the secret room like two black-clad, stealthy panthers. Except we weren't wearing black, unless we counted our boots, and the boots were not stealthy—more like clunky.

The plan was set. Unlike Dad, who had theorized that the room was probably just a cozy library where Randal could put his woolly socked feet up and wiggle his toes in front of a toasty fire, I suspected something else entirely. I was willing to bet that Randal had bigger secrets. Billionaire secrets. *Privacy* was another word for hiding place. Katsu had discovered something, and I needed to know what.

While Kyle went to borrow an extra set of keys from the mechanic he had been working with that morning, I waited outside Randal's private room, making sure Katsu didn't return. Finally, red-faced and panting, Kyle came racing around the corner, skidding down the hall in his nonstealthy boots.

"Slow down," I said, casually glancing around, like I wasn't looking. I was the lookout, which meant I stood outside the room and acted nonchalant.

"I thought you said to hurry," he countered, a line of sweat trailing down his temple.

"I did. But it's the first law of spying—act like you belong, and no one will question that you shouldn't be doing what you're doing. Running just makes you look suspicious, like you don't want to get caught."

"Right . . . spymaster." He dangled the keys, a wry smile on his face.

"How did you get the guy to give them to you?" I asked.

"I told him that I needed to get into the supply cabinet for extra toilet paper. I don't think he believed me, but no guy questions another guy's need for toilet paper."

Kyle tried three or four keys before finding the right one. He glanced up and down the hall one last time and then carefully unlocked the door. Together we slipped inside. The smell of rubber cement filled the room. I felt for the light switch and turned it on. Immediately, my heart sank. The room was nothing more than a comfy nook, complete with bookshelves and a gas fireplace.

This was terrible! Dad had been right. Two leather wingbacks sat in front of the hearth. Nothing strange. Nothing secret. But we were inside now, so I closed the door behind us in case someone came down the hall.

I groaned, utterly mortified. "It's just a plain old library. Randal probably comes in here to read and relax. What a waste of a locked room. How could I have been so wrong?"

"You give up fast." Kyle smirked and studied the room.

"I wasn't giving up," I said. "But look around. It's pretty obvious that this is not a great secret."

He tapped his temple. "To the untrained eye, maybe."

"What does that mean?" I asked.

"Something isn't right." Kyle crept around the perimeter, examining the walls and the floor.

The space didn't seem that unusual. It contained all the library essentials—bookshelves, two chairs, and a fireplace.

The only strange thing was the size. "It's smaller than I expected." I walked from one side of the room to the other, and it took me only a few steps.

"Exactly." Kyle pointed at me. "And Randal doesn't do small."

"Randal does big—really big. And what is that rubber-cement smell? It really stinks." I wrinkled my nose.

Kyle sniffed. "It's coming from somewhere close."

The heat kicked on. A vent rattled, causing me to jump.

"Nervous?" Kyle asked.

"No," I lied. I was hoping he couldn't hear my heart pounding in my chest.

"Let's scope this place out. Something seems fake, like a stage."

There was a needlepoint pillow with seals stitched on it placed on one of the chairs. A knitted mauve throw was crumpled up on the ottoman. I ran a finger along the edge of a brass lamp.

"What if this isn't the whole room?" Kyle stepped over

to the bookshelf. "There could be an entire other room behind it." He ran his hands down the shelving unit.

"You mean . . . there's a room within a room?" I pictured the map of the station I'd drawn in my notebook this morning and realized he was right. According to the layout, this room should be as big as the rec room—twice as big as it was.

Kyle shifted books around, trying to see behind them. "It should be on the other side of the shelves."

"How do we get to it?" I asked.

Kyle shoved the books back. His face twisted up in concentration. "There has to be a trigger. Some way to get behind the wall."

"A secret panel?" Excitement filled me. This was a puzzle—like a real-life video game. "How do we find the trick to opening it?"

"See anything that looks strange or out of place?" Kyle asked.

I studied the room again. Totally normal. It even had a fake fireplace. *That* was it. "The fireplace is gas. It's not real," I said. "Randal seems like he would have a *real* fireplace, with wood. Not a fake one. Unless he didn't have a choice."

I shifted the items on the mantel, but the fireplace didn't budge. I flicked a switch on the wall and the flames in the hearth jumped to life. "See? Gas. Makes lighting a fire a cinch," I said. I turned off the artificial flames and kept looking. But nothing budged.

"Wait—the switch," I said. "There are two of them." One turned on the fire. But what about the other one? Kyle reached over and flipped the switch.

Silently, the fireplace swung forward, revealing a secret door and a small opening.

My heart raced. "This is it!" I couldn't believe it. "We've found a secret room!"

"Hurry up. We don't have much time."

Kyle and I slipped through the small door and into Randal's secret room.

This was more like what I had expected. There was a giant polar bear rug on the floor, its mouth wide in a vicious roar. A huge stuffed tiger was mounted on a giant log suspended from the ceiling in the corner of the room. Randal had displayed a collection of his kills. Tiny golden plaques labeled the trophies: caribou, snow leopard, and an arctic fox.

One wall was covered with shelves filled with strange fossils. There were also dozens of sharp teeth and claws. Dad had told me once that a lot of rich collectors buy up fossils from different dig sites and keep them as souvenirs. Randal had his own treasure trove.

But the fossils weren't the main attraction. A table about the size and shape of a Ping-Pong table dominated the space. On top of it was a huge model of a miniature world: a winter wonderland. In this snowy landscape, tiny people wore fur coats and were surrounded by dozens of tiny animals. The fake snow glittered. There was a glassy water area with ice floes and polar bears and seals swimming and resting on the chunks of floating ice. At first I thought the model was cute. Maybe creating miniatures was Randal's hobby. But then I saw the creatures with curved tusks. The woolly mammoths. This landscape was from the past—a reenactment of a long-ago world populated with giant beasts.

"Weird. I guess Randal has a lot of time on his hands," Kyle said.

"Wait—look at this sign." There was a hand-painted sign at one end of the table. It read "Clark's Mammoth Park."

"He has a great imagination." Then Kyle asked the question we both were thinking. "You don't think this is meant to be a real park? Do you?"

"It seems more like a fantasy." I reached down and ran my finger over the icy water and stroked the back of a majestic polar bear. "There are no more mammoths. They don't exist."

"Yeah, but this whole station is a fantasy."

I was still admiring the model of the Arctic when I said, "Maybe that's what Katsu was talking about with the DNA."

"What do you mean?" Kyle looked at me dumbfounded. "What DNA?"

"DNA is a map, a blueprint of an organism's makeup," I said.

"Duh, I know what it *is*, but what would Katsu want it for?"

Dad and I had watched *Jurassic Park* like a million times. We had even watched the sequels. *Jurassic Park* was his favorite movie. It was about scientists who collected dinosaur DNA that had been trapped in amber. They used the DNA to create live dinosaurs for a zoolike park where people could come and see the formerly extinct creatures. In theory, it was pretty cool. Who wouldn't want to see real-live dinosaurs up close? But in the movie, the dinosaurs escaped from their enclosures and ran wild, attacking the scientists and totally destroying the park. The lesson was that dinosaurs were extinct for a reason. Except, of course, not everyone got the message.

Dad had told me that some Russian scientists had dreamed of creating a park with live mammoths to help the local economy in Siberia. It was a way the scientists could bring tourists to the area, even though I couldn't imagine the icy tundra being a popular vacation spot.

That must have been why Katsu was after the mammoth's genetic code.

"He wants to make mammoths," I said.

"You mean bring back mammoths, for real? That's crazy." Kyle leaned forward and fingered a miniature beast.

"Is it really that crazy?" I asked.

With genetic material, Katsu could clone a mammoth. From the look of this model park, Randal wanted to bring back the mammoth. This miniature scene wasn't the past. It was the future.

"That's impossible." Kyle's brow creased. "It would mean some *serious* science."

"Katsu was talking about DNA on the phone with someone. It sounded like he had already gotten a lab ready. People are waiting for him to return from this trip. My dad once told me that scientists have been trying for years to gather enough viable DNA to clone a mammoth."

"So it *could* happen? He could really do it?"

"I guess he could," I said. "I can't really imagine a park full of mammoths. But look at this model. Randal has a lot of money. And with his money—and his ambition—it sure looks like he plans on trying."

Kyle picked up one of the miniature mammoths. Whoever built the model had created whole herds, including adults and their young. The snowy wonderland was also covered in caribou and polar bears. It was beautiful, but it looked eerie, hemmed in by fences and viewing platforms. Keeping all the mammoths contained would be a huge feat. They were migratory animals, and they wouldn't want to stay in one place.

"It's like a zoo," Kyle said.

"I can't see keeping giant mammoths in a zoo. Even one like this," I said. The model was beautiful but sad. I didn't want there to be living mammoths. They would be the only ones of their kind, kept in a pen, alone, out of their own time.

"Randal's crazy if he thinks he can really pull this off."

I remembered how Katsu had talked about Randal on the phone. He didn't think too highly of Randal, either. "Maybe this is a big scam, and Katsu is trying to steal the genetic material out from under Randal, preying on his dreams," I said.

"I could believe that. Legacy is really important to Randal. This park would be a whopping legacy."

"He has to know how crazy it is. Scientists have trouble cloning common animals that are alive today. It would be almost impossible to clone a whole extinct herd. He has to realize that this park could never happen."

"Guys like Randal don't know the meaning of the word *impossible*. Look how he built this station. And now that he's found a mammoth, who knows what he'll do?" Kyle said.

"I still don't believe it," I said. "If Katsu said he could do it, he must be lying. It's got to be a scam."

I almost felt sorry for Randal. Then I saw the claw of the polar bear skin rug and the room filled with trophy fossils, and I didn't feel so bad for him. Scam or no scam, he was used to getting his prizes, whether fossil, skin, or fur coat. Now he wanted the real thing.

I imagined that Randal, with his drive, would do whatever it took to build a park. But something still didn't make sense. Randal had just found the mammoth. How could he have planned all of this so fast—built a model and everything? Something didn't add up.

A banging sound filtered into the room.

"Did you hear something?" I asked.

Kyle peeked into the library. "Someone's unlocking the door!"

"Shut the fireplace!" I cried.

Kyle swung the fireplace closed, and we scrambled to hide under the model table. I dropped to the floor and crawled like a crab. My heart banged against my chest. It was hard to be stealthy and brave when you were about to get caught for breaking the rules. We were in big trouble.

I slowed my breathing, trying to calm myself. Kyle and I stared at each other as we heard the secret fireplace panel creak open, and then footsteps scuffed across the floor. A voice hummed a tune right there in the room with us. To me, it sounded like Katsu. Kyle put his finger over his lips, and then he held out his hand. A tiny mammoth sat in his palm. He had forgotten to put it back! I hoped Katsu didn't notice that one of the herd was missing.

My nose itched. I sniffed. Kyle's eyes widened. I held my breath, trying not to sneeze. Who knows the last time someone had dusted here. The humming stopped. All I could see were large boot toes poking under the table.

The sound of dogs barking drifted into the room. Katsu

hurried from the room, and we heard the door slam behind him.

Kyle and I were in the clear. I let out a gasp.

"They can't be back yet—it's too early," Kyle whispered. "What do you think has happened?"

"I don't know. They're supposed to be at the site all day." Suddenly, panic flooded through me. Digs were dangerous. Anything could have happened. What if Dad was hurt?

"We've got to go see," Kyle said.

Even though we were alone, we tiptoed quietly out of the secret room and then out of the small library and into the hallway.

There was only one sled in the compound. I looked through an ice-crusted window and saw that Dad was already off the sled and running into the building. He disappeared into the changing room.

Kyle and I followed him over to the lab building. The door banged open, bringing a gust of icy air shooting through me like a dozen arrows. Immediately I could tell that it had been a bad day at the dig site.

And I had a feeling it was about to get a lot worse at the station.

8

Tusk Troubles

The air in the lab was warm and muggy. I coughed, hoping Dad would turn around and tell me what had happened at the site to bring him back so early. But he just paced around the lab. He was fuming. He yanked off his hat and threw it to the floor. His goggles had left marks around his eyes, making his face look scarred and wild. His face was so red, it was practically a new shade. Red was the color of conflict, heat, and anger. Mars was the red planet, named for the Roman god of war. Zoey had told me the two moons of Mars were named fear and panic, and as I circled my dad, I felt like a small moon.

"I should have known! I should have seen something like this coming. Money must rot the brain—must make people do crazy things." His eyes roamed the room, unfocused. His fists were balled up. I had never seen Dad this mad.

"What's wrong?" I eased up beside him. "Did something happen at the site?"

He didn't answer. It was like I wasn't even in the room. I could feel the anger radiating off him.

"What's happened? What happened with the mammoth?" I asked, resting my hand on his sleeve.

When he finally looked at me, his eyes were sad, dark pools. "The worst thing possible."

The worst thing that I could think of was that the mammoth was rotten, having been exposed to the elements and then thawing. Or that scavengers had torn it to shreds and carried it away. I had heard Dad talk about expeditions where scientists went on grueling treks into the brutal Arctic landscape of Russia, returning home heartbroken, with only a piece of wrinkly gray skin the size of a doormat with a few wiry red mammoth hairs attached, because that was all that was left of the animal. All that work for a scrap of old, stinky flesh. Maybe all that was left of our mammoth was a clump of hair or a pile of bones. I wished he would just tell me.

Soon the other sled returned from the site. Ivan and West stumbled into the room, dragging a huge canvas bag behind them. They hoisted it up and set it on the table and then peeled the tough fabric back, exposing an enormous tusk. I rushed over to get a better look. Kyle came over also and stood next to me, and we both stared at it. His mom had followed Ivan and West into the room.

Looking at the tusk, I told myself that things weren't *that* bad—at least they had the ivory. Actually, I was surprised to see the tusk had made it back OK; usually that was the first thing to be stolen. Ivory was very valuable and often scavengers cut it off to sell for money. Randal had said that the tusks remained attached to the beast. He had showed us photographs and film footage at the welcome dinner. So where was the rest of the mammoth?

I ran my finger over the tusk. It was dark brown and mottled with tan and white streaks. I couldn't believe that I was looking at—and touching—a real mammoth tusk. It was beautiful and foreign, something I had only before seen in pictures, movies, or books.

"Nice, isn't it?" Dad asked. I felt everyone watching me, hovering closer.

"Yes," I said, but tentatively. Somehow I knew the question was a setup.

"Look closer." Dad had an angry smirk on his face.

West turned his back to Dad, avoiding his gaze. My stomach rolled over, and I leaned in closer to the tusk. Ivan handed me a magnifying glass. I held the glass over it and focused my attention. Again I ran my fingers over the smooth surface. The ivory looked good . . . too good. I realized why Dad was so upset.

"I get it," I said.

Dad nodded.

Randal hurried into the room at that moment, then stopped and cringed at the sight of the tusk.

"Good," Dad said, looking directly at him. "The man of the hour . . . Maya, tell Mr. Clark the problem with his *forgery*."

"This tusk is a fake," I said. "And not a very good one."
When Randal didn't respond, Dad slumped.

How could Randal have betrayed the whole expedition?
I wondered.

"A fake?" Katsu said. He looked around the room searching our faces, refusing to believe what I was saying. "This
can't be happening!" Spit flew from his mouth.

Kyle moved closer to the table. "How do you know?"

"There aren't any cracks in the ivory. If it even *is* ivory."
I felt terrible. It was obvious to me, and I don't even know
that much about mammoths. If an amateur like me could
spot the fake, then the forgery was pathetic. Randal hadn't
even tried to get a *good* fake.

"I thought that was a good thing. I've seen elephant
tusks that don't have cracks, and they're real," Kyle said.

"Very smart," Dad said. "Go on, Maya."

"Well, that's because for the most part, elephant tusks
grow straight. The elephant uses trees to sharpen its
tusks. Mammoth tusks grew curved because they didn't
have trees to rub them against to shorten and sharpen
them," I said. "The cracks are natural, expected." I knew
my tusks.

"Huh," Kyle said, and he actually looked interested in
what I was saying.

"When they grew curved, they had tiny cracks," I said.

"This *tusk* doesn't have cracks . . . and isn't even real
ivory." Dad pulled the tusk closer, took his penknife out

of his pocket, and dug a chunk out of the tusk with the blade, sending bits crumbling.

Karen reached out her hand and ran the broken pieces through her fingers, leaving white chalky dust behind on her skin.

"It's made of plaster." Dad shook his head. He turned to Randal. "Did you really think I was so stupid that I wouldn't know a fake movie-prop tusk when I saw it? You didn't even bother to obtain a real tusk. With all your money, that would have been easy."

Jake was making a wide circle of the room, catching all of the action on film. He had no shame. I wondered if he knew all about the fakes. Dad must have, too, because he looked right into the camera. "Do we have your industrious nephew to thank for the props?"

Jake suddenly stared at the floor, refusing to look at Randal. The grand adventurer had been caught by his own pathetic trap, and I wondered how he planned to charm his way out of this situation. I narrowed my eyes and waited for him to respond. The room grew quiet.

Randal finally spoke. "You exceeded my expectations. I knew that you would find out about the mammoth sooner or later. I thought that we would be further along with the dig and that by then it wouldn't matter." He leaned against the table, head held high, confident even in disgrace.

"'Further along'?" Dad yelled. "'It wouldn't matter'?" I could tell he was trying to compose himself, but he blew up anyway. "There's no mammoth! How could that not matter? It is the only reason I came here!"

"This is an insult!" Ivan bellowed. "It's a ruse. You have lied to us, Randal."

Katsu's face was pasty. There went his grand plan for the DNA. There was no mammoth, which meant no clone, no need for a laboratory, no Mammoth Park. The mammoths would stay frozen in the past.

"I should have seen it," Dad went on. "The way the tusks were sticking out of the ice perfectly. Staged like a movie set. Massive ivory curving upward out of the frozen ground."

"We all wanted to believe it." Karen rested her hand on his shoulder, but Dad pulled away. He wasn't done with Randal yet.

"Did Jake get it all on film? All our ooohs and ahhhs? All of our excitement and thrills? You had us fooled. You played us. How could you do this to us?" Dad tapped his chest and then pointed at the others. "We're scientists. This isn't a joke. It's not a rich man's game to us."

"That is where you are wrong," Randal said quietly. "I brought you all here for a reason. This isn't a game to me, either. And the ice is not empty." His eyes suddenly sparkled mischievously. "You are correct that there is no mammoth, and I was a fool to think that such revered scientists would fall for such a ruse. But let me assure you that the expedition isn't over. In fact, the real expedition has just begun."

"What do you mean, the *real* expedition?" Katsu asked.

"Not me," said Dad. "I've had enough. I'm going home."

Katsu held up a hand. "Let him speak. I will listen to what you have to say, Randal. One chance." Katsu made a one sign with his finger.

"Please, Jason. Just listen." Randal was almost begging. "I am sure I can change your mind about me."

Dad stopped short of leaving the room, but he didn't turn around.

"Next to my family, this station is the most important thing to me," Randal said. He squared his shoulders. "To explore the Arctic wilderness has always been my dream. I read stories of great ships running aground in the icy waters and men struggling to forge through, living and dying to explore the great frozen cap. We're floating up here, just floating." His voice now was deep and booming, like an actor's. He paused for dramatic effect, then cleared his throat. "I believe with all my heart and soul that there is . . . greatness . . . under that ice, waiting for us. I found something there at the foot of the mountains."

"Do you know how ridiculous that sounds?" Dad asked. "It's a childish dream. You had no right to do what you did. We all have dreams. Yours are no more important than the rest of ours."

Ouch. Dad was angry. I didn't agree with Randal's methods. But we all had the same dream, didn't we? We all wanted to make a great discovery. Something about that made me sympathetic toward Randal, even though he had fooled us.

I pulled on Dad's sleeve, and he looked at me. "Maybe we should hear him out," I said. "Give him a chance to explain what happened. He did fly us all the way up here."

"That's right. I did," Randal said. He smiled at me, and I felt a little like a traitor. "You have a very bright daughter."

"She has a big heart," Dad said, some of his anger melting away. "All right. Go ahead and explain."

Randal rubbed his palms together. "Last month I did some virtual exploring using ground-penetrating radar, and some interesting data showed up."

"Cool!" Kyle said. "I've heard of that tech. Everyone is using it, from scientists to police."

"Really?" Dad said, his interest piqued. "What kind of data?"

"A mass. Take a look if you don't believe me." Randal pulled a folded-up document out of his jacket and spread it on the table for everyone to see. "It's right there in the permafrost."

The scientists crowded around the table and leaned over the document. The data looked like a bunch of charts and graphs with jagged lines. Jake and his camera hovered over the table like an annoying insect.

"That could be anything," Dad said. "It might not be a mammoth. It might not be organic. It could even be junk." He had gone cynical again, and who could blame him?

"You want us to believe that there is something there in the ice? Frankly, I don't trust you."

Randal leaned his head back. "I haven't given you any reason to trust me. *I* wouldn't trust me. But imagine the rewards when we unearth the discovery—the academic credit you have longed for will be yours, Jason. Not to mention the financial freedom to do anything you want—travel the world, fund expeditions. Never write another grant application again. Imagine it." He was practically pleading with Dad. "You all deserve this kind of success," he said, looking around the room at each person.

"It's a fool's errand. We could find nothing and waste your money and resources." Dad sighed. But something in his voice had changed.

"Then I am fairly warned and it will be my money to waste. My eyes are wide open. I know the risks."

Ivan and Katsu walked toward the door and engaged in a rapid, whispered conversation. Ivan shook his head, his brow furrowed. His voice was harsh, but when they were done talking, Katsu stepped forward. Ivan didn't look happy with the decision.

"We are here, so we will stay," Katsu said. "Though I agree with Doctor Parson. I am skeptical. But promises have been made." Katsu narrowed his eyes at Randal. "And promises must be kept."

I didn't like the sound of that.

Randal nodded to Katsu. Then he turned his attention

back to Dad. "Please, Jason. Continue on this journey with me," Randal said.

"Why don't we give it a try and see what it is?" I said to Dad. I didn't trust Randal, either, but I didn't want to go home with nothing, not even a few days in the Arctic. "We came all this way. It'll be like a vacation. We could stay a week and then go home."

"See, your daughter is game. You've traveled too far only to return home without even a few tales of adventure. I will show you the scenery when not working. See the land and meet the people."

Dad wasn't so easily swayed. "This is not Maya's decision to make. I'll have to think about it and let you know. A week isn't too long to stay, but that would be the longest I could invest."

"Let me know tonight. If you choose to leave, I can have Justice fly you out in the morning."

Karen stepped forward. "Randal, Kyle and I will be staying. I don't agree with your methods, but I understand that you did what you did to keep the project going. It was misleading, but we've all made mistakes before."

I looked over at Jake, who was fiddling with his camera. He had not filmed the latest events. That's when I connected what my dad said about the tusk being a movie prop and the model mammoth park in Randal's secret room. It was a pretty big coincidence that Randal created these grand plans to build a park and then miraculously found a frozen mammoth. Was the whole secret room staged? It had been pretty easy for Katsu, Kyle, and me to break into the locked room. Who was conning whom?

And what had Randal *really* found buried in the ice?

✦ ✦ ✦

Kyle followed me back to my room and sat down on his mom's bed.

Dad appeared a moment later and hovered in the doorway. He had a weary look on his face. I jumped up off my bed and hugged him. "I just want everything to work out," I said.

"I know you do. I'm sorry you have to be a part of this."

"I wanted there to be a mammoth." Maybe deep down I still held out hope.

"You know what they say: 'You don't find the mammoth—the mammoth finds you.'" He sighed. "It's my fault."

"It's not your fault, Dad. It's Randal's fault. He did this. He's to blame."

"No, no blame game. Tomorrow we start over." Dad ruffled my hair.

"We'll see what finds us," I said.

"OK. We can stay a week. We'll have some fun—go dogsledding, maybe build an igloo. And then we'll head home next week. I'll take a look at the dig site just to see what's there. Probably nothing, but you never know."

"Sounds good to me," Kyle said. "I'll talk to West.

Maybe Maya and I can go to the site and help out. We won't get in the way."

"Please, Dad? I really want to see the site. It won't hurt anything since there's no mammoth." I didn't mean for that to come out the way it sounded, so final, so much like a judgment.

"Yes. If you want to come, then sure." He leaned against the door frame. The nervous energy that had caused him to zing around the station that morning had all burned off. His anger was also gone. "If Karen says it's OK for Kyle to go, then it's fine by me. This is an opportunity for the both of you to see a dig site, even if there isn't a real mammoth. I'm going to go early. How about you two come up after lunch tomorrow and check it out?"

Maybe this trip would work out for the best. We could have a fun vacation and then head home. No problem.

9

Warnings

After dinner I was sitting at the computer in the comm, keeping an eagle eye out for Katsu. I didn't want him sneaking up on me and overhearing my conversation, especially since it was about him.

It was weird to be staring at Zoey in her bedroom while I was here at the station. Was this what it was like for Mom, seeing me at home cuddled up in my bedroom when she was traveling? I had a flash of homesickness, but I brushed it away. I was so relieved to see my best friend that I opened my mouth and poured out everything that had happened in the past twenty-four hours. I told her about the mammoth and how Randal had used fake tusks to lure us to the Arctic. The expedition was in total ruin, and I would probably be home in a week.

Then I said, "What did you find out?" I was still curious to learn what Zoey had managed to dig up on Ivan and Katsu.

"Well, you're up there with some heavy hitters." Zoey's fingers flew across her keyboard as she talked. "Katsu is the real deal. He's one of the top geneticists in the world. Problem is, he's a radical."

"A radical what?" I asked. The only thing radical I had noticed about Katsu was his radical addiction to hand sanitizer.

Zoey glanced into the lens. "For starters, the institute that he was working for in Japan fired him."

"People get fired all the time. That doesn't make them radical. What was he working on?" I was playing devil's advocate. I needed to hear solid proof about someone before I believed anything too extreme. All part of being a scientist.

"Cloning, genetic manipulation—all that fun stuff." A huge smile spread across Zoey's face. She loved intrigue.

"Are you serious? He's too radical for the cloning people?"

"Yep. Seems like he's all about shortcuts and instant gratification. He wants to go down in history as the first person to clone an extinct species." Zoey looked right into the camera and gave me a devious smile. "It looks like his extinct species of choice is the mammoth."

"Randal has a model of a mammoth park in his secret office." I shook my head. "Are you sure? Can mammoths really be cloned?"

"Looks like it. The science is solid. All that's needed is viable DNA. This is awesome! I'm so jealous."

"Well, don't be. The jig is up. There's no mammoth DNA to use for the cloning because it's a fake . . . I can't believe Randal faked the tusks." I shook my head again, the disappointment still raw.

"So what does Randal think he's going to find?" Zoey asked.

"He still *says* he wants to find a mammoth. But it seems fishy to me."

"What else could it be? Another fossil?" Zoey asked. "Maybe something crash landed from outer space, like a satellite or a spacecraft."

I laughed. "That would be cool. But I doubt it. I'm thinking it's just another animal fossil. Who knows?"

"I can dream." Zoey shoved a gummy bear into her mouth. "But Randal had better hope it's more than a dream."

"What do you mean?"

Zoey tapped on her computer keyboard. "Randal is in some serious trouble. I looked up Ivan, and trust me, you don't want to mess with him. He's part of a tough Russian crime family. Looks like they invest in companies doing scientific research, experiments, and drug trials. Some people think they develop drugs on the black market— that sort of thing."

"You mean he's not really a scientist?" The situation was getting worse.

"No, he's a scientist all right, but his family likes to make a lot of money, and they don't like to follow any rules."

"I bet they invested in Randal's company," I mused aloud. "But what are they going to do now? Do you think he's in danger? They wouldn't hurt him, would they?" Or anyone else, for that matter . . . like the scientists helping him?

"Let's just say he'd *better* find something in that ice. Something to make up for there not being a mammoth," Zoey said. "I'll be happy when you get back home safely."

A door slammed behind me. I jerked around in my chair.

Kyle was standing there, still in his outdoor gear. "Maya—come quick!" He doubled over and sucked in mouthfuls of air.

"What's wrong?" More drama, probably.

Then I heard a loud growling coming from outside. Kyle and I raced over to the window. A gray plume of smoke billowed across the sky. The rumbling grew louder. "It's the helicopter!" he yelled. Panic shot through me. Justice flew the helicopter, and I didn't want anything bad to happen to him. Suddenly, we could see it, hovering in the air, weaving unsteadily toward the landing pad.

"Sounds like something's wrong with the engine," Kyle said, clutching his face mask in his hands.

The helicopter disappeared behind the hangar, smoke spiraling upward.

"We have to do something. See if we can help," I said.

I turned to shut down the computer. "Zoey, gotta go."

I didn't wait for Zoey's response. The last thing I saw was her eyes wide with concern before the screen went black.

"Come on!" Kyle said.

I grabbed my coat, and we raced to the hangar. By the time we got there, the helicopter had landed. The acrid smell of smoke filled the air, but at least the helicopter hadn't crashed. Justice and a mechanic were already checking the engine. I was surprised to see Ivan looming around the hangar with his luggage. His arms were crossed over his massive chest, and he had an angry scowl on his face. He wasn't hiding the fact that he wanted to leave the station immediately. Kyle and I hung back when we saw that he and Randal were having a *discussion*.

"You can't hold us hostage! That's illegal," Ivan said, his brow twisted. "I'll call the authorities if you don't let me leave immediately. This is an outrage. First, you lie about the discovery and now you try to force me to stay here at the station."

"Calm down, Ivan. No one is holding you hostage," Randal replied. "As you can plainly see, we've had some technical difficulties and will have to postpone any outgoing flights. You are more than welcome to find other means of transportation off the station if you wish."

"That's impossible, and you know it." Ivan paced back and forth, his gaze shifting around the hangar nervously. "I must go. I can't stay here."

Ivan had been tense from the first moment I saw him

in the helicopter. I don't think the Arctic agreed with him.

Randal had little consolation for the big man. "If you want Justice to fly you out, then you'll just have to wait."

"It will take over a week to arrange for another flight to come here and take me to the nearest hub," Ivan complained. His panicked eyes did not match his gruff exterior.

"I'll do all I can to get the helicopter up and running before then. Just stay for the week and see what turns up." Randal buried his hands in his pockets.

"You're treading on thin ice, Randal. My family is not happy, and you don't want to anger them. When they find out we have been scammed, you will be in big trouble."

"Really? I thought your family would appreciate my techniques. Seeing as how they are quite knowledgeable in the art of scamming." Anger flashed over Ivan's face, but Randal continued calmly, "I'll deliver on my promise."

With that comment it was clear that Ivan did not intimidate Randal. Personally, I would be very afraid of him. Ivan was a giant and he had fists the size of grapefruits, and now he was trapped at the station like a wild animal in a zoo. And from what Zoey had said, Ivan's family knew how to get what they wanted.

Randal rested his hand on the Russian's shoulder. "We will find something under the ice. I know it. Just be patient. One week—remember? One week was all I asked."

He may have asked, but it was clear none of us really had a choice, especially now that the helicopter was down.

A smoky gray cloud hovered in the air over us. No one was leaving the station. We were all grounded.

Ivan was furious. "You'd just better hope that there is a mammoth or something with viable DNA in the ground. You are in debt to my family, and it's not the type of debt you can pay off with your millions. Get something we can use in the lab or I will take *your* DNA." Ivan drilled his finger into Randal's chest.

"I promise you, you won't be disappointed," Randal replied.

Ivan grabbed his suitcase and barged out of the hangar.

If Randal was shaken, it didn't show. He tipped his cap to us and headed over to the small office inside the hangar to speak with Justice in private.

I looked at Kyle. "Randal is in deep."

"This week is going to be interesting, that's for sure."

"Why would he go to all that trouble designing a park when he knew there was no mammoth?" I asked.

"Maybe he didn't know. Maybe he really thought he could just venture out and find a mammoth. Guys like that think that with a ton of money they can do anything. Remember all the trophy fossils we found in his secret room? He's probably been dreaming about his theme park for years."

"I hope he finds something, or Clark's Mammoth Park is going to turn out to be a pretty scary place," I said.

"More like Randal Clark's tomb," Kyle added.

10

Good Dogs and Bad Dogs

The scandal of "Tusk-gate" wasn't over. Not by a long shot. Dad was one of the nicest guys in the world, but he wasn't a doormat.

I knew that he had woken up early and headed out to the dig site with Karen and Ivan. Kyle and I were to join them at the site that afternoon.

A web of cold air clung to me, but I ignored it. I was trying to acclimate, like Justice said. I pretended that I didn't notice the way the cold sank through neoprene, fleece, and cotton until it rubbed against my skin and stole my warmth. I shifted from foot to foot and shook out my arms. There were no birds overhead. I imagined they had been absorbed into the white cottony blanket of the sky.

I stared at a chain-link fence standing guard in front of me.

West's face appeared in the door to the dog hut, and he yelled, "Don't touch the fence with bare skin! No fingers, noses, cheeks . . . and no tongues!" He pointed a gloved finger at Kyle, who burst out laughing, and I wondered where he had put his tongue before.

West continued. "No pressing up against it. The metal will stick to your skin—rip it clean off."

I eyed the fence from a safe distance. The cold was still there, lingering, acclimating to me.

Finally, the door shot open and the dogs spilled out of the warm hut. A pack of lean and lanky huskies barked and yapped, their pink tongues lolling out of their open mouths. Smoky breath plumed from their snouts. They bounced and jostled for our attention, banging up against the fence until West hurried over to let us in. Kyle and I went inside the enclosure and were immediately mobbed. Tails whipped back and forth. Dog bodies wove their way between the two of us as we petted and rubbed their furry backs.

Kyle dragged one dog around by a knotted rope that the dog clenched tightly in his jaws. The wild crystal-blue eyes of another dog stared at me. I knelt down and was overrun with dog love, licks, and kisses. West let Kyle and me jump around with the dogs for a while before motioning for us all to come back to the warmth of the hut. Once inside, I pulled off my gloves and sunk my fingers into their furry coats.

Then I saw the runt off in the corner by herself, pushed to the back of the pack. I was drawn to her right away. Her fur was all white except for a splatter of brown spots and speckles that made her look like she had been splashed with mud. I moved slowly in her direction. I held out my hand for her to smell, and she eased toward me, low to the ground, tail wagging wildly. Once she smelled me, she licked my fingers and let me run my hands through her thick, soft fur.

"She likes you," West said.

"Will she be one of the dogs pulling the sled today?" I asked hopefully.

"No, she doesn't do much pulling. Too small." He patted the haunch of a much bigger dog.

"Oh," I said, disappointed. "What's her name?"

"She doesn't have one."

The dog's amber-colored eyes stared up at me. What had looked like the brown splashes of a mud puddle reminded me of the cinnamon sugar that Mom used to sprinkle on toast to make it taste sweet and crunchy when it came out of the toaster oven. "How about Cinnamon? That's a good name." Naming something gave it strength, made it more whole. Cinnamon was a fiery color.

"For a sled dog?" Kyle knelt on the floor, his arms around two other dogs. "She needs a tough name. Like Ginger Snap! That's a tough-dog name."

"That's good, too. But I still like Cinnamon. Gives her a spark. What do you think, West?"

Cinnamon rolled over on her back, exposing her white belly.

"Not bad." West grinned at me, knowing what I was up to. "Since you're taking the initiative on giving her a name, why don't you get the brush out and give her a good brushing? That coat of hers is one big mat."

"Cinnamon!" I called to her as I dug a comb and brush out of the supply cabinet. She jumped to her feet and raced over to me. I rubbed her neck, getting a face full of dog licks. "I think she likes her new name." I dragged the brush through her tangled fur, and she yapped and squirmed.

"Don't get too attached. She's probably not going to stay with us, seeing as she's not as strong as the others," West said. He was holding a string of harnesses on his arm that must have weighed a ton. Strength seemed to be an important quality for West.

"Sure, she might be small, but she's smart," I said. A wad of shedded dog hair flew in the air as I brushed out her matted fur.

"She might be. But on a dog team, you need strength. No weak links. That little girl has a lot to prove if she wants to stick around." West flexed his arm and carried the harnesses to the other side of the dog pen.

"So where is she going if she can't stay here?" I asked. I held the dog in my arms, raking my fingers through her speckled fur. They couldn't just send her away. She wasn't that small. And what was wrong with being small? Nothing, that's what.

Kyle stood and rocked back on his heels, a big black-and-gray husky tangled up in his legs.

"Can I keep her?" I blurted out suddenly. Right away I knew Dad would kill me. First, no tusks, and now I had put in a request for a live animal. "Please?" It was crazy, but I didn't want her to go. I felt an instant connection with her. She was meant to be mine. I just knew it.

"You would have to ask Randal," West replied. "After yesterday, he might be in a generous mood. But you might also want to ask your dad. I don't know how he would react to a dog suddenly joining you. And then you'd need to ask if it's OK with Justice. But I don't see why he would mind." A dog poked his muzzle in West's hand, looking for a treat.

"I'll ask, so don't send her away yet," I said. "I think she likes me." Cinnamon had snuggled inside the crook of my arm and was wagging her tail.

"Two girls sticking together," West said. "I'll see what I can do."

Justice entered the hut, looking cool in his aviator sunglasses. "Who's ready to hit the powder and go for a run?"

"We're ready!" Kyle yelled.

Dog barks filled the hut.

"Justice will be driving the sled out to the site. He trains all our dogs." West gave Justice a pat on the back.

"What a cool job," Kyle said. "I'd love to be outside flying the helicopter and working with dogs all day."

"I've been raising dogs my whole life. More of a love than a job. My ancestors have lived in this area for generations. Dogs are as important to us as people. They're members of our family."

"Even the runts?" I asked. I nudged West with my elbow. He and Justice exchanged a smile.

"Well, all of the dogs have a place. Maybe not at the front of the pack, but we find roles for them. Sometimes the role is just as a companion. But that can be an important job, too." Justice scratched the top of Cinnamon's head and she wiggled out of my arms. She leaped and jumped and yapped, but she looked tiny in comparison to the other dogs.

"When we hitch the dogs up, can I drive?" Kyle begged. "Please?"

"We'll see," West said, and winked at Justice.

Justice went outside to harness the dogs and get the sled ready. Kyle and I followed right behind. The cold nipped at my exposed skin. The dogs danced on the snow. Kyle and I piled onto the back of the sled with Justice. The air was crisp and sharp and clear as glass. Through my goggles, the sky looked like cloudy marshmallows hanging low above our heads.

The trip out to the dig site was about ten miles. I tucked my head down and enjoyed the ride until Kyle pulled on my sleeve and pointed off in the distance. Silvery domes littered the landscape, clustered together like shiny igloos.

"That's where you both are going to be staying tonight," Justice said.

Finally, it was real. I was going to my first expedition site.

A huge white tent, barely visible from a distance, was where the dig was set up. When we reached it, the tent was buzzing with energy, people talking and working. It was like walking into a dream. The site was organized chaos. Dad and Randal were having a discussion, which was a nice way of saying that they were disagreeing. Ivan and Karen were also taking sides in the discussion. Equipment was everywhere. A generator buzzed in the background. To make the scene even more hectic, Jake was circling the group of scientists with his camera.

"We've arrived," West announced.

"Hey, you made it." Dad waved us over.

"Good. We can take a break and give the kids a tour of the site." Randal patted Kyle on the back. "Take a good look around. One day you could be leading your own expedition."

One side of the tent had been secured to an icy rock wall. A large crevice in the surface looked like a giant pick had taken a bite out of the ice. I peered through the jagged opening and saw the rough sides of walls that opened up into a small cave, protected by layers of clear tarp. My pulse quickened, for inside lay the mysterious mass. Randal directed our attention to where he planned on excavating. He put his arm around Kyle and showed him where they were removing sections of the permafrost in hopes of unearthing the mass. A table was covered in maps and tools. I tried to get closer to see what was going on, but Jake pushed his way forward, nosing his camera in to get a shot of Randal and Kyle. I tripped and bumped into his leg. He glared at me as if I were the most annoying person on the planet; when I tried to stand a little closer to Kyle, Jake yanked my hood back off my head, and I stumbled backward.

"Hey, no wannabes in the shot," he said.

What was he talking about? The last thing I wanted was to be on film, but with him constantly shoving that camera in everyone's face, it was hard not to be caught in one of his precious shots.

"You're ruining the close-up. Look, I know it's fun to be in a movie, but I need this to be real, and a little girl doesn't add much to the credibility of the dig. Now move it."

What a jerk. Who cared about his stupid movie? I shifted closer to Karen, but Jake moved also and sighed, annoyed. "Your big head is in the way." He reached out and pulled my hat off. I hadn't had time to braid my hair that morning, and when he pulled my hat off, my white hair exploded in a mass of wild frizz.

"Wow! Holy Yeti head! Someone has crazy hair," Jake yelled. "Let me get a shot of that. Weird. Is it real?" Jake reached his free hand out and messed up my hair.

"Get off me. And, yes, it's real." I stepped out of his reach.

I tried to grab my hat out of his hand, but he pulled back and shoved his camera in my face. I scowled into it. Kyle and Karen looked away and went back to inspecting the maps, trying to ignore Jake. But I felt everyone staring. Randal looked at me for a second and muttered something that sounded like *fascinating*. Dad grabbed my hat out of Jake's hand and gave it back to me.

"Back off," Dad said to Jake. "Keep your camera out of the way. And don't go near my daughter again. With or without your camera. Got it?"

"Hey, I go where my uncle goes. You don't have any say." Jake smirked. "I was just joking around with her. Have a sense of humor."

My cheeks flushed. I wished a crevasse in the icy floor would open up and swallow Jake and his camera whole. Why did I let a guy like him bother me? I was too embarrassed to stay inside the tent where everyone was planning and joking, so I went outside to hang with the dogs and get some fresh air. I approached the back of the sled and saw an Inuit woman sitting there. "Hi," I said, sitting down next to her. "I'm Maya."

She smiled warmly at me. Justice glanced over at us. "This is my grandmother, Jada," Justice said. "She likes to come visit the site some days."

"I like to see the mountains," she said. Jada was sitting on a pile of furs on the edge of the sled. A fur-lined hood ringed her face and a fur blanket lay over her lap. She must have been used to the harsh weather, because she didn't seem to mind being outside.

"Would you like to warm up in the tent?" I asked.

"No," she said. "I want some quiet. It's too loud inside."

She stretched her blanket over my legs and then looked off into the distance. She was staring at an icy mountain ridge. It reminded me of a glass castle. I sat in silence and stared out over the landscape, the distance growing outward like a mirage. It was calming. My anger at Jake began to melt away. I must have been breathing heavily, because Jada patted my hand with her fur mitten.

"This is a place of great spirits. It is important to my people." Her voice was strong. "Stories are important to us. They give our past meaning. Our ancestors live on through the stories."

The dogs barked and jumped. Justice unhooked Cinnamon. He had let her come along since he knew that I liked her, and she bounded over to me.

"Jada, the dogs say they want to be in a story," Justice said. His dark eyes glittered in the sun.

Jada tucked a bit of my hair that had escaped back under my hat. She and Justice must have heard the whole thing.

"I hate my hair. It's a joke," I said. I had never said that to anyone before. It seemed childish, and I didn't want to act like a baby in front of Dad and Randal. But it was hard being different, especially when everyone could see it so easily.

"It is you. Part of your story." Jada rested her furry mitten on my shoulder.

"My story?" I asked. I didn't feel like I had much of a story to tell. My life was as blank as a white page. I knew that I wanted to go on expeditions, but I didn't know what I wanted to study. I just wanted to hurry into the future, when all those questions would be answered. I wanted something to happen that would tell me what I was meant to find. "I don't know my story," I said.

"We all have stories. We just need to tell them," Jada said.

"I don't think I have one yet."

Jada patted my leg. "You are an old girl. That is your story. You are an ancient spirit living inside a young body. Ready to take her place in the cold, icy wilderness." Her smile caused a flurry of wrinkles to crease her face. "You are wise and powerful." She paused for dramatic effect. "You are the protector of the small."

Cinnamon lifted her head as if she knew the story had just reached the part about her.

"But you are strong," Jada continued. "The wind knows you. The bears and the wolves know you. They know when you are near, the darkness will fall at your feet."

Justice glanced over and shook his head. "Jada, no young girl likes to be called old."

Jada made a clicking sound with her tongue and patted my leg. "It's an honor. Old means wise."

She was giving me a story to make me feel better. *Old girl.* Was that me? I didn't feel like an old girl, but I guessed I didn't have any choice. My story had picked me.

✦ ✦ ✦

In the end Dad won the argument, which was about how to approach the mass under the ice, and we headed back through the narrow opening and to the cave with the equipment. The side of one wall had been sheared away, bringing a dark shadow to the surface. The cave was hardly what I pictured a cave to look like. I expected a large glittery domed interior, but the ceiling of this cave was jagged and slanted. The opening was narrow near the front, and it felt like we were walking down a thin hallway of ice until the cave opened up. The floor was a thick layer of uneven, rocky ice. I had to watch my feet to keep from tripping.

Someone had set up a bank of solar lights in the cave, and the ice glowed in the darkness. "It's over here." Dad motioned toward one of the walls of ice.

"That has to be it—I can see a form." Kyle pushed his way to the front. He was even more excited than Dad.

"We need to go deeper. We need to see what it is." Randal paced the cave. "I must get a view of it."

✦ ✦ ✦

The scientists worked for hours, tirelessly trying to carve out bits of the facade. Swinging an ax or hammer was not a good idea, since the metal reverberated on the ice. Instead, chisels were used to delicately chip away at the surface. Bit by bit, they worked to free the mysterious mass from the ice. We still didn't even know what it *was*. It could have been nothing but a trick of the light. Maybe it was just a shadow frozen in the permafrost, like an ice spirit caught in time and space. But there was always the possibility it could be something more.

One of Mom's favorite excavation stories was about a Mongolian princess found buried in the frozen ground. When the princess was dug up, the scientists learned that she was not some delicate fairy-tale princess but the leader of her tribe. She had the image of a deer with smoke spiraling up from his horns tattooed on her skin. A necklace of bone hung around her throat. The princess was a warrior.

When her body was brought to the surface, it immediately began to decay. With the air eating away at her skin, decomposition occurred at a furious rate. The earth was trying to reclaim her body. Only in the ice was the discovery safe. Once a body was removed from the airtight ground, it was a race against time to learn its secrets.

After a few hours, we began packing up for the night. I went to see how Dad was doing. The generator hummed from outside the cave, and cords snaked underfoot through the entrance. The hours at the dig had been long, the work grueling. Dad was hunched over, examining the progress. I pushed forward to get a look. The shadow in the ice was starting to take form. I nudged in front of Jake and his camera. I could be pushy, too.

"Stop," Dad said, holding up his hand. Everyone froze.

"Is that . . . what I think it is?" Ivan said, examining the ice block. "Could it really be?"

We all moved closer.

"Look at the shape," Dad said. The figure was not large, but it looked taller than it was wide. Not as big as a mammoth. Jake looked at Kyle and then back at the shadowy ice mass.

"It's too hard to tell, but it looks like it could be an organic form," Ivan said.

"You mean it could be an animal or a *person*?" I asked. A chill washed over me that had nothing to do with the climate. I couldn't believe the idea that we could be finding a real person from another era in time. This was a major find.

"We don't want to get ahead of ourselves here," Dad warned, but it was clear that something lifelike—human-like—was taking form through the ice.

Jake and his camera stuck to the thing like glue. "Speculate, man. Give us your best scientific guess. What are we looking at, Doctor?" His voice deepened as he shifted into interview mode.

"We are looking at a section of frozen permafrost. There is something inside it, but right now I can't tell." For the first time, Dad turned to the camera and suppressed a smile. "It doesn't look like an animal, and I don't see a skeleton or fossilized bone."

"Come on, Doc," Jake pressed. "You gotta give me something."

"I won't speculate." Dad focused back on the form.

"Is it human?" Jake asked. "'Cause it looks like it could be a person."

Everyone was silent. Jake had stated the obvious. He put his camera down for a second. "You can look at some of the shots I took. Through the lens it looks like a human figure. It's certainly not a mammoth."

We all huddled around Jake as he uploaded a file to his laptop, and we watched the playback of the film. He was right. Seeing the ice wall cropped through the lens, the form looked even more like the shadow and shape of a person. For a second, I was both thrilled and scared.

"We don't know what that is," Ivan said, and he walked to the mouth of the cave to get some air. "It could be anything. We need to get closer."

"But it looks like a human. What else could it be?" Jake watched the film over and over.

"We don't want to decide what it is until we know for sure," Dad said. "Yesterday we thought we had a mammoth, and now you're showing me signs of a humanoid being. I want to be sure. I don't want to get excited and find it's another hoax."

Jake rolled his eyes. "Uncle Randal just wanted to get

you here. Give him a break. This is his dream. And with the nerd patrol breathing down his neck, he really needs to deliver something big." Jake motioned to Ivan, who was hovering at the edge of the cave, looking pale and jittery.

"You OK, Ivan?" Dad asked.

Hunched over, Ivan waved. "Just a little claustrophobic, that's all."

Dad turned back to Jake. "We all have dreams," he said. "And I'm sorry, but I have little sympathy for your uncle. He asked for this when he faked the tusk. He could have been honest."

"OK, Mr. High-and-Mighty, would any of you have come up here if you knew that all Randal had was an image?"

"Probably not," Dad said.

"See? My uncle *had* to lie. Otherwise, you wouldn't have come. Everyone wants a sure thing these days. No one is willing to take any risks."

"Randal didn't need to lie," I said. "He could have told the truth, and maybe we would have come." I looked at Dad. "Right?"

"Randal could have hired an excavation team to do what we are doing now. He would have found a team eager to get paid to excavate the site," Dad said.

"He wanted you. He wanted the credibility of real scientists working on the project, not just a bunch of hired hands to do the work."

Dad was quiet. I nudged him with my elbow and smiled.

"Look, I probably shouldn't be telling you this," Jake said, leaning in conspiratorially, "but Randal wants you to be the one to write about the find. He was hoping you would write a paper for the science journals, maybe even write a book."

"Why me?" Dad asked.

"Randal read some of your proposals on mammoths. He said you have passion. That's important to him."

Dad hid a smile. It was true—he did have passion for anything concerning mammoths. So maybe Randal wasn't that bad after all. At least he was a good judge of character when it came to my dad.

Did Jake mean it? I wanted to believe that Dad's work was getting noticed, but it sounded like Jake was trying to manipulate him.

Karen spoke up. "We just want to be sure before we rush to judgment. That's all." She watched the film again.

"I know what I see, and it isn't an animal or a skeleton," Jake said, pointing at the screen. "It has the shape of a person with arms and legs."

"Is it really a person?" I asked, looking up at Dad.

"It might be." Dad moved closer to the form in the ice. He was quiet, and I wasn't sure that I liked that. "To know for sure, we need to get deeper into the ice, closer to the form—without breaching the subject."

"Awesome." Jake beamed. "This is better than a woolly

mammoth. This could be a real human life captured in the ice."

I remembered the doll that Mom had found in the Amazon. It looked human, like a tiny girl, but it wasn't. This thing in the ice—could it really be a person, or did it just look like one?

11

The Dome

I stretched out on my bunk inside the dome where Kyle, Karen, and I were spending the night. Cinnamon was curled at the end of my sleeping bag, keeping my feet warm with her furry body. Today had been a good day, minus the Jake incident. The mood had lifted dramatically, and the expedition had gone from a complete academic loss and professional embarrassment to stratospheric potential. Simply put, we had found something buried in the ice, something potentially different, new, and exciting, something that could be evidence of an ancient human being. It was no longer a scrambled-looking blob on a computer screen. It was real. This was the kind of feeling Mom must love, the feeling that all the hard work and traveling away from friends and family was worth it.

The dome was amazing. I thought it would be like sleeping in an igloo, but it was almost like a little cabin. It consisted of one big room that had been divided into sections with our personal gear and equipment, and we each had an area in which to sleep and store our stuff. The floor of the dome was insulated, making it warm enough to take off our boots and coats. Karen had brought a thermos of hot chocolate and poured it into two metal cups. Kyle and I sipped the hot chocolate while our socks dried on the small space heater. Hot-chocolate brown was the color of comfort and sweet yummyness that warmed me from the inside out.

Kyle had piles of comic books poking out of his backpack. His mom had made him leave his computer game back at the station. I really hoped we weren't going to play cards. The only games I knew were Go Fish and gin rummy, and both were embarrassing. The first game because it was for kids and the second because retirees played it. My grandpa taught me how to play, which on the upside meant I was pretty good at it. Luckily, Karen was prepared with the night's entertainment.

"Hey, Maya, come sit on my bed. I thought the three of us could hang out and do some storytelling. We can make up stories about the specimen found in the ice." Karen patted her blue neoprene sleeping bag. She had a big goofy grin on her face. I had seen the look many times when my parents wanted to have fun with an activity that was secretly educational.

Kyle fell back into his pillow. "Aw, Mom. Do we have to?"

"Yes, it will be fun. We have the whole night, and in case you hadn't realized, there is no television and no computer. We'll actually have to talk to one another. Back in the olden days, people told stories for entertainment."

Karen waved the thermos at me, luring me over with more hot chocolate. Then she pulled a bag of mini candy bars out of her backpack. Bribery with chocolate always worked.

"OK, but what if in my story the person isn't a real person?" Kyle asked. "I like fantasy. I don't do history or real life."

"Whatever story you want to tell is fine. Whatever is real to you will be real to us. You get to make it up. You get to decide every detail." Karen beamed. She knew she had him.

"Sounds like fun," I said, plopping down on her bed.

"I'll start while you two think up your stories." She cleared her throat and turned off one of the lights, leaving only the single glow of a lantern to illuminate the dome. She lowered her voice and began. "We have discovered the remains of an Inuit father from thousands of years ago. He was on his way home from a day of hunting, three downy geese hung from his back, their lifeless necks dangling. His heart was filled with pride. He had food for the next week. His wife would be happy. And then out of nowhere a wind rose up, blinding him. He dug a ditch in the snow to protect himself, but he became trapped in the man-made snow cave. The temperature plummeted. Chilled to the bone, he grew tired and weak. A fever gripped him, showering him with a cold sweat. He drifted off and fell asleep forever, dreaming of his wife and children and the life he left behind."

"That's really good," I said, and I meant it.

"Your turn," Karen said.

I hesitated. "Maybe she was a warrior or a hunter," I said. "She was tracking a herd of caribou and she broke through an ice forge. The water swallowed her up and froze around her."

"She?" Kyle said.

"It could be a she," I said.

"It looked like a dude. I don't think it was a girl."

"It's her story, Kyle," Karen said. "Maya can tell it however she wants."

I continued. "She's from a tribe of hunters, and . . . um . . . she was frozen in the ice capsule, cursed forever by a witch. She was cursed to be alone until another hunter came to set her free. The hunter was a man who prowled the night shaped as a wolf."

"Good. Very imaginative. I love the wolf man. Your turn, Kyle."

"Maybe this place is a graveyard and there are more people trapped in the ice. Like an army of warriors. Like the clay warriors in China. And the warriors will be awakened to fight in an epic battle," Kyle said.

The idea of an icy graveyard was creepy. I didn't like the idea of there being lots of people captured, frozen in time. It was different when they were animals. There were mammoth graveyards all over the place, but digging up a real graveyard . . . that gave me the heebie-jeebies. I wanted there to be just one person, which would make it seem special. Because the person we found was one of a kind.

"What else could it be, Mom?" Kyle asked.

"It could be a shaman from an Inuit tribe. He was out talking to the mountains, listening to the wind. He was on a pilgrimage to the icy wilderness. And he stopped to rescue a wounded bird that had broken its wing and fallen to the earth." She scrunched up her face and paused to think. "And a storm flew in, fast as a hawk. Snow thunder rumbled, and then lightning struck the ridge above him, sending a shower of ice and snow down on top of him, trapping him forever in an icy prison."

"That's another great story. You're really good at this." I smiled at Karen.

"She makes up stories all the time. It's kind of her thing," Kyle said.

"What are shamans really like?" I asked.

"The few I have met were wise tribal men and women. Some are healers or mediators. They are very spiritual. One even brought messages from the spirit world back to the living." Karen's face came alive when she spoke. "They speak to the spirits and convey wisdom, sometimes solving problems for their communities. They tell stories, like we just did, and help hold communities together, making sure traditions are passed down," Karen said.

"Sounds cool," I said.

"Have you thought about what you would like to do when you grow up?" Karen asked. "Maybe you'd like to follow in your mom's or dad's footsteps?"

It was a question I dreaded. I didn't know what my discovery would be. "I've got some ideas, but mostly I want to find something no one's seen before." I rubbed a thread of yarn between my fingers. "I want to go to the best school, get grants—that sort of thing—so I can be in the right place to make a discovery. But still, I'm not sure." If indecision were a color, it would be a pale one, faded like old blue jeans.

"Not school again." Kyle rolled his eyes. "After this trip you'll never want to go back to school."

"You don't need to decide right away," Karen said. "You have a long time to figure out what calls to you." She squeezed my hand.

I had always wanted to travel and be like a gypsy, but I guess I never thought about what it was I was hoping *to find.* I thought again of the doll that Mom had found in the rain forest. It wasn't a real person, but it was part of a real person's possessions, carried from mother to daughter. It was precious. And I knew that Dad wanted a mammoth. But what was it that I was looking for? That was the real question. Right then I didn't know the answer.

"Maybe the frozen dude is Thor." Kyle raised himself up from his sleeping bag. "Or a Viking whose ship was shattered in the icy sea, and the Vikings came ashore to hunt bears and caribou. And then this one Viking guy walked out over thin ice and it cracked, and he broke through the surface, plummeting down into the icy water beneath. And he was frozen like an ice cube." Kyle exhaled. "And his Viking shipmates left him as a sign that they were here."

"I thought Thor had a hammer. He would break his way out of the ice," I said, just to be a pain.

"The hammer got too heavy. He couldn't lift it, and he died with it in his frozen hands," Kyle said. "He's been waiting for centuries to be pulled from his icy grave."

The shadow had taken on a life of its own. We all wanted the figure in the ice to be someone special, to fit our hopes and dreams: a warrior princess, an Inuit shaman, or a Viking hero trapped in the ice. Whoever or whatever it was, it was waiting for us to free it.

Like Dad had said, you don't find the mammoth, the mammoth finds you. And though we didn't find a mammoth, *something* had found us. Something wanted to be freed from the icy world that held it prisoner.

12

The Discovery

The next day Kyle and I entertained ourselves by riding the dogsled with Justice and the snowmobiles with West. Learning to ride a snowmobile was a blast. Kyle got really good at it. West even set up an obstacle course for us to race on. We rounded the domes, wove in between crates, and maneuvered our way around a super-skinny snowman wearing a long red scarf looped around his neck like five times, compliments of Karen. Once we had the course down, we began the races.

We formed two teams: Team Yeti and Team Shark Bite. West and me versus Kyle and Justice. I pulled my snow-mobile up to the starting line, which West had drawn in the snow with his boot heel. I stared through my yellow-tinted goggles at Kyle. The whole world glowed gold. Gold was the color of competition, of winning, of crushing my opponent, leaving him in my snowy wake.

West raised his arm. "Get ready!" he yelled.

"You're going down, Yeti girl," Kyle said.

"In your dreams, shark boy." I revved my engine, leaning forward in the seat, preparing to fly.

"Get set! . . . Go!" West yelled and dropped his arm.

I gunned the engine and took off. Kyle won the first two races, but the third one was all mine. I could feel it. I navigated my way to the inside track and skirted the domes. At the orange cones I pulled ahead of Kyle. Bits of snow and ice flew through the air. I narrowly dodged a stack of crates and headed out across the flats toward the snowman. I felt free, tearing through the wind, plowing over bumps. Making a tight turn, I took a chunk out of the side of the super-skinny snowman, who was getting skinnier and skinnier with each race, since the closer we got on the turns, the more of his body got trimmed off by the nose of the snowmobiles.

My pulse raced. I was close to the finish, but Kyle was gaining on me. I had a few yards' lead to spare and then I would be home free. Kyle swerved his snowmobile to go around me, but I stayed focused on the finish line. I dug in and plowed ahead.

Justice waved me across the finish line. Victory was mine! Score one for Team Yeti. Kyle pulled up alongside me and shook his head, but after a moment he grinned and gave me a thumbs-up sign.

After the races we ate lunch and warmed up inside the domes, and then Justice took us over to the excavation site. By the time we reached the site, the sky had darkened. The cave glowed faintly from the outside, and my heart raced with anticipation to see how far the team had gotten. Justice needed to get back to the station to feed and put the dogs away for the night.

Randal met us at the perimeter of the site.

Before we could make our way into the cave, Ivan came staggering from the cave opening with a terrified look on his face. His neck warmer was pulled down, and his skin looked ghostly pale. His goggles dangled from his wrist, and his eyes were wild with panic. I wondered if he was having another attack of claustrophobia.

"Go on, you two. I'll handle this," Randal said.

Kyle and I pulled back and gave Ivan a wide berth. Randal approached the disoriented scientist and asked, "What's happened, Ivan? Has there been an accident?"

Ivan's gaze drifted over to him. "We . . . found something," he said, shaking his head. "I won't go back inside. We should leave. We can't move it."

"What is it?" Randal clutched the man's gloved hands, and excitement burned in his eyes. "What have we discovered?"

Ivan crumpled to his knees on the icy ground.

Observing the man's distress, Randal pulled a two-way radio out of his pocket. "Justice, this is Randal. Over."

Static burst from the radio, and Justice's voice answered: "Copy."

"I need you back here at the site immediately. Ivan needs to be transported back to the station. Over."

"On my way. Over." The radio crackled again, then went silent.

Randal knelt down to Ivan's level. "Have a seat. Justice is coming to take you back." Ivan made his way into a tent and then over to a crate to sit down. Kyle and I followed. A small space heater hooked up to the mobile generator took the chill out of the tent. Once Ivan had sat, Randal wasted no time bombarding him with questions. "What did you see?"

Ivan shook his head. His breathing was short and raspy.

"What is it?" Randal clutched Ivan's jacket, his eyes widened, desperate for information. A nervous shiver went up my spine as I tried to imagine what could have scared the big man.

Ivan tilted his head toward Randal, and after a few excruciatingly long seconds, he said, "We found . . . an *angel.*"

The hairs prickled on the back of my neck. "Did he say angel?" I asked Kyle.

"Yeah," Kyle said, eyes wide.

"What?" Randal asked, clearly not having expected that response.

"A fallen angel," Ivan whispered through chapped lips. "It's in the cave, trapped in the permafrost."

"You're mistaken," Randal said, shaking his head. "It can't be. We'll just take a look and see what it *really* is. You've been working too hard, and the Arctic doesn't agree with you."

Ivan rose to his feet, more steady than he'd been a

moment ago. "It's true. It's true." Spit flew from his mouth. "I know what I saw."

"I'm not suggesting you're seeing things. I believe you *think* you saw an angel," Randal said. Well, actually Randal *was* suggesting that Ivan had imagined an angel. But if it wasn't an angel, what had made Ivan think it was?

"We must not move it," Ivan pleaded. "We need to leave it. Bad things will happen."

"Now you're just being superstitious." Randal let out an exasperated sigh. His patience with Ivan seemed to be wearing thin. "Nothing bad is going to happen. The site is perfectly safe."

Ivan didn't look well. He slumped back down onto the crate. I pulled a bottle out of my pack and gave him a drink of water. I hoped Justice would hurry up. Randal must have been thinking the same thing, because he pulled out his radio and told Justice to pick up the pace.

"You believe me, don't you, children?"

Ivan's gaze latched on to me, and I didn't know what to say, so I nodded. "Sure," I said. But really I wanted to see this angel and understand what he was so upset about.

"Yeah, me too," Kyle said.

Ivan reached over and pulled on one of my braids that hung down outside of my hat. "White hair. It's not normal in someone so young."

I snatched my hair out of his hands. "Hey, no touching."

"Ivan, leave the children alone," Randal said.

"It must have fallen from the sky." It took me a second to realize Ivan wasn't talking about me but about the discovery.

"I need to know what's happened in the cave," Randal said to Kyle and me. "You two wait here."

Fat chance of that happening. I wasn't about to stay out here in the tent with Ivan acting so strange. I was eager to see what had happened. I waited at the tent flap for Randal to make his way into the cave before motioning for Kyle to follow me. "Let's go. I'm not staying here."

"Right behind you," Kyle said.

After making our way to the cave entrance, we passed through the narrow crevice. My gloves scratched against the rough surface. The walls felt like they were closing in on me, and then suddenly they opened up and we were in the cave area where the excavation had been established. I found a spot in the corner of the site, which provided Kyle and me with a perfect view. Excitement buzzed around us. Randal was talking to Dad in hushed tones. Jake was milling about with his camera propped on his right shoulder like an extra appendage.

"Let's see this discovery, shall we?" Randal announced, rubbing his gloved hands together.

"This way." Dad directed Randal toward the rough block that they'd been working on earlier.

"I see that I have chosen the right man for the job," Randal said. "You have done exemplary work over the past few days."

Kyle and I followed a few steps behind. The buzz of the generator grew. A flicker of light from a solar lamp cast an eerie glow on the cave walls. My heart raced as my eyes scanned the icy surface.

I couldn't believe what I saw.

There was a big hole in the ice wall where the shadow had been the day before. It looked like some giant monster had taken a bite out of it. A huge chunk of ice rested on the cave floor. The block was crude: rough and cracked. They must have freed the shadow from the rocky ice wall, and now it sat like a giant glass coffin with a figure sealed inside.

"What is it?" I whispered to Kyle, mesmerized by the flickering shadows playing on the ice.

"I think it's . . . I think it's really a person." Kyle nudged me with his shoulder.

I couldn't deny it now. Through a spiderweb of cracks on the icy surface, the figure looked like a person trapped in a giant ice cube. It had a face. More important, it had flesh. I had seen enough dug-up mummies and ancient bodies to know that this was no mummy. The flesh is the first thing to go, since flesh is mostly made of water, and once a person dies, the body pretty much dries up the same way a grape shrivels up into a raisin. This person was no raisin.

"It looks almost alive," I said. A pang filled my stomach.

Kyle furrowed his brow. "Almost. But it's been buried in the ice for who knows how long."

"Look at the skin. It doesn't look dead."

"I know. But it's been encased in solid ice."

"It's not all shriveled up and decayed. How can the skin live?" I asked.

"The ice is somehow preserving it."

I couldn't hold my question in a second longer. I stepped forward so that the scientists saw me. Kyle followed behind me. My dad frowned, but I knew he was too busy to give me a lecture. "Will someone please tell us what it is?" I asked. "You must have some idea."

Jake and Dad exchanged a look. Randal stood marveling at the block of ice, and for once he was speechless.

"Well, you have to tell us now. We've all seen it." I stared at Dad.

"We're not sure," Dad responded.

"It's a breakthrough. That's what it is," Randal said.

"It's a lot to take in, Randal." Dad patted him on the back of his puffy brown snowsuit. "The point is we have potentially made what could be a groundbreaking discovery. We need to eliminate all possibilities before we get too excited."

"It's beautiful. It's the most magnificent specimen I've ever seen." Randal looked over his shoulder at Dad. "I had no idea . . . No idea." He gave a half-choked laugh, and glanced at Jake. "It's better than we imagined. And now it is ours."

"But what is it?" Kyle asked.

"Tests will have to be run . . . scans. An MRI will need to be done." Dad looked at the ice. "It appears to be humanoid. A young humanoid male."

"A boy," I said.

"If that's a person, then what are those?" Kyle pointed to the back of the form. Two huge arched objects filled the icy slab behind the figure. The frozen boy had two massive wings attached to his back, covered with hundreds of creamy, parchment-colored feathers.

"They look like wings," I said, stating the obvious. That was when I realized it hadn't been the boy who had startled Ivan—it had been his *wings*.

"What kind of a person has wings?" Kyle asked.

No one answered, but we all had an idea.

Randal stepped forward. "We must begin to study him."

"We will, but we must be cautious. The body might be a real specimen, or it might be another imitation," Dad said, lowering his voice.

"Can't be. Look at the wings," Jake said.

"Wings can be faked," Dad said. "Like tusks."

"I wouldn't fake this," Randal said. "I couldn't even dream of finding something like this." His voice drifted off as he stared.

Karen shifted. "Many tribal communities used feathers

as decorations for ceremonial garb. Feather headdresses and costumes are not uncommon throughout history. We don't even know how old the find is, let alone if the wings are a part of his musculature. We'll need carbon dating."

"Tribal is a good hypothesis for the wings." Dad paused and scratched his chin. "They could be just for decoration."

"They look too real," Jake countered. "And if they are for decoration, then why are they white and not colorful?"

"We won't know until we investigate further," Dad said.

"The wings could be mechanical!" Kyle blurted out. "Maybe they're man-made, out of metal or something, and they work like a hang glider."

"Whatever it is, it will be investigated to the fullest. It could be a modern-day missing person. Someone's family could be looking for him. Wings or no wings."

"No way," Jake said. "First, any lost kid in this area would have sent out a major search party and made all the papers, even if the kid went missing decades ago."

"You confirmed?" Karen asked. "It's not a lost child?"

Jake set his camera on the table. "Yesterday, after we saw that the shape looked human, I did some research. A lost person was the first thing I checked for. Last thing we needed was to discover a poor kid in a costume. I even contacted the nearest paper and the police."

Karen frowned, unconvinced, and Jake rolled his eyes,

obviously highly annoyed with all the questions. But Karen didn't back down. "This is important. We aren't filmmakers. We're scientists. We must research every possibility."

Jake sighed. "I researched thoroughly. I could ask some more, if that will make you feel better."

Karen eased up on Jake. "No, I should do it. It's my responsibility. You're the filmmaker. I'm the anthropologist. I'll start researching and questioning the locals to make sure it isn't someone's missing child or a cultural icon. It could be a statue—a mannequin made for a celebration." Karen began to gather up her gear and walked over to Kyle and me. "Are you two ready to go back to the dome?"

"Can I stay, please?" Kyle said.

Karen pulled Kyle's neck muffler up high around his face. "You'll have plenty of time to see the discovery later."

Dad turned to me. "Karen's right. Time to get you two settled in for the night."

As we were walking out, we met up with Justice, who had come to take Ivan back to the station. Dad paused at the mouth of the tent. "I forgot my pack," he said.

"I'll go get it," I said. "It'll just take me a second."

Once through the crevice again, I saw my dad's pack on the ground. Randal and Jake were over by the discovery. Jake was talking a mile a minute. "Think about it, Uncle Randal! Think about the prestige, the notoriety. You'll be famous. Famous!"

"Famous . . ." Randal's gaze drifted as if he were focusing on something far away.

"It's a game changer," Jake said.

"The project has all been worth it," Randal said. "Years of work for this one moment."

"I never doubted you, Uncle Randal," Jake said with pride.

"We've finally found our Icarus," Randal said.

I grabbed the pack and snuck back down the tight, icy chamber. It was clear that the boy in the ice, *their Icarus*, was not as big a surprise to Randal as it was to the rest of us.

141

13

Arctic Fever

I was glad to be back at the station the next day. Spending time at the dig site felt like being on an island in the middle of a sea of snow. It was fun, but the place was too cut off from the rest of the world. I didn't know how Randal lived up here all year round without the rest of us around. The snow and cold were starting to get to me. I was always bundled up, wearing three pairs of socks and big boots, and Karen had lent me a pair of her fingerless gloves to wear when I was inside. It was a bad sign when you needed to wear gloves indoors.

The following morning, Randal decided that the discovery should be moved back to the station. It took the guys all day to move the block of ice back to the lab. They built a sled that could distribute and carry the ice slab's weight and then pulled it with snowmobiles across the snow. Kyle said they had to go really slow, so as not to tip over or drive the nose of the sled into the ground.

Back at the lab, we decided to call the winged boy Charlie, instead of referring to him as "the ancient thing" or "the ice angel" or "the humanoid being with prehistoric avian-like appendages." (That's what Dad kept calling it, and it didn't exactly roll off the tongue.) Kyle wanted to call the creature Thor, but that idea got voted down. Somehow no one was buying that the creature was a Viking.

One of the labs had a walk-in freezer, and Charlie was kept inside like a slab of frozen meat. I had my hat, gloves, and coat on with the hood up as I peered into the ice block, trying to get a good look at Charlie in his lozenge of ice. I couldn't wait for them to thaw him out so that we would know for sure what he really was.

Karen thought Charlie was an ancient life-form, so old that no one knew it ever existed, like a first-generation Inuit, or even more ancient, due to the wings. She was even willing to admit that it might be a cross-species.

Dad thought Charlie was some kind of hybrid human-bird creature, a missing link, similar to how the birds descended from dinosaurs. Why not have a half-man, half-bird creature?

Kyle was going with alien. Maybe he was right and Charlie was shrink-wrapped in starlight, and had been left behind by his mother ship or fallen from the sky.

Ivan was convinced Charlie was an angel, an icon that should be left untouched. Katsu, on the other hand, was just glad to have a specimen to study.

I wasn't sure what Charlie was, but I knew there was something very special about him, and it wasn't just the wings. He shouldn't look as good as he did.

While everyone had a different opinion about what it was that lay frozen in the ice, no one could deny that we were on the verge of making an amazing discovery.

+ + +

Over the next few days, the scientists conducted endless tests on Charlie—at least the tests that could be done through the block of ice. Katsu wanted to drill down through the ice and take samples from Charlie's skin, but Dad was adamant about not thawing him out until he could be moved to a proper facility that could handle the body once it hit the air. Remains were fragile. But I think Dad was just trying to hold on to the moment. For now, Charlie was perfect, lying in his cold glass coffin like a prince. He was what we imagined and had hoped for, and if we breached the ice, we might lose him forever.

Sometimes when no one was around, I would brave the freezer and talk to Charlie like he could hear me. It was hard to explain the feeling I got, standing next to the ice. The only way I could describe it was warmth, which sounded crazy. How could something so cold and frozen make me feel warm inside? All I knew was that my heart welled up when I was around him.

Perched on a stool, I talked. I hoped he could hear me. I told him all about Mom and about the Amazon. I figured talking about a warm place kept my mind off the fact that my breath plumed out in smoky whirls. I described how the rain forest was always damp and hot and how the air was filled with moisture.

The Arctic was the opposite. Even with all the snow, the Arctic had the rainfall average of a desert, so it was very dry and cold. We were in a frozen desert. I liked the contrast of the snowy landscape to that of the sandy desert. They were both treacherous, but for different reasons. Nature was heartless, and Charlie was proof. Somehow he had perished just like the mammoths.

The lights in the freezer lab flickered over my head. The *genny* was acting up again. That's what West and Justice called the generator that powered the station. Ever since we had brought Charlie back to the lab, the genny wasn't happy.

Then the lights went out completely, plunging the ice-cold room into darkness. My heart leaped. I wasn't afraid of the dark, but this was *really* dark: not one flicker of light. The room was sealed tight and was pitch-black—starless-space black—and I was alone with a frozen body.

I reached out and touched the block of ice, trying to feel around it, so that I could make my way to the door and get out of the room. No panicking, just slow and steady. I ran my gloved hand down the side of the ice.

"Charlie, it's time for me to go. The generator just went out and there aren't any backup lights in here." Talking to him soothed me.

I breathed deeply, but the freezing air chilled my throat. The darkness made the room seem colder. I could feel the cold air rise up off the surface of the table and the block of ice itself. The chill wrapped around me. My eyes were wide. I searched the darkness for the door. For a brief second, I thought I saw something glimmer inside the block of ice, a greenish-blue flame that danced across the night sky.

At first I thought I was seeing things, until the light grew, like a tiny flame or a little green lightning bug, glowing from the center of the block of ice. The warm glow seemed to be coming from inside Charlie. I pressed my face closer to the surface of the ice. The light swirled and bloomed like a star twinkling in a far-off galaxy. It was beautiful. A warm sensation spread through my body. The flame grew and grew.

But as I looked closer, the generator kicked back on and the overhead lights blinded me with brightness. I blinked furiously and rubbed my eyes. When I looked again, the glowing light inside the ice was gone. I sucked in a lungful of cold air and almost choked. Fear of what was happening overtook me, and I ran for the door and out of the freezer.

I raced into the main lab, knocking over a tray of metal instruments. I gathered them up as fast as I could, but before I left the lab, I looked up. The freezer door was ajar. I dove to close it but not before peering inside. I was unable not to look. But Charlie was as still as stone.

I hurried back to my room. Maybe I was getting sick. I felt my forehead, almost hoping to feel the flush of a burning fever, but my skin was cool. As I was walked down the corridor that led to the bunk area, I noticed a thread on the floor, and I knelt down and picked it up. I ran the woolly thread between my fingers and recognized it as yarn. I followed the length of yarn down the hall and around two corners as if I were being led by a trail of bread crumbs to something or somewhere special. When I looked up, I realized the yarn had led me to my own room.

Tentatively, I stepped inside. I couldn't believe my eyes. Karen was sitting on her bed surrounded by a giant web of yarn, strung around the room from wall to wall, woven into a matrix of colorful threads. She had hooked the yarn to the dresser and doorknobs, bedposts, and lamp stand. It looked like a giant knit star.

"What are you doing?" I asked, my gaze gliding over the yarn maze.

"I made it," she said proudly. "Isn't it beautiful?"

"Well, yes," I acknowledged, tentatively stepping into the matrix.

It must have taken Karen hours to make. She looked pale. A line of sweat ringed her hairline. The room felt warm and smelled slightly of damp sheep. Her fingers nervously tied tiny knots in a tangle of orange yarn balled up in her lap.

"What is it?" I asked.

"It's a pattern I saw in a dream, or a vision, maybe."

"What kind of dream?" This was getting more interesting by the second. Was Karen seeing strange things, too?

"I've been working really hard. Reading a lot." She rubbed her eyes. "I think I must have dozed off at the computer. I saw this pattern outlined in light, against a black sky. Crazy, huh?" She smiled tiredly.

"No, I don't think that's crazy at all." I stepped over the lines of yarn and made my way over to sit on the bed next to her. "Are you feeling OK?" I asked, half joking, and felt her forehead, which felt fine to me.

"I don't think I have a fever," she said. "Unless it's some new Arctic fever that plays strange tricks with your mind."

"You seem all right to me. The matrix really brightens up the room," I said, trying to be positive.

"You know the weirdest part?" she asked.

"No, what?"

"I think Charlie was in my dream. I could have sworn I saw him." Karen tossed the ball of yarn into her bag.

"Really?" I said, remembering the glowing light inside of the ice.

"I guess I should clean this up. Unless we've both turned into spiders, a web of yarn makes it hard to move around." Karen stood and fingered a strand.

"Let me get a couple of pictures first." I said, grabbing my bag and digging for my camera. "It really is beautiful."

Perhaps it should have been scary to see such strange things, but I didn't feel afraid. I looked up at Karen and was glad that I wasn't the only one seeing strange yet magical things.

14

The Curse of the Mammoth

Most scientists didn't believe in curses. A curse tended to get in the way of valuable research time.

Many ancient civilizations did believe in curses, probably because the people took death seriously. (Who wouldn't?)

When I was seven, my hamster, Lady Snuffles, died. (Don't be sad. She lived a good life. Carefree, lots of treats, and endless wallowing in shredded newspaper.) My parents and I had a little ceremony and buried her in a shoe box in the backyard. I wrapped her tiny body in an old pink washcloth and put a small troll doll in the box, so she wouldn't be lonely. I also dropped in some hamster treats, so she wouldn't get hungry, and a jingle bell that she liked to play with, so she would have fun. I did this for me, really, because Lady Snuffles was not going to wake up and get the munchies or need a little entertainment. She was gone.

This was something I had in common with the Egyptians. Dad used the tragic death of my hamster as a teaching moment. (That type of thing was what professor parents lived for.) The Egyptians buried their kings with everything they might need in the afterlife. They also sealed the tomb with a curse. Anyone who disturbed the tomb, or at least touched the sarcophagus, would be cursed: Horrific things would happen to him or her. The Egyptians didn't want people digging up their kings, their ancestors, or their pets. They had a point. I would not like it if someone dug up my hamster to inspect her bones. Creepy!

What was an ancient civilization supposed to do but invent curses to keep grave robbers and scientists out of their ancestors' tombs? And it wasn't just ancient civilizations that believed remains should be left alone; there were many people who believed a curse would follow anyone who removed fossils or bones from their resting place.

It was getting harder and harder to deny the strange things going on in the station. The lights were the most noticeable. First, they just flickered. Then, they went to what West called a "sustained flicker," meaning they went off, came back on, and went out again, all in an interval of a few seconds—which was what had happened when I was in the freezer with Charlie. Next, the lights went out for an hour, which triggered the backup generator. This freaked out everyone because, if the power kept shorting out, Charlie could be put in jeopardy. This kind of didn't make sense to me at first, since he was frozen and it was freezing outside. I told Dad that we could just put Charlie outside and he would be fine, but Dad said that keeping

Charlie at a constant temperature was crucial. Any thawing and refreezing would damage him.

West was working double-time on the genny. It was a top-of-the-line model, he said, and he couldn't find anything wrong with it. But something *was* wrong with it. I was in the rec room with Kyle when the lights went out again. The backup generator came on, and the room glowed with murky auxiliary lighting. We decided to head down to the end of the hall where the generator was located. That's when we heard yelling coming from the maintenance room. I could hear both Ivan's and West's voices sparring back and forth.

When we got there, sparks were flying from the doorway. Kyle shielded me with his arm as we peered inside. The generator hissed and sizzled. A popping sound, followed by a series of sparks, filled the dim room. West's sleeves were rolled up, and he was covered in grease. A side panel of the generator was open, exposing metal guts.

"Shut it down! Shut it down!" West yelled, and Ivan turned the power off.

"What are you doing in here?" West asked Ivan. He wiped his greasy hands on a rag. "The mechanical room is for maintenance personnel only."

Ivan mopped sweat from his brow. "I smelled smoke. I got worried, so I came to check it out."

"Smoke? Is that right?" Clearly, West wasn't buying it.

"You smelled smoke from all the way in your room? I think that's unlikely. The bunks are nowhere near here."

"I'm telling the truth. I was lying on my bed and I had the strangest dream about fire and ice." Ivan shoved his hands in his pockets. "When I woke up, I had this overwhelming feeling that something was happening. I couldn't sit still, so I decided to look around."

So Ivan was having strange dreams and feelings, too. Interesting.

A thin wisp of black smoke rose from the generator.

"That doesn't look good," Kyle whispered to me.

West glared at Ivan and said, "I don't think it's a coincidence that you just happened to be here when the generator gave out." He tossed the rag into the trash and stared at the broken genny. "It's a good thing we have a backup."

Ivan looked from West to me and Kyle, hovering in the doorway, and then back to West again. "What are you suggesting? Are you implying I sabotaged the generator? Because that is an outrage. I would never hurt the mission."

"'The mission,'" West said dismissively. "This isn't about continuing the mission, it's about you returning home and ending the expedition. I've known guys like you. Tough on the outside but weak on the inside."

"Don't you see what's happening?" Ivan's voice cracked, and he threaded his thick fingers through his hair. "Don't you feel it? The expedition is cursed."

"Cursed?" West snorted. "Superstition doesn't fly with me. This generator was sabotaged—and by a man, not a curse. We all know that you want to get out of here. And if the generator fails, we'll have to abandon the station." West shrugged. "Sounds like a strategy to me."

Ivan thrust his chest out and got up in West's face, which I figured was not a good idea. The two men started circling and then pushing and yelling at each other. Anger poured out of them. It was like watching two rams lock horns.

"Stop it!" I shouted, and I tried to wedge myself between them. Ivan's elbow accidentally hit me in the shoulder, throwing me backward to the floor. His eyes went wide.

"Hey! Watch it!" Kyle knelt beside me. "Are you OK?"

"Look what you did!" West yelled. "Hurting a kid." His face was twisted with anger, and he shoved Ivan against the wall.

I winced. I wanted to stop the fight, not make it worse.

"I'm not hurt. I'm fine," I said, stumbling to my feet. We needed to focus on what was going on, not argue with one another. "Enough yelling," I said.

"Stop fighting!" Kyle shouted. He stepped forward and held up his hands. Suddenly, a stream of white light erupted from one of his fingertips.

"What is *that*?" I said.

Kyle reached out his hand, and the thread of light

coursed out of his finger, traveled across West's arm, and hit the far wall, dancing across the surface.

We all pulled back, amazed.

"Hey, look! I can make it move!" With a twitch of his finger, Kyle sent the energy swirling around the room like a glowing ribbon of light.

"It's got to be coming from the generator," West said.

"The generator's shut down," Ivan said, a look of panic in his eyes.

"Do you feel that?" I asked, pressing my chest. A sensation of calm and peace filled me.

"Stop this!" West grabbed Kyle's arm and shook him. The light zapped out.

Kyle yanked his arm out of West's hand. "You broke it," he cried.

"You could have been hurt—electrocuted, even." West took Kyle by the shoulder. "Are you sure you're OK?"

"Fine," Kyle said, though I could tell by the tone of his voice he was disappointed that West had stopped the light show.

"It was so . . . real," I said. I pulled up my sleeve. All the hair on my arm was standing straight up. "I could feel it."

"Is that what magic feels like?" Kyle asked, wiggling his fingers.

"No! That was nothing strange," said West. "Nothing magical or supernatural. It was just good old Tom Edison and Ben Franklin. Lightbulbs and electricity." With that, he turned and stomped out of the room and headed down the hallway.

Ivan hurried out behind him, pale as a ghost.

"Keep telling yourself that, West," Kyle said after the man had gone.

Something strange was going on, and Ivan was right— we could all *feel* it.

✦ ✦ ✦

Kyle went to his room and I went to mine. Karen wasn't in bed yet. Unable to sleep, I lay in bed and stared at the underside of the top bunk. Finally, I pulled back the covers, slipped out, and went to the lab to look for Dad. At this hour of the night, I became aware of the emptiness of the hallway, which was the color of lumpy oatmeal— unofficially, the color of blandness. But the situation at the station could hardly have been described as bland. Not anymore.

I found Dad sitting on a stool, staring at the computer screen. He had dark circles under his eyes.

He jerked up, surprised to see me. "Maya, what are you doing awake?"

"I couldn't sleep. The Arctic is giving me insomnia," I said. "Why are *you* still up?" I asked, turning the conversation back on him. "You look tired."

"I couldn't sleep, either." He ran his hand through his hair.

"Why not?" I climbed up onto the stool next to him.

"I had a really weird dream last night."

"Maybe you should talk about it," I said, wondering if strange dreams were contagious. "Sometimes if you tell someone your dream, it makes it less scary."

"How did you get so smart?" Dad asked, a faint smile on his face.

"Osmosis."

"It's kind of cool, really, when I think about it." He shrugged.

"Tell me."

"I had this dream that I was awake—but I had to be dreaming." Dad shook his head. "It just felt so real. I went to see Randal, and we were standing in his library. All of a sudden, the wall with the fireplace on it flipped open, revealing a hidden room."

Dad had discovered Randal's secret room in a dream! How could he have known that it was there? Kyle and I hadn't told him about the room or the miniature park. "What happened next?" I asked.

"Well, Randal and I walked into the room. He had a table covered with a big display, but we got distracted, because it started snowing—right there inside of the room. Wild dream, huh?"

"Yeah—really wild." Snow was better than water, I thought.

"And then Randal and I were standing in a frozen landscape, and there were mammoths." Dad's face lit up.

"Whole *herds* of mammoths lumbering along a snowy plain. There were mothers and calves. And I saw caribou and polar bears."

"Sounds like you walked into a dream come true."

"Exactly. It was the most amazing dream I've ever had." He twisted up his face. "Except it was cold, really cold. And that was strange. I have never had a dream that was so lifelike."

Listening to Dad talk about his dream, I was hit with a flash of inspiration. "It's like a *dreamscape*. A place that feels real but is so fantastic that it has to be a dream."

"That's right. Then it got a little scary. The animals were getting close to us. Too close for my taste. I didn't mind watching them, but the last thing I wanted was to get trampled by a woolly mammoth, dream or no dream. Except that when I tried to run, to escape, and get back to the station, there was a fence all around us, and Randal and I couldn't get out."

A fence. The image of the model mammoth park filled my head. There were fences penning in all of the mammoths. It was as if Dad had shrunk down and gone into Randal's model.

"I was cold—and awestruck at being in another world with the mammoths. I could feel their thick woolly hair and hear their calls and snorts. I love mammoths, but they're wild creatures and very protective of their young."

"Sounds intense." I didn't know what else to say. I

wanted to tell him about the light show that had happened to Kyle in the genny room and about seeing the light inside of Charlie, but I was too nervous.

"I guess people have dreams that feel real. I was literally caged like an animal in a zoo, but the snow was alive, swirling with energy that came from all around us. The feeling was overwhelming. It was magical. "

"How did you get out? I mean, how did the dream end?"

"That was strange, too. Randal kept yelling, 'The dream is over. I know you're out there. I'm here to help you.' And then the mammoths lumbered off and the snow stopped falling. And we were back in Randal's library. The fake fire was blazing and the dream was over."

"Wow—that was some dream." I felt like a traitor. I should have said something. One thing stood out in my mind and that was the *feeling*. Both Dad and I had felt an overwhelming sense of magical energy. It seemed like everyone was having strange dreams. The visions were spreading through the station like a virus.

"Speaking of dreams, you should head off to bed. How about I tuck you in?"

Dad got down off his stool and walked me back to my room. I crawled under the covers. My bedsprings creaked. I punched my pillow over and over and tried to clear my head. I told myself that sleep would make things better.

But I was wrong.

15

The Snow Ghost

I woke up in the middle of the night to the sound of someone calling my name. Sitting up in bed, I listened hard. I heard it again, but I couldn't tell where the voice was coming from. Was it Kyle, or was I just imagining it? Didn't Karen hear anything? I crawled out of my sleeping bag and crept over to her bed. She was sound asleep, so I jostled her.

"Karen," I whispered, but she rolled over and faced the wall.

I pulled on my pants and boots and tried not to trip over the remnants of Karen's yarn matrix. With my sweatshirt hood pulled up, I peered out of the room. The hall was dimly lit and totally deserted. I inched down to the guys' room. Dad's familiar snores drifted out from beneath the door. He was sleeping, and since there was no light on, I was sure that Kyle was sleeping, too.

The howling wind seemed to carry my name to me over and over. A chill climbed up my back. I shook it off. It was nothing, I told myself. *Just go back to bed.* But I had come this far.

I went to the nearest window and peered out through the snow-crusted glass. A figure was hunched on the icy ground. The relentless wind battered the crumpled form. Whoever it was appeared to be wearing a big puffy coat . . . just like the one that Randal always wore! My heart raced in my chest. Had he stumbled outside and fallen? He could be hurt. A person wouldn't last long outside in the cold and the wind.

I couldn't just stand there and do nothing. I had to help him. I *should* get Dad, but I didn't know how long the person had been out in the snow. Dad would take forever to wake up. Plus, he always needed a reason to take action. He would want to know why I was awake this late, why I was wandering the halls, why there was someone outside at this hour, and so on. I didn't have time to explain or to persuade him to hurry up. More important, Randal—or whoever—didn't have time. I needed to move.

A line of coats hung on hooks by the door. I grabbed one and pulled it on. It was a man's coat that engulfed me and practically dragged on the ground. The sleeves hung below my hands. I didn't have gloves, but I had put on my boots. I grabbed a pair of goggles and pulled the hood up over my hoodie. It would have to be enough.

I passed from the warmth of the hallway into the mud-room. The cold grabbed at me, tried to warn me off. If I thought too hard, I would chicken out and run back to the bunks and it might be too late. *Just go*, I told myself. I shoved the door open and plunged into the freezing darkness. I stepped into the windswept snow, and my boot sank about four inches, but I kept walking. A crust had formed, and with each step the ground crunched under my feet.

The wind attacked, yanking me off balance. I scrambled for the guideline and grabbed the blue rope through my coat sleeve. The line was a thick vein keeping me from being blown across the compound. I followed it as far as I could, keeping my eyes on the figure in the big brown coat. My face burned, so I pulled my sweatshirt up to cover my nose. I should have turned around and gone back, but then I thought I heard a groaning. He was alive! He needed me.

I had gone as far as I could with the line, but to reach the person I would have to let go and hope that I could make it to him on my own. On our first day at the station, West had told us all to always hold on to the line and never leave the path. The wind gnawed at my limbs with its needle teeth. If I let go of the line, I would be at the mercy of Mother Nature, and she had no heart. Her howling wind would eat me alive.

A groan echoed from the bundle on the ground, and I could have sworn someone said, "Help me." Randal! It had to be him. I let go of the line.

I steadied myself and crouched low to the ground. Then

I took off running, and the wind seemed to lift me, carrying me faster and farther. I tried to drop to my knees, and I grabbed at the ground with my coat-covered hands, but there was nothing to hold on to. Because of its slickness, the fabric slipped on the icy ground. I pulled my sleeve up, but the snow dissolved in my bare hands, like burning salt or sharp sand. Panic choked my throat, and I bit back a scream. I covered my hands and scrambled as fast as I could. I sucked in the cold air, and my lungs felt as if they were swimming in ice. But I had gone too far to turn back.

I crawled on all fours, so the wind wouldn't lift me up like a kite and blow me across the flats. Randal was much farther away than I had originally thought. Distances were deceiving in the Arctic. With my head down, it was hard to see clearly, but each step brought me closer to him.

The mass shifted, growing in size the closer I got. I sensed that he was about to roll over, so I hurried forward and finally reached him. I slammed hard into him. His body was solid.

It wasn't Randal.

When I touched the form through my coat, I realized it wasn't a person at all but a giant tarp strapped to the ground. No hunched body . . . no Randal. How stupid. I had crawled all the way out there for nothing. My face hurt. My throat burned. I felt like such an idiot. But I *had* heard him. The voice had been so clear in my mind. Had I been sleepwalking out in the cold, and had I finally woken up, stranded on a tarp island, yards away from the safety of the station?

I felt exhausted, like I had just run five miles. My legs were weak. I pulled up the thin lip of the tarp and crawled underneath, wedging myself inside the tentlike space. I slumped to the ground and leaned against something hard.

The tarp was covering a stack of crates, which mercifully blocked the wind. I wanted to rest, but I knew I needed to get back inside the station, where it was warm and safe. I couldn't stay out there in the cold and freeze. But I was so tired.

Inside the makeshift fortress, my breathing was loud. Then I heard a grinding, beeping sound. It was something I had heard before—an annoying sound. I pushed myself up onto my knees and looked in one of the crates. Inside was one of the cameras that Jake was always carrying around or placing at the station to capture the action.

The camera was running. The lens stared out of a small hole in the tarp. Why would Jake put a camera out here in the middle of the night? The place was deserted. Was this a trap? Had Jake lured me out here? That was a crazy idea. He had no reason to trick me, and he had no way of knowing that I would wake up and stumble out there. The camera was pointed away from the station and out into the emptiness, the vast snowy wilderness.

What was out there? What was he trying to film?

I stared into the distance. The minutes dragged on. The darkness seemed to grow around me. The floodlights of the station flickered.

Something far away moved, but I didn't trust my own eyesight anymore.

The wind settled. The weather quieted down, and a silence fell over the world. It was like the start of a movie, when the lights are turned low. Then, at the very edge of my vision, something lifted up off the ground, as if a trapdoor in a stage had opened.

As I watched, a beautiful creature floated out. A gauzy, sparkly form of a woman with feathery wings of light flew upward into the black sky, then tumbled to the ground and leaped back into the air again. Light poured out of her skin. It was a greenish color that reminded me of the flicker of light I had seen glowing inside Charlie's ice block.

I closed my eyes and released the breath I had been holding tightly in my lungs. I was imagining it. She wasn't real. Just like the voice wasn't real. And Randal wasn't real.

But when I opened my eyes, the figure was still there, still moving, floating, flying across the snow-swept ground. I couldn't look away.

Was she human? Was she a ghost? A beautiful snow ghost?

At the bottom of one of her loops, the being seemed to catch my eye—though I wasn't even sure that she had eyes. The dark orbs where eyes should have been looked at me. But how could they? I was hidden completely under the tarp. There was no way that the figure saw me. Maybe, like an animal, she sensed me or smelled me.

The snow ghost hovered near my hiding place. Shivers ran up my back. The figure was greenish-white smoke in the darkness, a sheet of cloud cover, a night bird cut free from whatever storybook she flew out of. And she was coming closer.

She was almost close enough to touch me. Maybe I was dreaming that I was awake under the tarp, under the spell of the Arctic, under the magnetic pull of the earth. I didn't know what was real anymore.

Then West's harsh and frantic voice cut through the silence and boomed across the compound like the roar of a bear. Startled, I turned back to the station to see where the sound was coming from. He called my name over and over. His voice ricocheted off the darkness. Peering through the canvas tarp, this time I was sure it was really West coming to find me.

I scrambled, suddenly afraid that West had already left. I needed him to see me, to help me back inside. I stumbled out from under the tarp and waved my arms as if I were stranded on a deserted island and a plane was circling overhead.

I yelled, "Over here! I'm over here."

West turned and leaned into the wind, which was again

blowing hard, and made his way to the tarp. The wind, the snow, and the cold Arctic were no match for West. Not tonight.

I looked back out into the darkness, but the beautiful creature had disappeared. I had to have been seeing things, the same way that people trapped in the desert saw mirages of palm trees and pools of cool water when they were dying of thirst. An oasis. I was probably just seeing mirages of snow and wind and turning them into beautiful snowy creatures in my mind. Ghosts aren't real, whether they're made of snow or not.

I heard a buzzing in my ear.

The camera! The camera was seeing all this, too. If there was something out there that wasn't an illusion, then it would be recorded in digital form. Maybe that was why the camera was there. Maybe Jake was looking for the snow ghost, too.

West finally reached me. Without a word, he picked me up like a sack of flour, threw me over his shoulder, and trudged back to the station. He carried me all the way to the medical center. I tried to tell him that I was fine and that I could walk, but he didn't listen. He flung me onto a gurney. Dr. Kernel was there and waiting and immediately went to work.

She examined every inch of me, uncurling my fingers and checking my pulse, my temperature, my breathing, and my heart rate. I never had to wiggle my toes more in my life. I was covered in blankets that oozed electric heat. I felt myself starting to sweat.

Dr. Kernel's hair was back in a tight twist, pulling her eyes back. Her focus was like a laser.

I cleared my throat. "Do you think I'm crazy?" I asked. "I mean is there any logical, scientific reason for what just happened to me?" The blanket was heavy on my chest.

"Well, medically speaking, a person in your condition could be suffering from dementia, hallucinations, or simple madness," she said with a straight face.

"Is that what you think happened?" I asked, thinking to myself, *What kind of doctor says that?*

She smiled. "Gotcha. Come on, Maya. Look at it this way. You've never been in this kind of environment. You're young and curious—maybe a little *too* curious." She tweaked my nose. "But honestly, I think you're healthy. As for what you saw, I don't know. I only take care of the insides. I'll leave the outsides to Randal and his guys."

"Thanks," I replied, feeling a little better.

There was a lot of whispering out in the hallway. Now that I had been diagnosed as healthy, I wondered just how much trouble I was in. Could I be punished for trying to save a man's life? Yes. Oh, yes. Good intentions rarely got a person a get-out-of-jail-free card.

Finally, Dad was let in to see me. His hair was poking up all over his head and his eyes were bloodshot. He had been rubbing them too much—worried about me, I knew.

I felt a painful twinge in my chest that had nothing to do with the cold. I was the stress causer. He walked up to my bedside. "Maya, what happened tonight?"

I didn't know what to say, so I just blurted out the truth. "I woke up and heard something. Someone was calling my name. So I got out of bed. I didn't know what was going on. I just felt like I had to go—I had to get up."

"You should have gotten me," Dad said. "What happened next? How did you get outside?"

"I was looking around the station, and I wandered to the back door. I heard someone calling me from outside, and when I looked out the window, I thought I saw Randal collapsed on the snow. I was going to get you, Dad, but I was afraid it would take too long, and he would be dead by then of hypothermia or something. I didn't think." I clutched at the edge of my blanket, pulling it up to my face. A single hot tear rolled down my cheek. I felt so stupid. I had thought I was a hero, but I'd just caused trouble.

"So I grabbed a coat and ran out into the compound to try and rescue Randal. Only, when I reached him, it wasn't Randal at all. It was a tarp."

"I could have prevented this. Next time, come and get me," Dad said.

"I'm sorry. I promise," I said, sniffling.

"You were trying to help." Dad leaned over and kissed me on the top of my head. "You did a good deed. Or thought you were doing one."

Karen appeared in the doorway and hurried over to my bed. Her hair was a wild mass of curls. Kyle, who was right behind her, hung back, sitting on another bed in the room.

"I'm so sorry." Karen twisted the sleeve of her robe. Tears welled in her eyes.

"It's not your fault, Karen," Dad said.

"When I woke up and you weren't there, I was so worried," Karen said.

"You're lucky Karen woke up and got West," my dad said to me.

"Next time, wake me up. OK?" Karen squeezed my hand.

"I swear I heard him calling for help. I didn't think that I had time to get you, Dad." I realized how dumb that sounded. Why would a grown man like Randal ask *me* for help? He wouldn't.

"She took action. I like that. I'm glad she's got my back," Randal said from the doorway. Jake weaseled his way into the room. His goggles were perched on his forehead, and his face was red from the cold.

"What did you do to my equipment?" he demanded. "I had cameras set up for a night shoot, and then all of a sudden West is running around yelling for you. And where do they find you? All over my stuff, that's where."

Randal put his hand on Jake's shoulder. "Not now, Jake. She's had a scare, a tough night."

"*She's* had a tough night? What about me? My night has been ruined," Jake said.

"I didn't touch the camera. I didn't move it." I wanted to tell someone about the snow ghost, but Jake was too angry. He would just yell at me and tell me keep away from his stuff. So instead I said, "Did you see anything on the camera playback? Was anything out there?" The camera would prove that I saw something.

"I haven't had time to go through all the footage." He narrowed his eyes at me. "So I can't tell yet."

"Did you trick me?" I asked. "Did you have something set up out there? Some kind of special effects, like a film projector, flashing images on the snow?" I didn't trust Jake. He was just the type to pull some elaborate hoax to embarrass me.

He snorted. "You've got to be kidding. I wouldn't waste my time with tricks. I'm a serious filmmaker."

"But I saw something!" I shouted.

Everyone was staring at me, and I went mute. My throat tightened.

Jake glared, like he wanted me to shut up. "Probably a lot of snow. And wind. That's all." He turned and left the room, but I think we both knew we shared a secret.

"Get some rest, everybody," Randal said. "We have another big day tomorrow." He followed his nephew out of the room.

"Did something happen outside?" Dad asked.

"I saw . . . lights." I didn't know how else to describe the beautiful woman.

West stood behind the doctor. "We're all chasing mirages. I told Jake that there was nothing out there. But does he listen to me? Nope."

"Mirages?" Dad asked.

"The snow plays tricks on the eyes and the mind. Plus the extreme cold causes people to see all sorts of things in the snow. It's not real. *Some* people don't believe it and want to keep on looking," West said.

"Jake's an explorer, too. He just uses a camera instead of our type of equipment," Dad said.

"A *remote* explorer—that's what he is. It's not real. It's virtual. I told him to stow his gear before someone got hurt, but I thought it was going to be him. Not one of the young ones," West said, looking at me like I was the runt of the litter.

"I'm not hurt. I'm fine. What was Jake trying to capture on film?"

"Don't you worry. Nothing to capture," West said.

But I didn't believe that. Not with what had happened the past two days. There was *a lot* to capture.

16

Dreamscape

My leg rubbed against the blue nylon rope as I trekked between buildings. My arms were loaded down with books about the Arctic, covering every subject from climate and weather conditions to indigenous species, and also the natural and anthropological history.

It was the morning following my late-night adventure. After asking Randal if he had any reference books I could look at, I was told that I could help myself to the stash of books in his *secret* library. Now I was headed back to my room to do some serious research. There had to be a logical explanation for what I had seen in the night, and I was determined to find it.

Kyle raced up beside me. His eyes widened when he saw my load. "Need some help with your homework?"

I eyed him skeptically. From everything he had said, books gave him a rash, so I was surprised he wanted to help me. But my arms were starting to crack under the weight, so I said, "Sure. If you really mean it. I have a ton of research to do, and I could use the extra pair of eyes."

Kyle took the top four books off the pile, and I sighed

with relief. With my free hand, I reached down and grabbed the blue guideline. A devious grin spread across Kyle's face. "We're about to have a lesson . . . just not the kind you were expecting."

I had made a huge mistake. Kyle dropped the books into the snow. They sank down, right through the crust.

"Hey! What are you doing? You'll ruin them!" I said.

He grabbed the two books still in my hands and tossed one onto the pile and held the other one out to me.

"Is this what you want?" He mischievously wiggled the book and pulled it out of my reach when I dove for it.

"Stop it. This isn't funny." I regained my footing.

"No, it's not funny. It's ridiculous!" He examined the spine. "This book is about the Arctic." He shook his head, mystified.

"So? I'm doing research. I like studying. I want to learn about this place and what I've gotten myself into." I stood my ground.

"That's the problem." He took a few steps backward, still holding the book out to me like a taunt. "Look around you. *This* is the Arctic. It's not in here," he said, tapping the cover of the book. "You bury your head in a book so hard that you forget to look up. Look up, Maya! Look around you." He spun around with his arms extended. "What are you scared of?"

"The Arctic doesn't scare me." My stomach sank when I thought about what happened the last time I let go of the rope and wandered out into the blinding snow. "I don't want to make the same mistake I did last night. I could have been really hurt." My gaze drifted out over the snowy compound.

"That's why this is so important. You can't let what happened keep you from taking risks. Plus, trying to save 'Randal' was really brave. You shouldn't be ashamed." Kyle raised an eyebrow and held up the book. "Come and get it . . . brave girl."

"You are such a pain." I felt the blue line under my glove. But maybe he had a point.

"I know. But I'm also right here, and I won't let anything happen to you." He held out his hand. "I promise."

I dropped the rope and took a tentative step toward him. "There. Are you happy now?"

Kyle pulled down his mask for a second and winked at me. "Something is wrong with your book." He dropped to his knees in the snow and the book fell to the ground in front of him.

I sighed. What was he up to now?

"It's moving. It's fighting me, Maya!" He was trying to hold on to the book, which did appear to be fighting him, dragging him across the snow on his knees.

I ran to his side and tried to grab the book, but he hopped forward, the book stretched out in his hands. I scrambled to get a hold of his sleeve, but he was quicker and jumped up, holding the book higher in the air.

"Maya, I think your book wants to fly. It wants to be free!" He yelled and leaped around the compound with the book in his arms, trying madly to contain it. He looked so crazy that I had to laugh.

"No! Don't let it go. I need it!" I yelled, chasing after him, joining in his game.

He dramatically pulled the book down to his ear, as if listening to what the book had to say. "It hates being inside the stuffy library. It wants to experience life. Have fun. Get out into the world." His arms shot out; the book was back in the air.

"But it's a book. It can't fly." I followed him, unable to stop smiling under my face mask.

"I can't hold on to it. It's going . . . It's going . . . It's gone!" With that, Kyle hurled the book up into the sky. It came crashing down to the icy ground with an explosion of pages. The spine cracked and a chunk of pages went flying into the air.

"Kyle!" I yelled. "You broke it."

His eyes went wide and the two of us raced around the compound, trying to snatch up the loose pages that were blowing everywhere. We grabbed as many as we could, but a large swath of pages fluttered across the snowy compound, blending with the white landscape, almost invisible.

Finally, we collapsed on the snow, exhausted from running around, our arms filled with pages. "Well, at least some of them made it to freedom," he said, motioning toward the horizon.

"I think that was the last chapter," I said. "I'll never know how the book ends."

"That's the point!" Kyle elbowed me. "Now the Arctic can read about itself."

I smiled. Maybe he was right. Maybe flying off toward the horizon wasn't such a bad thing—as long as you didn't go out by yourself, with no way of getting back to safety.

Kyle picked up the books he had dropped and walked me to the main building.

"You really have a thing for flying, don't you?" I said, remembering how he had wanted to help Justice with the helicopter.

"Yeah, it's cool. And I've never had this kind of access to a pilot and helicopter before."

"You could get your license and be a pilot one day," I said.

"Maybe." He got quiet and stared down at his boots.

"What's wrong?" I asked as we made our way inside. I started pulling off my gloves and hat.

"It's nothing," he said, stripping off his face mask.

"It doesn't sound like nothing." I hung my coat on a hook.

He sighed. "It's just this wild dream I had last night, but . . ."

"But what? Tell me about it," I prodded, my interest piqued.

Kyle sat down on the bench in the changing room. "It

was great. The best dream ever." His face lit up. "When the dream started, I was flying in the helicopter and something went wrong. Justice and I had to eject—which I don't think is even possible in a helicopter."

"In a dream helicopter, maybe," I said. "Um . . . so far this doesn't sound like a great dream."

"Wait—it gets good. See, I saw Justice float to the ground in his parachute, but I didn't have one and I panicked. Then I did the only thing I could—I flailed my arms. And suddenly I was flying!"

"Cool. I love flying dreams." I sat down next to him on the bench.

"But that's what was weird. It felt so real—like it was more than a dream. And it got even better."

"What happened?" I asked.

"I grew wings! And flew even higher and faster. I was soaring like a bird."

"You had wings . . ." I said enviously. That *was* a great dream.

"Really big white ones. Just like Charlie's."

"Sounds magical."

"It was the best feeling ever," he said.

✦ ✦ ✦

That day, the battle over Charlie was in full force. Katsu and Ivan wanted to break the ice and get a sample of real solid flesh and bone, but Dad and Karen wanted to wait until more research could be done. They wanted to transport Charlie, ice and all, back to the States. Randal was in the middle. He saw both sides, but he had a contract with Katsu, so it wasn't looking too good for Dad and Karen. Plus, Randal didn't want anyone taking Charlie away from him, so getting samples was the obvious solution to the problem.

In the afternoon, everyone took a break and Kyle went to check out the hangar, so I was alone in the lab when a burst of static filled the room. It started as a low humming sound, like someone had left a radio on. I looked around the room, but I couldn't find a radio. Was it coming from an intercom system? I couldn't tell. The longer I listened, the more it sounded almost like a muffled voice, a scratchy one on an old radio. I searched the lab for a stereo system, or for a computer that had been left on, but I found nothing. It was starting to grate on my nerves.

"Maybe it's a ghost. Maybe the station is haunted," I said aloud.

It was probably nothing.

I don't know why, but I opened the heavy door to the freezer. The seal broke and a wave of frosty air floated out. I wasn't wearing my coat, so I stayed in the doorway, rubbing my arms and peering inside. No change with Charlie. No glowing light.

The noise got louder and turned into a buzzing sound, like a swarm of electric wasps. Overcome with dizziness, I leaned on the door frame. The buzzing noise kept getting louder and louder. I put my hands over my ears. The annoying buzz was too much to handle—I had to leave the lab. So I tried to shut the door to the freezer. I pushed hard on it, but before it closed completely, the ice encasing Charlie cracked.

As I stared, mesmerized, an enormous fissure appeared, and then the crack spidered out over the entire surface of the frozen block. The buzzing sound grew louder and then changed, shifting like a radio changing frequency. Huge chunks of ice broke off, fell to the floor, and shattered. What was left of the block began to melt rapidly. Water beaded up and dripped down the surface, pooling on the table. But the room was still cold. I stepped inside to get a better look. This couldn't be happening! But the ice kept melting, and the puddle on the floor kept growing and spreading.

After the ice shattered, the noise receded. I stood there, stunned. It had happened so fast, I didn't know how to react. Had I done something to cause the ice to break? But I hadn't even touched it or been anywhere near it.

Water continued to spill off the table in a wave that rushed toward me. Within seconds, I was standing in a foot of cold water. The ice had melted in a huge rush of water.

This was impossible! Ice didn't melt that fast, and it didn't just crack and break apart, especially in a climate-controlled freezer.

I had no idea where all the water was coming from. There couldn't be that much, unless a pipe had broken. I looked around, trying to rationalize what I was seeing. But if a pipe had broken in the freezer, the water would be frozen, or at least would have started to freeze. I backed up, bracing myself against a table. I had to stop the melting. I just didn't know how. Fear washed over me. The water was rising higher and higher.

I raced out of the freezer toward the door leading out of the lab.

As I got near it, I turned around, taking in one last glance of the ruin left behind. The freezer door was wide open. The ice block had completely melted, and there on the table was the body of the boy we called Charlie.

His arm twitched. His fingers stretched. His torso shifted. I tripped, bumping my hip against some shelves. I couldn't believe what I was seeing. My heart pounded in my chest.

Charlie sat up on the table and stared at me with huge black eyes. He opened his wings wide into the air. They were white and enormous, and they arched over his head. His mouth opened wide like a fish's and he gasped, taking in huge breaths of air. A glowing bluish-green light bloomed inside his chest, exactly like the flicker of light I had seen inside the ice before. He lifted his chin and looked right into my eyes, pleading with me. He needed me. I could feel it. I could feel the glowing warmth in his chest. It was life.

Charlie was alive, and he was trapped in the ice.

I tried not to panic, but the water had covered my shoes and soaked my jeans, and it was still rising fast. A sharp, tingling pain raced up my body from where the icy water soaked through to skin. I ran the last few steps to the door of the lab, but the water flooded the room, pushing so hard against the door that I couldn't open it inward.

I was trapped. I banged my clenched fists against the door. My throat was raw from screaming, but no one could hear me. No one knew I was in trouble. Hot tears streamed down my face as the water lifted me off my feet, throwing me against the door.

The water was up to my neck now, and I tasted salt. I kicked with my legs and the water lifted me up. I tried to swim, grabbing on to anything I could find to keep my head up, but I couldn't hold on. I went under, sliding below the surface as I watched, helpless. Panic exploded in my chest. I was drowning in the middle of the day, in the lab, in Randal's million-dollar research station. It made no sense. It couldn't be real.

It became harder to move my legs. The water felt thick, like gelatin, and it was hardening. And then the water surrounding me froze solid, and I was encased inside an icy block, suspended.

My arms were outstretched and my legs were captured in a bent, kicking pose. My hair floated out in thin white wires, each strand trapped in the ice in a brittle web. It would have been a pretty thing to see, like a tragic fairy tale, a scene of a girl frozen forever.

Was that how it would end? Would I die like this, like a baby mammoth swallowed by the melting ice? Would my father excavate my frozen body like the woolly mammoth that had always eluded him? I was the ice girl, the old girl, and I was trapped.

But I was still alive. My heart still raced in my chest and air still filled my lungs. I was still aware of everything around me. I could see the lab and hear the faint buzzing sound. A computer blinked from the workstation where it sat. The lights still shone brightly from the bank of overhead fluorescent fixtures. Why was I not dead? It was too real to be a dream. I had to think of something, *do* something to help me get free. I was frozen, just like Charlie.

If I could turn my head, I would look back at him, but I was stuck.

Was Charlie somehow doing this? Was he sending me a message?

And if he was, could I send him one back? Could he hear me or sense me?

I had to try to do something, even if it didn't work. I focused my thoughts. I called out to Charlie silently. *Please hear me. Please let me go.* I screamed in my mind.

Charlie, stop!

For a few moments nothing happened. Loneliness overwhelmed me. The stillness was terrible. My mind raced and then bumped around in my head like a trapped insect looking for a way out.

Then slowly the buzzing sound receded, and the ice softened its grasp on me. I could move my body a little—a finger and then my foot. The ice groaned. It was breaking up, melting, disappearing as quickly as it had come.

I slumped to the floor, and within just a few minutes the water had receded like a mysterious tide that had never been there. The floor was completely dry, and I lay shivering on the cold tile. I wanted to get up and run away, run back to my room and pack my bags and leave the station.

But I struggled to my feet and walked over to the open freezer door, and I saw what I knew I would see. Charlie hadn't gone anywhere. He was still trapped in the block of ice. I leaned against the door frame. The block hadn't miraculously melted at all, filling the lab with water, drowning me, and freezing me into a human ice cube. It had been an illusion, some trick played on my mind.

I didn't know how it had happened, but I think it was Charlie, and I think he was trying to send me a message, and that message was, *Help me.*

I couldn't explain any of it scientifically. The only thing I knew for sure was that I understood how Charlie felt: alone, trapped, helpless, but aware of everything going on around him. I had to do something to help him. Longing bubbled up inside me, pushing against my heart. It ached for the boy trapped in the ice. I wanted to tell Dad—but he was so busy, so excited to have found Charlie. Everyone was.

Anyway, what would I tell him? I felt like I was slipping. I knew what I had seen. I had felt everything, and I knew it wasn't a dream. Was the weather affecting me, or was I just going crazy? Maybe Dr. Kernel was right and I was delusional, seeing things. No one would believe me, especially after the incident with the snow ghost. But still, no matter how hard I told myself to be logical, the sense I had about Charlie wouldn't go away.

I went back to my room and changed into my pajamas and put on two fresh pairs of socks, sweatshirts, and scarves, because even inside it was never really warm without at least two layers of clothes. I huddled on my bunk and decided to wait until I could figure things out.

Something weird was going on. There had been all the strange events—the flickering light, the power outages, the strange feelings and emotions and dreams. All the events had one thing in common: They all began when Charlie arrived.

After my experience in the lab, I just wanted to go to bed, but I was too anxious, too jittery for sleep. Time at the station blurred together, days and nights. Once the discovery of Charlie was made, Dad had postponed our early departure, and now we were back to the original timeline of a month's stay before I had to be back for school. No wonder Ivan was having a hard time acclimating to the

Arctic. I was feeling off balance, too, like nothing around me was real, but only a snow-swept mirage.

Once I had warmed up a little, I got up and went back to the scene of the strangeness—the lab. Randal, Karen, and Katsu were there, all in the freezer, so I waited. I sat at the desk and watched as the computer screen filled with Charlie's test information—information that was impossible for me to decipher. I shifted in my chair and my foot hit something on the shelf beneath me. I saw a flash of silver at my feet. Katsu's silver case. It sparkled like a silver fish, a lure, a hook. Silver was the most unsympathetic color in the spectrum. Shiny and impenetrable, it was a logical color. It was a little bit science and a little bit sparkly. Silver was tough and glamorous at the same time.

There the case sat, all alone on the shelf. Anyone could unlatch it and take a quick peek inside. No one would know. I inched the case closer to myself with the heel of my boot. Then I saw the lock. It probably wouldn't open. That would be the test; if it was unlocked, I would peek, if it was locked, I would leave it alone. Let fate decide.

I crouched under the table and flicked the clasps. They opened with a pop. My pulse quickened. All I had to do was lift the lid and look inside.

The lid sprang open, and I saw that the case was lined with thick gray insulated foam. Nestled in the lining on one side were sharp surgical instruments for cutting, slicing, and piercing, along with a tool that looked like a small electric drill. The other side of the case was filled with empty glass vials. I felt sick to my stomach. And then I felt a hot anger slide over me. I knew what the tools were used for. Katsu was going to hurt Charlie. He didn't understand what he was doing. He didn't realize that Charlie was special. I couldn't let Katsu use his *tools* on him.

I felt the air around me move and I bent down to close the case, but it was too late. I hadn't even heard the door to the freezer close. My nose twitched. The scent of hand sanitizer filled the room. I raised my head and swallowed hard.

"It is a collection kit," Katsu said. His voice was calm, kind. If he was angry with me for snooping, he didn't show it.

"Oh, sorry," I said, trying to smile. "I was just curious." I lowered the lid.

"Of course you were. You are the daughter of a scientist. I would expect nothing less. You want to know what is happening around you."

Scientist. Didn't he mean *lightweight*? I thought, remembering what he had said about Dad to his colleague on the phone. He didn't take anyone here seriously.

"What's it for?" I asked.

"I am going to use the tools to drill down into the ice and take samples from the winged specimen." His eyes sparkled. "Such a marvelous creature. One of a kind."

Was that how he saw Charlie—as a *specimen*?

"You mean you're going to cut him up and take little pieces of him back to your lab to study." I thought of Randal's secret room, filled with trophy fossils. Katsu wanted to collect Charlie and keep him as a prize.

"Exactly. Now you see. Now you know what I'm going to do. It is the way of the scientist. We study. We learn." He reached down and took the silver case from my hands.

What I saw was a torture kit. Katsu didn't have sympathy for a discovery like Charlie. My eyes burned. I wanted to heave that silver case into the cold snowy sea outside the station door, or to call up an ancient Inuit god to blow it far, far away, or to summon a giant mythical thunderbird to swoop down from the heavens and snatch it up in its beak and fly away. My fists were tight balls. I couldn't look Katsu in the eye.

He seemed to sense my unease. "It won't hurt him. He isn't alive. Believing such foolishness is the first mistake of a young scientist."

I sighed.

"I don't mean to offend. We all make that mistake. We personify creatures. Make them seem human. Give them names and imaginary lives with families and friends. But this creature is not real. Charlie is not a person anymore. He is a specimen, and that makes him so much more special and important." Katsu squirted more hand sanitizer onto his palm. The scent of alcohol filled my nostrils.

"How do you know?" I said, finding my voice. Frustration was building in me. I had to do something to make him understand.

"You are right. I don't know for sure. There are no guarantees. But I will take that risk. I will study him."

"What will you do after you take samples?" I asked.

"I will bring him back from the dead." Katsu chuckled. "Not literally. But I will make more of him. Make many Charlies. For the world to see."

More Charlies? It wasn't polite to call a person crazy to his face, and probably not a good idea to do it behind his back, either. But I had to admit that what Katsu was suggesting was a little out there.

"That's impossible," I said.

"No, it is possible. I will make it happen. It is my science."

"But it's not right." My face felt hot, and panic filled me. "You can't. You can't do that! I won't let you!" I yelled, and grabbed the silver case from him and tucked it under my arm.

"You are too young to see the possibilities of the future and what we plan to build." He held out his hands. "Give me back my case."

"No. I saw Randal's mammoth park. I saw that you wanted to clone mammoths. Now that you don't have one, you're going to use Charlie." I felt sick to my stomach. I looked around the room, trying to figure out my next move. No way was I surrendering the case.

"I know this is hard to accept. Long ago science was

feared. It was too unbelievable. It was likened to sorcery. Maybe it would be easier to see what I am doing as a kind of magic."

"Magic isn't cruel. I won't let you hurt Charlie," I said, and ran for the door.

"Maya!" Randal's voice boomed across the room. "Stop this. Right now."

I stopped and slowly turned around, feeling a mix of shame and anger. Randal's face was filled with disappointment. But he just didn't understand. None of them did. They didn't know what I knew about Charlie.

Karen and Randal had come out of the freezer into the lab. A worried look filled Karen's face.

"Katsu said he's going to drill," I said. "Going to take samples of Charlie. Is that true?"

"Yes," Randal replied. "We will start tomorrow with the procedure."

"But you can't. You can't hurt him." My voice was thick in my throat. I walked back to the desk and dropped the case onto the cold metal surface, giving Katsu a dirty look. "Please, Randal," I said, going over to where he stood and grabbing him by the arm.

But he just he patted my hand and peeled my fingers off. "Maya, you're acting irrationally. I thought you were more mature," Randal said.

"Charlie won't be hurt," Karen said. "He won't feel a thing. He's not alive anymore. He just looks like a real boy because he's suspended in the ice. It's what makes him so rare, such an important find." Karen stroked my hair. "There's no one like him in the world."

"That's what I tried to tell her, but she doesn't understand," Katsu said. "It's a mistake to bring children into the field. They see everything as a pet or a friend." He frowned, looking down at me.

"That's enough, Katsu." Randal motioned to the door. "Let's go to my office and discuss the procedure for tomorrow."

The two of them left, shutting the door behind them, leaving me alone with Karen. I knew from the look on her face that there was little I could say to persuade her to save Charlie. But I had to try.

"You don't understand. He's real—Charlie is alive." My voice cracked. "I can *feel* him. I don't know how else to explain it. But I feel him here." I tapped my chest.

"Oh, Maya. He's not alive. He's been preserved in the ice and only looks real. He has not been alive for a very long time."

I shook my head. "You have to believe me. He's alive inside the ice. He's not dead."

"I'm sorry. I know that you and Kyle have grown attached to Charlie. But you must remember what we are here for. Your dad and I study the past. We learn about boys like Charlie to help us understand where we came from. He's very important. Think of him as a hero, giving us valuable insight into what his life was like many years ago."

I knew Karen was just trying to make me feel better, and I knew that under normal circumstances she was right. But she didn't know that Charlie was real. How else could he have shown me that vision? Why else was he messing with the electricity and sending everyone strange dreams?

I had to find Kyle. We had to do something, anything, to stop Katsu before he cloned Charlie. We had to prove to Randal that Charlie was behind the dreamscapes that we were experiencing. He was not a specimen suspended in the ice; he was waiting to be freed from his frozen tomb before Katsu got a chance to use his shiny drill.

One thing I had learned from my parents was that scientists appreciate logical analysis. When faced with a dilemma, they needed proof—irrefutable, verifiable facts. Dreams, visions, and gut feelings are not facts. As much as I *knew* they were true, I couldn't prove it yet. If I wanted to help Charlie, I would have to prove with cold, hard data that he was alive.

I couldn't get the image of Charlie sitting up on the metal table in the lab out of my mind. His gaze locked on to mine. His wings stretched out, ruffling the air. Mostly I felt pain— his pain, his fear, his panic to be freed from the frozen block of ice. I had a problem to solve. I had to help Charlie.

There was only one person who might have the proof I was looking for. He might even have it on film.

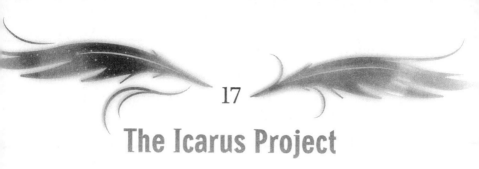

17

The Icarus Project

Kyle and I huddled over a cup of cocoa, discussing the events of the past few days. I had decided to confide in him.

"The weirdest thing happened to me," I began.

"Does it have to do with Charlie?" Kyle had a serious look on his face. "Go on."

He listened as I told him about seeing the glowing light inside Charlie, about freezing in midair in the lab and how I felt a strange presence, but not a scary one, just like someone was there with me.

And then Kyle did the coolest thing ever. He believed me. He didn't think the glowing light was weird at all. "What do you think it was?" he asked.

"I think it was Charlie," I said. "Who else would it be?" I ran my hands through my tangled hair.

"Well, I don't know." Kyle eyed me strangely. "Are you feeling OK?"

"Yes, I'm fine. Why?" I asked a little too quickly.

Kyle held his hands up. "Don't get so defensive."

"What? Do you think I'm crazy?" I asked.

"No, I've just never seen you so passionate about anything," Kyle said. "I think we need to check it out."

I took a deep breath and told him about the camera under the tarp and what it might have captured. I hated to admit it, but Jake and his camera were my only hope to save Charlie. I didn't think it was a coincidence that the snow ghost I saw had wings just like Charlie's. If Jake got the winged creature on tape, then maybe we could use it to keep Charlie at the station, to protect him. Maybe we could get some endangered-species status or at least persuade the scientists and Randal to see him in a new way—more than just a specimen. It was worth a shot.

"We have to get a look at the tape," I said to Kyle. "I have to find out if the camera captured anything."

"We could sneak into Jake's room and watch the playback on his computer. He uploads all the film he shoots every day so he has a backup."

I nodded. It sounded like a plan to me.

✦ ✦ ✦

Jake's room was surprisingly neat. His bed looked like you could bounce a quarter off it. There was a dresser in one corner and a laundry bag hanging on a hook. A neat L-shaped desk took up most of the room. Two large computers sat on the desk. Someone had labeled and tied up all the wires. Numerous cameras and tripods were positioned around the room. The floor was spotless.

"Wow, he's got two computers." Kyle rushed over to the desk and plopped down in the swivel chair. "Must be nice to have a billionaire uncle."

"Let's just hope Jake's as good a filmmaker as he thinks he is and got some good footage." I wiggled the mouse, and one of the computer monitors jumped to life. A smirking image of Jake's face appeared on the screen. He was staring *right* at us.

"Do I look like an idiot?" the Jake image asked. "Hands off my computer!"

My hand jerked off the mouse, and I stepped back.

Kyle snorted. "It's just a security screen," he said.

"I should have seen that coming." I pulled up another chair and shook off my nerves.

"Jake's big head is pretty scary," Kyle said, taking the mouse.

"Password," the image said.

"What do you think the password is?" Kyle asked.

"Try 'arcticninja.'" I raised my eyebrows playfully at Kyle and he burst out laughing.

"Are you kidding me?"

"No, I saw Jake type his password the other day when he was showing us the film on his laptop of Charlie back in the cave. He was so excited that he didn't see me looking." I smiled, satisfied that I got the jump on Jake.

"Very stealthy of you." Kyle typed in the password, and

we bypassed the security screen to Jake's desktop. "Now we need to find the film," Kyle said, and he started looking in different folders.

"I bet the files are date- and time-stamped," I said. "Find the one for two a.m. on the day I was outside."

"Wait," said Kyle. "What's this?"

"What's what?" I asked, scanning the folder.

"It's called the Icarus Project."

"Everyone knows Icarus. Next to Achilles, he's everyone's favorite character from mythology." I leaned forward to get a better look at what was inside of the project folder. "The winged boy who fell from the sky," I said.

"Right. I love that myth. Icarus's dad wanted to save his son from captivity and made him a pair of gigantic wings so he could fly over the prison walls. Except Icarus didn't listen to his dad's warning, because he was excited about flying, and he thought he knew better than his dad. He flew too close to the sun, and the wax holding the wings together melted. He plummeted to the sea and drowned," Kyle said.

"So why would Jake have film footage marked 'Icarus Project'?" I asked.

"Get this—the dates on these film clips go back for months, not days. Whatever they are, Jake's been working on them for a long time."

"Before we were even invited to the station, before we found Charlie. Open one."

Kyle randomly clicked on a file. I leaned in to see what it contained, and a small video screen popped open and began to play. Randal was sitting in one of the leather chairs in his private library. His face was red and flushed, his hair a wild mane. A mug was clenched in his hands and he was taking long drinks of the steamy liquid between speeches. One thing about Randal was that he could talk and talk and talk. Here he was discussing a major sighting. He wasn't sure what it was. He kept saying that it flew, that it had wings, and that it had come in the night.

Kyle and I skimmed through a half-dozen videos that Jake had filmed of his uncle. Many of the older videos chronicled the building of the station, which went back years, but the interesting ones came after the first *sighting*. This wasn't the sighting of Charlie under the ice. This was something they saw in the night sky—maybe even the snow ghost that I had seen. From what we could tell, Randal had been tracking the flying creature, following it. In one of the videos, filmed inside a dome, Randal sat on a crate, wearing his trademark puffy brown coat and discussing the being he had just seen. He had gotten close to it, really close, and he described the creature as miraculous, an advanced life-form. The word that stuck in my memory was *otherworldly*. He thought the snow ghost creature was an alien life-form—from another world, another planet, far away.

We found another video of Randal's "nightly sojourns,"

as he called them. He and Jake were tracking the snow ghost across the ice.

Randal had apparently tracked the creature's movements for years, finally establishing the dig site where the creature was seen most often. He speculated that the creature was searching for something—and whatever it was, he wanted to find it. Once he focused on a location, Randal used radar technology to find the mass, which he figured was the thing the creature was looking for.

He had never been looking for a mammoth—but he needed a credible scientific team to verify his findings, and so he had concocted a mammoth "discovery" to lure scientists to his compound in the Arctic and help him dig up the mysterious mass that would turn out to be Charlie. The model mammoth park in his secret room—all fake, designed to keep us off the trail of the real discovery.

I felt numb, but I still wanted to have proof of what I had seen out on the snow. I needed to see the snow ghost again. "We have to hurry," I said. "Did you find the film from the other night?"

"Right here."

In a few seconds we were watching the sky around the snowy compound. We fast-forwarded through a couple hours of wind sweeping over the desolate area, blowing gusts of snow. Nothing exciting at all . . . until an image of me stumbling under the tarp, yelling for Randal, appeared on the screen. My entrance had been less than graceful.

I cringed. "Wow, I look like a crazy person," I said.

"You sure do. Especially in that giant coat and goggles."

"You don't have to agree with me." I nudged Kyle with my elbow.

We watched and listened as I dug around the crates and looked for Randal, until I realized the mistake I had made. Then I talked to myself for a few minutes. That's when the wispy snow ghost appeared out on the ice.

"Look!" I said.

The camera had indeed caught brief glimpses of the image as it floated in and out of view.

"Pay dirt!" Kyle said.

The creature was a beautiful ghostly form with wings, just as I remembered. At first it looked as if threads of light from the aurora borealis had spooled down from the sky as a wave of translucent light danced over the compound. The greenish-blue light was the color of pure energy. But the closer the figure got to the camera, the more pale and ethereal she became. As the creature turned in the sky, the huge white wings became visible. Wings just like Charlie's.

"Look at the face," I said. The winged creature had soft features, beautiful and alien—sparkling large eyes, and long glowing arms. A glittery aura surrounded her.

"It looks like a girl," Kyle said. He blushed. "I mean, a woman."

"It does. Like a woman with wings." I glanced at Kyle.

"And Jake captured it all on film, which is proof that this is real."

"We aren't imagining this," Kyle said. "She's not in a solid form like Charlie," Kyle said. "He's got a body, skin, all that. She's more like . . . energy."

"It makes sense now why Jake won't tell anyone what he filmed. He wants to keep this a big secret." I watched the creature float across the screen. She was weaving between the buildings of the compound, and I could see why Randal had hypothesized that she was looking for something.

This was what Jake and Randal were hiding. That's what they didn't want Ivan and Katsu or even Dad to find out about. They had another Charlie—but this one was alive.

"They want to keep this quiet," Kyle said.

"Think about what this would mean for the station. Think about all the money and prestige from all the interviews and appearances." I couldn't believe what we were seeing. The creature was so beautiful, so exciting—and Jake had captured her on film. "Not only do they have the film, but they also have a real specimen."

"I bet they don't care what happens to Charlie, because they hope to capture more of them. Who knows how many more there are out there?" Kyle said.

"This whole expedition has been a con job, a scam from the beginning. Randal brought us out here to do his dirty work, but he's saving the real discovery for himself. I think we should go tell Dad." I hopped up.

"Not going to happen." Jake stood in the doorway with his arms crossed over his chest.

My stomach lurched.

"Um . . . Hey. What's up, man?" Kyle asked.

"What's up is that I just caught you two snooping around my computer. Trying to steal my files." Jake barged into the room, pushed Kyle's hand away from the mouse, and turned off the monitor.

"We weren't stealing," I said. "Well, OK . . . you're right about the snooping part. But if you and Randal had just told us what was on the film, none of this would have happened."

"Let's get one thing clear. I don't answer to you." Jake's words were full of bravado, but his face looked drawn and tired.

"But we can help you and Randal," Kyle said.

"We don't need your help."

"I think you do." I tried to reason with him. "Katsu and Ivan are going to experiment on Charlie. They don't know what he is—but you do. Don't you care?"

"It doesn't matter what I think. A deal is a deal. And Randal promised Katsu he could have the mammoth's DNA, and since there is no mammoth, that leaves the kid in the ice with the wings. I can't stop them." Jake sighed and slumped down on his bed.

"But you have the film. You could use it to persuade them to leave Charlie alone."

"The films are a secret. No one is going to find out. It's all we have." Jake ran his hands over his face.

"Then why did you do all this, if not for Charlie?"

"Look, the Icarus Project isn't over when you all leave. Katsu and Ivan get their DNA samples. Your dad and Karen will write their papers. I make a film. Randal gets all the fame and glory, vetted by top scientists so people know it's for real. That's how it's going to work."

"But Charlie is special. Really special." I paced the room. "We have to help him. We have to keep him safe."

"I get it—you're a softhearted girl. But it's OK. Katsu just wants to draw some blood and take tissue samples."

"He's going to clone him," Kyle said.

Jake rolled his eyes. "You two worry too much. Cloning is never going to happen."

"Katsu will try. He always wins. Remember, he's Doctor Victory!" I yelled.

"Calm down." Jake held out his hands. "I'd like to help. But there's nothing I can do."

The loud roaring sound of an engine filled the room. It was coming from outside the compound.

"What's going on out there?" Kyle asked.

"Let's go see," I said.

The three of us raced out of the room and down the

hallway. The sound grew louder and louder. I ran to the door but didn't bother to get my coat. I cupped my hands and peered out of the window toward the hangar.

"Looks like Justice got the chopper working again."

"You know what that means," Kyle said, shaking his head. "It means that Ivan and Katsu will be packing up and leaving."

"And they're going to take Charlie samples with them," I said.

I couldn't let that happen. Not after seeing the film of the other winged creature. We hardly knew anything about him. We had to do something drastic. I stared down Jake. "You can either help us or not. But they can't hurt Charlie. Not after what I saw on the film."

"Yeah, we're not letting them experiment. Are you in?" Kyle asked as Jake looked out the window.

"I'm not in until you tell me exactly what this big plan of yours is," Jake replied. "If the plan is convincing, then *maybe* I'll help. And you'll have to tell me what's in it for me."

"Well, for the first part of the plan, you need to get everyone out of the station for a few hours," I said. "Can you do it?"

He put his hands in his pockets and eyed me suspiciously. "Sure. Randal wants to start dismantling and packing up the dig site. I can encourage them to head out this afternoon. That should give you some time. Why? What are you going to do?"

I had only one idea, and it was a big one. Katsu left me no choice. I just hoped that when everything was done, I wouldn't regret my decision.

18

Operation Defrost

My plan was simple, but the decision that led to it had been brutal. I was going against everything my parents had taught me about excavations, but I couldn't ignore my heart anymore. Like Icarus, I had to take the risk and fly higher, no matter what the personal cost.

All I could think about was the air. Air was the enemy of scientific discoveries. If I was wrong, then once the ice was breached, the air would eat away at Charlie, destroying the discovery. But I was counting on the fact that once Charlie was thawed out, he would no longer be seen as just a *specimen* to study, but as a boy. A living, thinking, feeling creature. I had to melt as many cold scientific hearts as I could.

✦ ✦ ✦

Charlie had been placed on a wheeled metal platform to make it easier to transport him in ice form. Kyle and I wheeled the ice block out of the freezer and turned the heat up really high in the lab. Kyle helped me position the table over a drain in the floor. Once the thawing began, there would be a lot of water, and we didn't want it pooling and making a mess.

Even out in the warmth, it was going to take a long time to melt the ice. It took Dad an entire day to thaw out a frozen turkey last Thanksgiving, and Charlie was a lot bigger than a turkey. After a few minutes, the surface of the ice was glassy and slick with moisture, but not dripping yet.

"That was not easy," Jake said, joining us in the lab. "Do you know how hard it was to get Katsu to go with the rest of the team to the dig site and help pack up the equipment?" He sighed.

"How did you get him to finally go?" Kyle asked.

"I lent him one of my cameras and asked him to document the teardown of the site." He shrugged. "Everyone likes being a director."

"I think Katsu just hates manual labor. Helping to pack up isn't any fun—it's work," I added.

"And lots of work. We should have at least five or six hours before they come back, so I hope that's enough time." Jake strolled over to the ice block and peered in at Charlie.

"Let's speed up the process," Kyle said.

We found some heat lamps in the rec room and set them up over the body. The lamps were like small suns melting away the ice, this time setting the boy inside free.

"This is going to take forever, heat lamps or not," Kyle said. "What else can we do to thaw the little guy out faster?"

"What about chiseling him out? That way we don't need to thaw the whole block," Jake said.

Dad would kill me if he knew what we were doing. This was probably not the best or most scientifically approved method of extracting a frozen person. Probably the exact opposite. But now that we'd started, I was desperate to free Charlie. Being here in the lab with him, I felt connected to him. A shiver went up my spine.

"Smart thinking," Kyle said.

"But we should do it slowly, just in case," I said. "We don't want to hurt him. He could go into shock if we wake him too fast."

Jake rolled his eyes at us. "I hate to tell you both this, but Charlie—whatever he is—might not be revivable or even alive under all that ice. And we don't have a lot of time until everyone gets back. So I say we break the cube open. Why wait? If he's dead, he's dead. But if he is awake, he's awake."

"Way to be blunt," Kyle said, giving Jake a dirty look.

"What do you mean, dead?" My stomach twisted. There was no way that Charlie was dead. He was *otherworldly*. Maybe it was ridiculous to believe that Charlie was alive inside of the ice, but I know what I had seen in the dreamscape: a living, breathing boy with wings. I couldn't give up hope. "He can't be dead." My voice was quieter than I had expected. I was more than hoping for the impossible. I was betting on it.

Jake and Kyle exchanged a look that meant *she's in denial*, but I didn't care. I had looked into Charlie's eyes when he sat up on the table. I knew that he was inside the ice, desperate to get out.

Kyle ran the nozzle of the wet vacuum around the giant melting block. "This is going to take a long time."

Jake twirled a chisel around on his finger. I hated to admit that Jake was probably right about breaking the ice. We needed to thaw Charlie out and fast.

"OK, but don't chip away too much. Go slow."

Jake smiled and grasped the handle of his chisel like he was about to bash the block to pieces.

"Shouldn't you be filming this?" I asked, taking the tool out of his hand. I didn't trust him with that look in his eyes. He would probably take a chunk out of Charlie if he wasn't careful. Jake scowled at me but grabbed a tripod and began to set up his camera equipment to capture the entire event.

Kyle and I traded off being lookout, just in case. The station was quiet. When it was my turn to chisel, I found that the ice was rough and thick. But slowly, Charlie emerged. It was like watching a body float to the surface of a frozen pond. After chipping away for what felt like hours, there was only a thin crust of ice above Charlie's body.

I knew that the minute we broke through the ice we would know if he was alive. I also knew that the air would go to work on him. If he was just a body, he was going to start to decay. The discovery was huge; so much was invested—everyone's hopes and wishes. My heart raced. My hands were shaking. I put down the tool. The surface of the ice felt slick to my touch.

"Kyle, bring the lamp over." I set the heat lamp over Charlie's face and torso and waited. "We should let it melt. I don't want to cut him."

I picked at the ice by hand until my fingertips were numb. The ice crackled and flaked off. Finally, the surface chipped away. I wiped Charlie's face with a towel, then reached out to touch his cheek. The skin was cold but firm—not hard like I thought it would be. It was fleshy, like a living person's cheek. He was alive! I knew it.

"Come on already." Jake pulled at the hammer and chisel and hit the ice around the body like he was trying to remove ice and snow from his car. "Let's just do this."

The ice split and fell away from Charlie's left side, crashing to the floor. I backed away as Jake broke the ice from Charlie's other side. The only ice that was left was a thick bed beneath him.

I inched closer and wrinkled up my nose. He smelled a little like a wet dog. Underneath his body was a layer of soggy feathers, the tarnished color of old newspapers. There had to be hundreds of them. Kyle touched one, and it fell off in his hand. Charlie's legs and body were covered in a strange gauzelike fabric. I was glad he was wearing something, even though it did resemble ancient mummy wrappings. His chest and arms were bare.

"Is he breathing?" Jake asked.

Charlie's eyes were closed. His lashes were crusted with ice. I was afraid to try to wake him up. I put my head down on his chest, but I didn't hear anything. I shook my head, and my heart sank.

"Use a mirror," Jake said. "There's one over there." He pointed to the cabinet.

I grabbed the mirror and put it in front of his lips, but nothing happened. "I just want him to breathe. Charlie, breathe," I said.

Kyle put the heat lamp over his face. "Maybe he just needs to warm up some."

"He's a Popsicle," Jake said.

"Breathe," I whispered, and blew in his face. Nothing happened. He was not moving. I brushed his face with the towel again and picked the crust of ice from between his lips. I wedged his lips apart. "Breathe." I blew again on his face, but nothing happened.

"Sorry, kid," Jake said. "Tough break. He looks good, though. I would swear he was still alive."

"Get some more towels. I'll dry him off," I said. I wasn't giving up yet, as futile as it seemed.

"I'll help clean up the water," Kyle said.

I dried Charlie's face and body, soaked up the water with towels, and tossed chunks of leftover ice into the big metal sink. One more time, I thought. The mirror shook in my hands. My fingers were numb. My heart was broken. Wishing didn't make someone come to life—I knew that. But I made one last plea.

Charlie, it's me, I whispered inside my head and held the mirror up to his parted lips.

A tiny cloud of breath formed on the reflective surface.

My heart leaped. "He's alive! He breathed!" I spun around.

Kyle raced to my side, and Jake almost fell over trying to get his camera focused on Charlie.

"What do we do now?" Kyle asked.

"We warm him up," I said. "Get the blankets!"

We wrapped Charlie and cleaned up the piles of ice. Jake carted the biggest chunks outside. What water didn't go down the drain got sucked up by the wet vacuum. I turned up the electric blankets on Charlie. The heat lamps were still going full blast.

We waited. His skin was warm to the touch, like he had been sitting under an electric sun or toasting on a beach. The warmth made him feel more and more alive. He had to wake up. He *had* to.

"Wake up, Charlie!" I whispered. "I know you're in there. I know you can hear us. We heard you. We heard the messages."

Jake picked his camera up from the tripod and hovered around Charlie, trying to get a good angle.

After about a half hour, Charlie's eyes suddenly fluttered open and he sat up. His hair was down to his shoulders and was wavy and dark brown, almost black. His eyes looked like bright blue marbles, but they had a glassy look, like he had just woken up from a centuries-long nap—which is exactly what had happened. He tilted his head to the side and stared at me like I was the weirdest thing he had ever seen. Then he reached out and touched my hair.

"Snow ghost," he said.

We all laughed at once. Charlie was alive! He was real and he could talk—he could even speak English! But underneath that, I shivered. How had he known about the snow ghost? I hadn't called it that to anyone.

"No, I'm Maya. I'm a girl, not a ghost."

Charlie's lips parted. "Girl." He moved his legs, pulling them free from the ice bed. His wings stretched out and lifted up off the wet, slushy table. He ruffled them and shook bits of clinging ice and water free. They were magnificent, better than I had hoped. He shook them like a dog would shake after a bath, and we all got a little wet. The gauzelike cloth was still covering his legs and middle.

"Your wings," I said. "Are they real?"

Charlie just stared at me. I didn't know if he fully understood what I was saying.

I looked at his back. "Are you hurt?" I asked.

"Do you think he understands us?" Kyle asked.

"Who knows? Plus, he just woke up from a deep sleep. Who knows where his mind went?" Jake said.

"We still don't know anything about him," I said.

After his first few words, Charlie wasn't doing much talking. His eyes were wide, and he seemed to be taking us all in. I think we fascinated him as much as he fascinated us.

"Let me get a shot." Jake nosed his annoying camera closer to Charlie. The lens focused in and made a clicking sound that Charlie clearly didn't like, because he swatted at the camera and made a weird noise and the camera shorted out.

"Hey, what did you do to my stuff?" Jake looked at the broken camera. "Man, this equipment is sensitive. It's not a joke."

Kyle and I smiled at each other. I wanted to high-five Charlie.

"Maybe you should go and get another one. You don't want to miss out on getting some good shots," I said.

"You're right. I need to get as much footage as possible."

"We can't stay in here. What if someone comes in and catches us?" Kyle asked.

"You guys take him to one of your rooms and keep him hidden. I don't want anything to happen until I can get more footage," Jake said on his way out the door.

"We should get him some clothes. He can't walk around in a toga. He'll freeze," Kyle said.

"He looks like your size, Kyle," I said. "Can we borrow some of your clothes?"

Charlie pointed at Kyle. "Clothes."

"Sure. I don't mind." Kyle motioned to the door. "Let's go."

One thing I tried *not* to think about was what I was going to tell Dad. I could worry about that later. Charlie was awake, and even more important, he was moving around. He was able to walk and though he wasn't exactly the chatty type, it was clear that he could speak, even if he just repeated the words we said to him.

This meant that I was right. He wasn't an old decaying fossil—he was something new. A surge of excitement filled me. I had acted on my instincts and taken a huge risk, and it had paid off. It would have been easier to play it safe and doubt myself, but I hadn't. I hoped Dad would be proud of me, because I was practically bursting. I felt light as a feather.

Charlie followed Kyle and me as we raced down the hall. I volunteered to keep him in my room. I had seen Dad and Kyle's room, and believe me, unless we wanted to hide Charlie under a pile of dirty laundry, the room I shared with Karen was the better option.

But getting Charlie into my room was a challenge. Everything caught his attention. He was like a little kid and a puppy rolled into one. He had to inspect everything, and I mean everything: the floors, the walls, the equipment, the windows. The fluorescent light fixtures that hung overhead were the most interesting thing Charlie had ever seen—or so I assumed. He reached up and tried to touch the glowing light until Kyle grabbed his arm. Charlie wouldn't move until Kyle told him what it was. "Lightbulb," Kyle said. "Hot. Don't touch it. You'll burn your hand."

"Lightbulb. Hot. Burn," Charlie repeated. Satisfied with this exchange, Charlie walked on, only to be distracted by a fly that was going the other way. Charlie darted back down the hall, chasing the insect. "Stop!" I yelled. "This is going to take forever."

"Forever!" Charlie yelled back.

Kyle pulled a comic book out of his pocket, rolled it up, and swatted the fly. He picked up the squished body and held it in his palm out for Charlie to see.

"Dead," he said. "Gone. No fly."

"Gone. No fly," Charlie repeated, watching Kyle's every move. They were obviously having some bonding time, murdering innocent insects.

It seemed that Charlie was a natural mimic, picking up everything Kyle and I said and echoing it. He sent us dreams, and he could pick up language—what kind of creature was he? I had seen a film on octopuses that showed them crawling across the ocean floor, seamlessly mimicking the complex surface. The creatures were amazing and had a natural, magical ability to adapt. Maybe Charlie had something similar.

"I'll grab some clothes out of your room," I said to Kyle. "You take Charlie to my bunk and keep him there until I get back."

"Deal," Kyle said. "Let's motor, Charlie."

"Deal," Charlie said, and dutifully followed Kyle, with the dead fly still in his palm. As I watched them walk toward my room, I wondered how I was going to find a shirt to fit over his wings.

19

Mimicking

I should never have left Kyle alone with a cool, magical, mystical creature.

After I had grabbed some clothes from Kyle's suitcase for Charlie to wear and made my way back to my room, I was faced with a terrible shock. There were comic books everywhere. Kyle and Charlie were sitting on my bed, with an open bag of cheese puffs between them. Charlie's cheeks bulged, and a ring of orange powder surrounded his lips. Broken cheese puffs lay scattered across my sleeping bag like orange caterpillars. Kyle was using one as a pointer on a page in his comic book. It was a scene out of a disaster movie.

I froze. My throat tightened, and my heart sank. No, that was an understatement. My heart crashed to the floor and broke into a million pieces, or more appropriately a million feathers, because that was what was covering the floor, the chair, the desk, and my bed—feathers. Beautiful, silky, creamy feathers.

"What happened to his wings?" I shrieked.

Charlie's wings were all over the place. A huge piece of wing was draped over the desk chair and another piece was hanging from the door frame.

"They kind of just fell off." Kyle shrugged. He didn't seem too worried.

I picked up a piece, imagining that it must have been painful for Charlie to lose it—except that Charlie was engrossed in the comic book and didn't look at all upset. "What do you mean, 'fell off'? Wings don't just fall off. They flap and lift and fly. They don't fall."

"I just figured that Charlie was done with them. Or that he was *molting*," Kyle said.

"Shedding some feathers is fine, but not both of his wings." I knelt down and scooped up an armful of wing bits. Tears filled my eyes. Dad was going to be furious. Somehow Kyle and I had just made a bad situation much, much worse. We had proved my father right. When the ice melted and Charlie emerged, things happened, things changed about him. It was like the air was eating him up, destroying what was beautiful and special about him.

Kyle noticed me crying and closed the comic book. "Don't you think you're overreacting?"

"No," I mumbled through my tears. "Those were his *wings*. And now they're gone." I fingered the silky feathers.

Charlie reached out a finger and touched my face. He began to mumble until Kyle said, "Tears. She's crying over the fact that your wings fell off."

"Crying. Wings. Off." He patted Kyle on the back and said, "Clothes."

I sniffled and handed him the clothes. "Well, at least now your sweatshirt will fit him." That was when I noticed that Charlie's hair was shorter and lighter. Sitting next to Kyle on the bed, Charlie looked about the same size, but just a few minutes ago, back in the lab, I could have sworn that Kyle was taller than Charlie. Now the two looked more alike.

I shook my head. I was probably just overwhelmed and imagining the similarities in their appearance.

Charlie put on the long underwear, the pair of pants, and the sweatshirt. I had also grabbed some socks. Kyle dug through his mom's bag of knitting and pulled out a hat and a scarf, which he wrapped around Charlie's neck. They both laughed, since the knitted scarf was a seriously long Technicolor snake that Karen must have been working on for years.

"My mom only knows how to knit hats and scarves," Kyle said. "And I don't think she knows when to stop."

I grabbed some gloves out of my backpack. "Here you go, Charlie. I packed an extra pair for Dad because he's always losing his." I handed him the gloves, and that's when I saw his hand. "What happened?" I asked, kneeling down and cupping his hand in mine.

Then it hit me all at once: the size, the hair color, and the wings falling off. Charlie was looking more and more like *Kyle*. Right down to his hand.

"What's wrong?" Kyle asked.

I pointed. "Look at his fingers."

"Weird." Kyle placed his hand next to Charlie's.

The last two fingers on Charlie's hand were missing, just like the fingers on Kyle's hand.

"I have a feeling this isn't a coincidence," Kyle said, curling up his fingers.

"I don't think so, either. I think Charlie is mimicking you," I said.

"Mimicking me? But how?"

"Maybe that's how Charlie adapts. He's starting to look like you. And he's picking up our language," I said.

Charlie mumbled something through a mouthful of cheese puffs.

I continued hypothesizing. "He shouldn't even be alive. He's survived being frozen in a block of ice and look at him now. He doesn't even have freezer burn. Anything's possible."

"We could ask him," Kyle said.

"Ask him what? If he's a magical creature, an angel, or an alien being?" I asked.

"Maybe we should just teach him how to talk first."

Jake raced into the room, camera in tow, panting. "Finally! I didn't know where you guys went." His eyes widened at seeing the mass of feathers. "Whoa," was all he said, and then he began filming.

The three of us decided that the best classroom for Charlie was the rec room, and so we spent the next few hours teaching him how to play Ping-Pong, throw darts, play card games, and arm-wrestle with Kyle. Then we taught him how to make a bologna sandwich, because no one could live off cheese puffs alone. Jake filmed everything and even seemed to be having fun for once. Then, since it was getting late, we decided to hide out in my room until the scientists got back.

I plopped down on the bed next to Charlie. Under one arm, he squeezed Karen's stuffed polar bear. I reached over and petted the bear. Charlie handed it to me.

"Polar bear," I said, stroking its fur.

"Grrrr," Kyle said. I smiled. Kyle growled like a bear again, and I pretended to attack him with the stuffed bear. "Tough bear," Kyle said.

"He's strong." I handed the bear to Charlie. "Polar bears live on the ice. They have to be strong to live in the Arctic."

"A strong bear." Charlie nodded. He went back to reading the comic book and stuffed another cheese puff into his mouth. "Lives on the ice."

"But you're strong, too," I said. "You lived inside the ice."

"I was no alive." He squinted up his face, searching for words to express what he was thinking. "I was asleep."

"You were sleeping," Kyle said. "How did you get there? Frozen in the ice?"

Charlie shook his head. "No, no."

"Did you fall?" I asked, but he ignored me. "You had wings, so it's natural to think you might have fallen while flying."

Charlie grabbed some more of Kyle's comic books. "More stories," he said. "More powers."

"He likes the superpowers." Kyle shrugged and smiled.

Charlie didn't realize that of all of us, he was the one with the closest thing to superpowers.

"What kind of powers do you think Charlie has?" I nudged Kyle, wondering if the thought had occurred to him.

"Well, he doesn't have superhuman strength, if his arm wrestling was any indication. I beat him easily." Kyle smirked.

"But he can change his own body. He mimicked you, didn't he?" I smiled. "And the dreams! He can create visions and dreamscapes."

"Dreamscapes . . ." Kyle said. "Yeah, that's a cool way to put it. He builds dreams. That's an awesome power."

The two of them went back to reading comic books.

✦ ✦ ✦

As evening approached, the others returned from the dig site. It was really hard to hide when everyone in the station was looking for us. I knew that escape or evasion was pointless, so basically we waited to be found. Karen saw Charlie first, and it took her a while before the shock wore off and she could form sentences. Between the room being covered in feathers and Charlie being dressed in Kyle's clothes, I think she was a little overwhelmed.

She paced back and forth. "This can't be happening. He can't be here. He can't be alive and well and walking around."

"I'm alive now," Charlie said. "No more sleeping." He laid his head on the pillow that was in his lap and made snoring sounds. Kyle and I laughed.

"He talks," Karen said. She made a nervous bark sound in the back of her throat. "He speaks English." Tears welled up in her eyes, and she practically hurdled Kyle and me to get over to Charlie. She ran her fingers through his hair the way a mom would do.

"Well, sort of," Kyle said. "I've been teaching him stuff. Important stuff. Like the entire history of the X-Men, and all their superpowers."

"That's nice. I think." Karen's eyes went really wide, and she practiced taking deep breaths. "I'll go get Jason. He'll know what to do. I'm afraid that Randal will be furious." Karen eyed Jake, but he just shrugged and kept filming. "Katsu is going to flip out, and so is Ivan. I have no idea how he's going to handle this. His sanity's already holding on by a thread."

"Everyone will have to deal with it," I said. "Charlie is a living being. Not someone who you guys can just plant a flag on and claim, like you just landed on the moon."

"Is that why you two did this? Because you think we were trying to claim him?"

"Well, aren't you? You all want Charlie for your own scientific experiments," I said. Even Dad wanted to study and publish papers about Charlie—to put his name on the map.

"We didn't want Katsu or Ivan or Randal to hurt him." Kyle sat on the edge of the bed. "Charlie's not a lab rat."

"I know. But until now he wasn't a living breathing person, either. We thought he was dead. We all thought that he was ancient, from another time." She shook her head. "It's just unbelievable."

"Please, Karen." I jumped up. "They'll take him away. Katsu will clone him."

"No, dear. Katsu only wanted to clone mammoths." Karen reached over and tucked a loose hair behind my ear. "I can't believe I just said that. Anyway, no one is going to clone a boy."

Randal stood in the doorway. His green eyes sparkled. He didn't seem surprised to see Charlie.

"We don't know that he *is* a boy, Karen. We don't know what he is, and now I must take him back to the lab with me," Randal said.

"No!" I jumped to my feet and charged toward Randal, blocking him from the room. "You can't have him."

Dad rushed into the room and held me back. "Maya, I can't believe you were a part of this. How could you have

224

done this to Charlie—to all of us? You put a major scientific expedition at risk." The look on Dad's face was utter disappointment. "I'm sorry, Randal. I take full responsibility for my daughter's lack of *judgment*." And when he said *judgment,* it really sounded like he meant *crime.*

"What do you mean?" I was utterly shocked. I knew that Dad was not going to be happy that we thawed out Charlie, but he was really angry.

"You could have hurt Charlie. He's not a toy or a new dog for you to play with," Dad said.

"We weren't playing with him." My face was hot with shame. Dad didn't get it.

"Yeah, we were teaching him stuff." Kyle came to my defense.

"Teaching me to be alive," Charlie said. He smiled a big goofy grin. "Like a polar bear. A superhero."

Dad helped Charlie off the bed. Disappointment filled his face.

"But, Dad," I pleaded. "It's not fair."

"No buts. This is serious, Maya." Dad turned his back on me. "We are going to take Charlie back to the lab, where he will be safe."

Safe? Hardly. The lab was the least safe place in the whole station. My stomach rolled over. How had my plan turned into such a mess? In trying to save Charlie, I had made the situation worse for him. Now he was going to be more trapped, more studied than ever. A wave of fear shuddered through me. I thought I was helping. I thought I was doing the right thing.

"We know about the Icarus Project," I blurted out, playing my last card.

Randal shot me a stern look. "Your daughter is resourceful."

"What's the Icarus Project?" Dad asked.

"It's nothing, just a name that Jake came up with for his film of the mission expedition," Randal said quickly. He was sneaky, pinning the name on Jake. He shot me a devious glance. "Let's not jeopardize all that we've worked for. This is an important opportunity for *your father*, Maya. You don't want to ruin this for him, do you?"

The conversation was over. Charlie was taken away.

My stomach ached. Technically, my brilliant plan had backfired.

Within an hour of Karen and Dad discovering what Kyle and I had done, Charlie was back in the lab behind a pane of glass. Only this time, the room was heated, and he had a cot to sit on. He was being observed. Jake, who was no help at all once the adults showed up, had set up a camera on a tripod and was recording Charlie's every move.

+ + +

The next day, Karen reassembled the pair of wings. All the feathers had been gathered up and spread out on one of the metal tables. Dad photographed them from every possible angle. Next, wearing gloves and using tweezers, the two of them examined the feathers one by one and clump by clump, cataloging the spectacular wings. Even in pieces, they were magnificent. They weren't the wings of an exotic bird but of a boy. I thought about telling Dad about Charlie's mimicking behavior, but I decided not to, especially with Katsu around.

I approached the table, but Dad was giving me the silent treatment. Actually, he was pretending to be hard at work, but he wouldn't look at me, and when I asked how it was going, I got no response. Karen gave me a weak smile.

"I'm really sorry, Dad."

No response.

I walked over to the window that looked into Charlie's room. In it, Katsu was pacing. They were watching each other closely. Katsu adjusted his glasses. He was cautious, his movements calculated. He wandered the room in slow loops, the way a shark would circle its prey. Charlie had a bright-eyed look on his face. The scientist wore a self-satisfied smirk, like he knew I was watching him. He put his silver case on the table and lifted the lid. The implements gleamed.

I had walked right into Dr. Victory's trap. He wanted his samples and now he was going to get them, thanks to me and my brilliant plan to free Charlie. I thawed out his specimen for him. I had made it easier. Now Katsu didn't even need to drill down into the ice.

He had won. Victory.

Katsu took a strange-looking piece of equipment out of his silver case. It looked like the kind of metal guns that the earring store had used when I got my ears pierced. I pulled on my earlobe, remembering the sharp pain as the gun shot the metal stud into my lobe. Was he going to pierce Charlie's ear?

"What is that thing?" I asked. My hands were pressed to the glass. Katsu took a small piece of plastic and loaded it into the gun. "Is it a tranquilizer?" I asked.

Karen looked up and then went back to her work. "No. That's a tagging gun."

"What's Katsu going to do with a tagging gun?" I asked, but knew the answer as soon as I said it.

"It has a GPS system in it. From what Katsu tells me," Karen said.

"Dad! He can't tag Charlie. Tagging is done to animals out in the wild, not to people," I said, my fists clenched.

Dad sighed. He probably sensed I wasn't going to accept silence anymore. "I know. But try telling that to Katsu and Randal."

"You can't let them do it."

"I can't stop them, either." Dad continued to pull the feathers apart with the thin metal tweezers.

Katsu held the gun in one hand and slowly, gingerly approached Charlie. Almost as if he heard my thoughts, his glance turned my way and a satisfied smile filled his face. I had given him Charlie on a platter.

Katsu took Charlie's head in his hand. Poor kid didn't even flinch. He let Katsu walk right up to him and touch his face. I hated Katsu. I hated science, and the cold metal table and the ugly cement floor. The computers and machines buzzed in the background, and I hated them, too. Katsu turned Charlie's head to the side and tagged him on his ear. I winced when the gun snapped and the tag went on. Charlie didn't seem to feel the pain of the metal point that drove through his flesh. But I felt it. I knew what it meant. It meant that Charlie was being claimed, tagged like an animal to probe and study.

The plastic dangled from the cartilage on the edge of Charlie's ear. It looked ridiculous. To Katsu, Charlie was just another specimen. Katsu didn't see a boy; he saw walking, talking DNA.

"I thought scientists were supposed to be good," I said.

"Not all of them," Dad said. "Scientists are people. Sometimes people do bad things or things that look bad from the outside."

"Is Katsu bad?"

"Yes," Karen whispered. My dad sighed in agreement.

"What about Randal?" I asked.

"Randal's not a bad man. He just lets his ambitions get the better of him. He made a bad deal, and now he has to honor it."

The truth began to sink in. Thawing Charlie out hadn't changed anything. I thought that if he was real and living, they would treat him differently, but instead they were treating him like an animal. But he was more than that. I thought about the Icarus Project. Randal had named his expedition after a boy from mythology, one who had escaped captivity by wearing a pair of wings made by his father. Charlie was Randal's mythical boy, and he wasn't about to let him go free.

I turned my back to the glass, unable to watch any more tests. "Dad. What is Charlie?"

"I don't know." He didn't look up.

"You must have some idea. I think he's special. He's a person."

"A *person* doesn't wake up from being frozen in the ice." Dad set down his tweezers and waved me over.

"Has Randal told you what his plans are? Is Katsu going to take Charlie away?"

"No, I think Katsu just wants to take some tissue samples—blood samples, hair samples. Things like that. He'll take the samples back to his lab and study them."

"You mean clone him." I sat on the stool next to him.

"No, Charlie won't be cloned. It's illegal to clone human beings." He rubbed my back, but it was little comfort.

"You just said that Charlie isn't human."

To that, Dad didn't have a response.

20

The Skeleton Site

I woke early the next morning, hoping for a chance to see Charlie before more testing began. The hallway was deserted. The doorknob to the lab twisted easily in my hand. The room was eerily quiet. No one was inside yet. The fluorescent light buzzed overhead. As I crept into the room, I saw that a stool was overturned. A trash can had spilled its wadded-up paper guts all over the floor.

The glass of the observation room reflected my face back at me. Charlie's room was dark. My throat felt dry.

"Charlie!" I darted to his room and flicked on the light. The door had been left wide open. Blankets were bunched up on the bed, leaving an empty white dent in the sheets where he had slept. One of Kyle's comic books was splayed out on the floor. I lifted it up, noticing a torn page. My heart pounded.

Charlie was gone.

I ran out of the lab and down the hall. My mind raced. I had to find him. I grabbed my coat, hat, and gloves and dressed as quickly as I could.

As I was putting on my coat, Kyle walked up behind

me. I turned and saw him just as he was shoving a piece of toast in his mouth. "What's going on?" he mumbled.

"He's gone, that's what."

He stopped chewing. "Who?"

"Charlie, of course! The lab's deserted!" I was so frantic that I could barely zip my coat.

"How do you know?"

"His room is empty and I found this on the floor." I handed Kyle the torn comic book.

"I gave him this." There were toast crumbs on Kyle's chin that he didn't bother brushing off. "I said he could have it because he liked it so much."

"That was the only thing left in his room," I said. The torn edge hung by a thread.

"He wouldn't have left it." Kyle gritted his teeth.

"I know. I think they took him away."

"They can't do that!" Kyle grabbed his coat and followed me out the door. "Where are we going?"

"The comm!" I yelled over my shoulder as the cold air hit me in the face.

✦ ✦ ✦

The comm room was crowded and noisy. West and Randal were there, hunched over a map that had been spread out on the table. Katsu and Jake stood nearby. My eyes locked with Dad's and he rushed over to me. "I'm sorry." He pulled me in for a hug. "I know Charlie was your friend."

Was? There was no *was* about it.

"Charlie *is* our friend," I corrected him.

The room went silent.

"What have you guys done with him?" Kyle's voice cracked.

"We didn't do anything. At least not all of us." Karen brushed Kyle's hair out of his face.

Dad put his hand on my arm. His fingernails had been bitten down to the quick. "Charlie's disappeared."

"What do you mean he's disappeared?" My anger rose. The room was too quiet. Everyone stared at us. I wished someone would just say something.

Kyle stared holes into his mother. "Charlie didn't just disappear," he said.

Karen's eyes were filled with worry. "When I went into the lab this morning to take over for the night shift, Charlie wasn't in his room. I thought that he might be in the bathroom, but he wasn't. I looked everywhere. But I couldn't find him."

"Karen came and got me, and we notified Randal," Dad said.

"You guys had him locked up," Kyle said. "That means someone had to let him out of the cell."

Karen frowned. "It wasn't a cell. It was for his own protection."

"Good job protecting him," I snapped.

"That's enough. It's not our fault that Ivan took him," Dad said.

"Ivan took Charlie?" I yelled. I looked around the room. With all the excitement, I hadn't realized that everyone was there except for two people: Ivan and Charlie. I would have expected it from Katsu, but not Ivan.

Dad ran his hands through his hair and sighed. Obviously, they knew more than they were telling us, and once Dad slipped, they had to tell us everything.

"Ivan's gone, too," Karen said. "We aren't sure exactly what happened, but we suspect that Ivan is behind it all."

Randal stepped forward. "I believe that Ivan has taken Charlie with him to Russia."

"He was pretty desperate to get off the station the past few days," Justice said.

I remembered the scene Ivan made in the hangar. The Arctic had not agreed with him.

Katsu cleared his throat. "Ivan has broken his word to all of us. He has no honor. I want to assure you all that I had nothing to do with his deception."

"He's gone rogue," Jake said, shifting his camera to his shoulder.

"How did Ivan get off the station without anyone knowing?" I asked.

"Ivan was on the night watch," Katsu said. "He could have easily woken the boy and departed while the rest of us were asleep."

"What about the tag and the GPS?" I asked. "Isn't that why you tagged Charlie—so you could keep track of him?"

"It has been disabled," Katsu said. "My Russian colleague is smart. Misguided but very smart."

"Rest assured we will do everything to apprehend Ivan and secure the specimen," Randal said. "West will instruct us on the course of action."

West squared his shoulders and directed our attention to the map of the surrounding area on the table in front of him. A grid had been drawn on the map. "I'm organizing a search of the area. No dome, igloo, icehouse, or doghouse will be left unexamined. I'm going to divide up the jobs, and we need volunteers."

"Ivan couldn't have gone too far without the chopper," Kyle said.

"That's what we're hoping," West said. "Justice is going to take the chopper up to get an aerial view and see if he can locate the two of them. We need people to observe what is happening on the ground to go with him."

"I'll go," Kyle sprang forward. Karen nodded.

"Do we know how Ivan and Charlie are traveling?" Dad asked.

"A snowmobile is missing from the shed. We think Ivan took it and went to town." West pointed out a route on the map. "I think Ivan was hoping to catch a ride to the airport from there."

"Then we need a ground search, too," Dad said.

West nodded. "We have two sleds."

Hands shot up in the air. West pointed, delegating jobs.

"Jake will take one sled. And Katsu and I will take the other."

"What about us?" I said. "Dad and I want to help, too."

West nodded at us. "We need a team to secure the dig site. You two can take the snowmobile out. I doubt they went there, but we need to cover all the bases."

"We'll do it," I said, relieved to help in any way I could.

Randal patted me on the shoulder. "See, dear, nothing to worry about." He cleared his throat and addressed the rest of the group. "I will be staying at the station to monitor the progress from here."

West handed out two-way radios. "Keep in radio contact, people. We don't want any surprises out there," he said.

Jake bounced up and down on the balls of his feet. "Let's get our Charlie back."

"What's next?" Kyle asked.

"We can start by helping round up the dogs. Justice needs all the help he can get right now." West shook his head.

"What do you mean?" I asked. Justice took pride in caring for his dogs. I couldn't imagine him needing our help.

"You'll see." West strode out of the room.

✦ ✦ ✦

The dogs were everywhere, running loose around the compound. Ivan had let all of them out of their enclosure. When Justice finally managed to get most of them rounded up, he prepared the two sleds to head out. Meanwhile Dad, Kyle, and I helped corral the rest of the dogs. Even my new pup, Cinnamon, had managed to escape her pen. After getting a leash on her, I slumped down on the ground next to the hut and stared out over the compound.

"Better get inside." Dad knelt down next to me.

I leaned back, too tired to get up right away. I scratched Cinnamon's head. "Why do you think Ivan let all the dogs out? That seems strange."

"I don't think Ivan knew what he was doing. Maybe he planned on taking a dogsled into town but found he couldn't handle the animals and decided to steal a snowmobile instead."

"Maybe."

The trampled snow of the compound was covered in boot and paw prints.

"Ivan was desperate to get out," Dad went on. "He wasn't thinking straight. Probably panicked and lost control of the dogs." He patted Cinnamon.

"Or maybe he let them out on purpose," I said, getting to my feet. An idea flashed in front of me as I stared at the ground. "Where's his trail?"

Dad hesitated. "His trail?"

"Ivan's trail. The snowmobile would have left a trail, right?" I asked. Dad nodded. "So where did the trail lead to?"

"West said that he couldn't tell for sure. Since the dogs

were out, they marked up the snow and disturbed the snowmobile tracks."

"Exactly! What if Ivan let the dogs out on purpose—to cover his tracks?"

"That's a good idea. But there's only one real way out of here and that's the airport. Ivan had to get to town somehow—so we know where he's going. There's no point in him hiding." Dad's conclusion was logical, but something wasn't right about the dogs.

"Except if he *wasn't* going to town . . ." I said under my breath.

Cinnamon barked.

"Come on," Dad said. "Let's get Cinnamon in her cage. We need to head out before it gets any later."

✦ ✦ ✦

Dad and I each put on another layer and suited up for the ride out to the site.

West gave us instructions before we left. "She's gassed up and ready to go. Take it slow and you'll be fine. There's a two-way radio in your pack. If you get into any trouble, just call Randal. He's here, monitoring everyone's progress."

"Sounds good," Dad said, adjusting his goggles for at least the tenth time.

"The site's a skeleton, since we packed most everything yesterday. Like I said, I doubt Ivan's there. Just ride out, take a look around, and come straight back."

"What do you mean, a skeleton?" I asked, sitting behind Dad on the snowmobile.

"We've been dismantling the site. There's still some stuff left, but for the most part our gear has been packed up. The site has pretty much been stripped bare—you know, like a skeleton."

It was sad to think we were probably not going to see much, but I was too worried about Charlie to care.

"Enjoy the ride, and I'll see you two later." West's stubbly beard, dark eyes, and broad shoulders were reassuring, as was his hard-as-nails stance. I felt better about Charlie just looking at him.

"OK, let's find this guy." Dad waved to West and started the engine.

+ + +

For the entire excruciatingly slow ride all I could think about was how scared Charlie must be, wherever he was. Dad drove the snowmobile like a turtle wearing snowshoes. The cold needled through my jacket. I held tight and kept my head down.

Then the domes appeared on the horizon, emerging out of the landscape, silvery as lost treasure. West wasn't kidding when he said the site was a skeleton. The main tent was still there, along with a few domes, but most of the camp had been dismantled and packed up.

The snowmobile slowed. I saw something out of the corner of my eye. "There!" I pointed over Dad's shoulder.

In the distance, near the dig site, was a snowmobile. My heart leaped. Black smoke spiraled into the sky from that spot like a harbinger, a warning, or a signal. Ivan and Charlie weren't supposed to be here. We had come as a precaution only. West was supposed to catch Ivan and save Charlie, not us. We weren't the heroes. But deep down I knew when I saw the dog tracks in the compound that Ivan had been up to something. He was too smart to make a mistake with the animals. He had a plan all along, and it appeared that going to town wasn't part of it.

Dad pulled up beside the other snowmobile and cut the engine. Ivan's snowmobile had apparently hit a large chunk of ice, because the front end was badly damaged. It sat there, abandoned. There was no one around. The site was quiet except for the gnawing wind that howled like a lost dog. I scanned the area. Where was Ivan? Where had he taken Charlie?

A scream shattered the cold air. Dad tensed and I gasped. We both turned toward the sound.

"It came from the tent," Dad said. "You wait here."

Was he serious? I was not about to sit by the snowmobile and wait. I crept along behind him, ignoring his order to wait behind. He tried to shoo me off, but I mouthed, "I'm coming."

Nothing remained inside the tent but a few crates, random supplies, and equipment too heavy to move by hand. And Ivan. He was crouched on the ground, hunched over like a shrunken troll. The fearsome man had been reduced to a frozen mess, clutching his arms around himself. His face was covered in a thin coating of frost and ice shavings. There was so much snow on his beard that it looked gray. With his goggles off and his face mask pulled down, his skin looked bluish. He'd been outside too long. His eyes were so vacant that at first I wasn't sure if he was alive. Dad grabbed my arm.

"Stay behind me. And keep quiet."

I nodded and receded into the shadows. Dad could deal with Ivan—I wanted to find Charlie. He had to be here somewhere.

Dad spoke in a low voice to Ivan. The large Russian's eyes moved toward him, watched him, while the rest of his body stayed perfectly still. I was afraid if I moved, I would startle the wild beast that lurked behind his shifting gaze. Of all the people at the station, Ivan looked like a strong one, but it seemed the Arctic had taken its toll.

But it wasn't just the Arctic. I knew better. It was Charlie that frightened him. He feared the winged boy and what he might represent. When Ivan saw Charlie, he saw an angel. He was in awe of the powerful, mystical figure, and also afraid of it. Ivan had reacted to him based on his superstitions.

That's when I saw the body. It was wrapped in plastic, lying in the hole where the ice block had been removed.

I could see a blurred face through the clear plastic. It was Charlie!

His breath formed a misty fog on the plastic surface. It reminded me of when he was frozen in the block of ice, and we didn't know if he was alive or not. Ivan had tied him up and put him in the hole that he had once been taken from. Madness. How could Ivan do that?

"Dad!" I screamed. "Charlie's here! He's alive."

"I know. Stay calm." Dad had seen. He knew Charlie was being held captive. Dad was a rock, the steady anchor of our family. He would handle this. I tried to calm my racing heart, but it pounded in my chest. My body trembled.

"Ivan, he's just a boy," Dad said. "Charlie won't hurt anyone."

"We must put him back where we found him!" Ivan said. "He isn't ours to keep."

Ivan hadn't taken Charlie back to Russia after all. He hadn't come to the dig site to hide. He came here to put Charlie back into the ground.

Ivan hiccupped. "He needs to stay right here. Terrible things will happen if we take him away."

"He can't go back into the ground. It's too late." Dad moved toward Charlie. Ivan staggered to his feet and then lurched forward.

Dad held up his hands and spoke to me quietly. "I'm going to help him get some air."

A tinge of fear bloomed inside of me. I wanted to get

Charlie out of the hole and go home. Dad slipped his knife out of his pack. I inched closer and drew Ivan's attention away from Charlie and Dad. Ivan's dark eyes followed me, tracking my movements through the tent. The star-shaped white scar stood out on his cheek.

"You shouldn't be here."

"Why not?" I asked.

"It's your fault." He speared me with his gaze. I was shaking with cold, and yet I was sweating under my snow-suit. "A little white witch," he said, pointing at me. "An old child is a bad omen." Ivan was scaring me, but I knew I wasn't the problem.

I took a deep breath. "You're being superstitious, Ivan. I'm not an omen or a witch."

Ivan snorted. "And a winged boy is just a boy. You and I don't believe that."

He had a point. Charlie wasn't just a boy. But he wasn't cause for such irrational fear, either.

Dad cut Charlie out of the plastic and untied him. The two of them crawled slowly out of the hole. Charlie was not smiling. He rubbed his wrists where the rope had left red marks in his skin. I went to him, but he pulled away, not recognizing me. "It's OK, Charlie. We're here now to take you back to the station."

Ivan jerked his head around and saw what Dad had done. "No, no, no! He can't leave here. He must go back to where we found him."

Dad pulled the radio out of his pack. "Look, Ivan. I'm going to radio Randal and have him send the guys out, and then we can all head back to the station together. We'll forget all this happened." Dad slowly backed out of the tent, pulling us along with him.

In a burst of movement, Ivan stood up from his crouch and lunged at Dad, grabbing the radio right out of his hand. He smashed it to the ground and stomped on it. The radio shattered. Now our only means of communicating with the station was gone.

"Ivan, no!" my dad yelled, startling Charlie.

Charlie darted out of the tent and Ivan staggered after him. Before Dad could join the chase, he grabbed me. "You stay here. Promise me, Maya! I can't keep track of you out there. Stay in the tent until I get back."

I nodded and waited just inside the flap. They were about thirty yards away when *it* happened.

Charlie ran and Ivan followed, but Dad caught up to them. Dad and Ivan struggled, pushing and shoving. Ivan towered over Dad, who was trying to hold the big man back from Charlie. Then Ivan pulled away and ran. Dad stumbled after him across the rough terrain.

Then I don't know what happened, exactly. I heard a loud noise like a crack. Then it was like Dad was moving in slow motion. His body fell forward with his arms outstretched, but his leg caught on something and it twisted underneath him. He went down. He hit the ice with a smack, and then he just lay there, motionless.

I screamed to him, but he didn't move.

I ran across the jagged icy surface as fast as I could.

Ivan didn't even stop. He headed straight to the snowmobile, climbed aboard, and took off. By the time I reached Dad, Ivan was driving away. Panic filled me when I realized that he had taken our undamaged snowmobile.

"Hey, wait!" I yelled. I ran a few feet, but it was pointless trying to chase a snowmobile. Then I fell to my knees by Dad's side.

The sight of the blood stopped me, sucked the air out of my lungs. There was red everywhere. Bloody red all over the whiteness of the snow. Red overwhelmed me.

Dad wasn't moving. I lifted his goggles. His eyes were closed, and blood ran down the side of his head. There was a rough chunk of bloody ice on the ground. He must have hit his head when he fell.

I turned him over onto his back. His leg was twisted the wrong way. I had a bad feeling it was broken. I swallowed and tried to breathe. *Keep breathing.*

I sensed a person walking up, and then Charlie was kneeling down beside me.

"Dad's hurt, Charlie. Get me a pack. Get the first-aid kit." My voice wobbled in my throat. I tried to swallow my emotions.

Charlie sprang to action, burrowing into the backpack and pulling out everything inside. I grabbed the kit and focused on helping Dad. I had to stop the bleeding on his head. It was so cold that the blood had crusted up around his hairline. I packed gauze over the cut and pulled his hat down over the quickly dressed wound. I had to keep him warm and protected.

"Help me get him inside one of the domes," I said. "Get something to help me lift him." I looked around for some abandoned material that would help us move Dad.

Charlie found an old sled that Justice must have left behind and he lifted Dad onto it. We slid him inside one of the domes. I felt relieved to be inside, even if there was no heat, because at least we now had some shelter. I cradled Dad's head in my lap and tried to keep him warm.

Charlie stared out of the small window. "He's gone. He's gone."

I guessed that he was talking about Ivan. I didn't know. I didn't care about Ivan or about Charlie anymore. I just cared about Dad. The radio was smashed, and I was stranded with my unconscious father, with no way to get word back to Randal and the station.

I sat shivering. All the supplies had been packed up. The dome felt like a hollow shell. Dad grew colder and colder in my arms. There was no heat, no generator, no power. But with Ivan probably headed back to camp on the snowmobile, they would soon figure out that we were missing. We should just wait it out . . . wait for help. But when was help going to come? How long could we last in this dome? Would we freeze before help came? When Dad and I didn't return, Randal would surely send someone— right? I half expected West to come bounding across the ice any second. I would be fine waiting. But it wasn't me I was worried about.

Questions raced through my mind. How long would Dad last without medical attention? How bad was his leg? And was I just going to sit there and do nothing?

Not a chance.

21

The Myth of Old Girl

It felt as if we were on the surface of the moon, desolate and alone, stranded among craters of ice. Charlie was no help. He perched himself on top of the silvery dome like an owl. He was the lookout, but for what I didn't know. He just stared up at the sky.

He was wearing white snow pants, boots, and a T-shirt. Apparently, the freezing temperatures, snow, and frigid wind had no effect on him or his skin. But that wasn't true for Dad or me. Dad's face looked pasty. Even with his face mask on, his cheeks were cold to the touch. His breathing was so shallow that not even a feather would float above his lips.

Fear gripped me. The air was rough and frozen in my throat. Without heat, we wouldn't last the night. I had to get Dad out of there and back to the station. As the sky darkened, our options dwindled. We couldn't stay in the tomblike death dome, which felt more and more like a silvery crypt where mythical snow princesses buried their fallen fathers.

The sled was our best bet. Charlie and I could pull Dad

back to the station. But the more I thought about it, the more problems there were with the idea. Venturing out in the snow without GPS or a guide was foolish. It was ten miles back to the station, a long way to travel by foot. We could get turned around and lost even as the rescue party showed up at the excavation site. Plus, Charlie and I were both pretty runty.

Still, my greatest fear was Dad dying during the night. I couldn't let that happen. I would rather freeze to death, pulling him on a sled, than stay at the skeleton site and die doing nothing. Besides, we might run into West on the way. He was probably about to send out a team to find us. Maybe Jake would film the rescue effort.

Dad needed help.

I bundled him up with extra blankets and covered him with a discarded tarp. I could barely see him under all the covering. The sled was ready. I just had to get Charlie to help me pull.

"Come down!" I yelled. "Please, Charlie. We need to go home."

"Home," he yelled back. "I want to go home!" His voice echoed.

A shiver went up my spine that had nothing to do with the cold. Charlie stood on the dome and leaped to the ground, landing in the snow a few feet away from me. Once he hit the ground, he began spinning around in circles with his arms outstretched, trying to catch snowflakes on his tongue, which would have been really cute under normal circumstances.

But not now. Not since our rescue plan had fallen apart.

"Aren't you going to help me?" I asked.

"Help me," he parroted. "Are you going to help *me*, snow ghost?"

Strange. There were times when I thought Charlie knew exactly what he was saying and then he would go back to joking around or mimicking my words. I couldn't understand it. "I'm not a snow ghost."

"I know you aren't a snow ghost." He tilted his head at me. "You are Old Girl."

I stood in the doorway of the dome. I didn't have time to *be* anyone. "Please, come over here and help me pull the sled." My voice caught in my throat. I swallowed hard. "We don't have time to play games. We have to go."

"I will help you. I will help you stay alive. Like you helped me escape the ice and the scarred man." Charlie helped me maneuver the sled out of the dome, and then once outside, he ran up behind the sled and gave it a strong push.

"Mush!" he yelled. "Mush!" One moment he was so serious and then the next he was playing in the snow like a little kid.

"Stop it! Just stop it!" I snapped. I didn't want to yell at him, but I couldn't take it anymore. "Be serious."

He raced up beside me and began pulling. The momentum was just what we needed, and the sled glided along

on the ice pack. We followed the tracks of the snowmobile. But the wind had kicked up, and I knew we didn't
have much time before the tracks would be blown away.
We just needed to keep going.

"What are you?" I asked. Through my ice-crusted goggles, Charlie looked perfect. His hair was fluttering in the
wind. His cheeks were rosy, his eyes bright. "You're not
like us. Look at you." I pointed to him. "You aren't even
cold. The snow doesn't affect you at all."

"I'm Charlie." He touched the tag on his ear. "I'm here,
now."

"But you're special," I said. "When we found you, you
had wings. You could fly. Then you changed your own
body to look like Kyle. You could do more than just pull
the sled if you wanted to."

"But I *want* to pull the sled," he said.

"You're stronger than me. You could really help us. You
could save my dad." My focus shifted to the ground and
every step I took.

"Save you," he said, and tilted his head toward me, but
I didn't look up. "Save you."

"Yes," I said. I was getting tired. White was a heavy color.
The sky settled on my shoulders like a great white stone.

"I'm young, too young," Charlie said.

"You're young? Like for your species?" It never occurred
to me that Charlie was young, like a puppy of his own kind.
No wonder his mind wandered.

"Species?" he asked.

"Species is a way to group creatures that are similar. They share the same basic biology. Like mammals or reptiles or birds. And humans, except we don't have wings. Like you did. You are special—a species like none other." I exhaled. My head ached. I couldn't think about it anymore.

We walked along in silence for a while. Every step was an effort. The ground was rough and uneven, even jagged in places. I kept picturing Dad falling and hitting his head. The cold knifed through my body.

Time melted, step-by-step. An hour passed, maybe two. We had slowed down. The sled got heavier and heavier. I had to conserve energy. I didn't know how much longer I could go on. Finally, I had to stop. I knelt down in the snow, exhausted. No one had come for us. I was alone with Dad and a strange boy. The white world surrounded me. I hated white. I hated the way it ganged up on me.

I didn't want to cry. Even under my face mask, the tears would freeze to my face, and I couldn't stand that. I tried to stand but sank back down. I crawled over to check on Dad. He was breathing, at least. That was something.

"Dad, I'm not strong enough. I'm not like Mom or like you. I can't make it."

"Strong," Charlie raised his voice. "You need *strong*?"

"I'm not talking to you," I snapped. My head fell to Dad's chest. "I'm sorry. I'm sorry, Dad."

"Strong?" Charlie repeated.

"Yes, I need to be stronger. But I'm not. I'm not strong. I'm tired and cold." I rested my head on the tarp. When I looked up, Charlie was gone.

Great. What a perfect time to abandon ship. Dad was still out like a light. I didn't know how long I had been walking or how far. I had to keep going, but I was so tired. My head sagged, my shoulders caved in, pitching me forward against Dad's chest. I closed my eyes and slid into the darkness.

My face was numb under my goggles and face mask. I wondered if my skin was windburned like West's face, the elements scrubbing away a layer of me at a time.

I don't know how long I had been sitting when I heard the growling.

When I looked up, I couldn't believe my eyes. Standing up on its hind legs was a huge white polar bear.

I didn't remember seeing or hearing it approach. It must have stumbled upon us. I had forgotten that it was migration season—something I'd read in a book, but that hadn't sunk in until that moment.

The great bear stood a few feet away from the sled. Even on its haunches, it towered over me. It roared, and a cloud of smoke billowed from its gaping maw filled with razor-sharp teeth.

My mind went blank.

I wasn't sure what to do. Roll up into a ball and play dead? That wouldn't be hard. I was halfway there already.

Besides, I couldn't run and leave Dad alone on the sled. So I just stared, and the bear stared back at me with its black, alien eyes that somehow looked familiar and kind. Maybe the bear was just curious and wanted to see who this strange creature was pulling a sled across its home.

The perfect ending to a terrible day. I was going to be eaten by a polar bear.

It dropped to all fours and ambled toward me.

"No!" I yelled. The bear could eat me if it wanted to, but I wasn't about to let it hurt Dad. "No! Go away!" I waved my arms, but the bear just stared at me. It roared again. Its hot breath was a puff of smoke in the cold air.

"Ya! Ya! Get out of here!" I tried to shoo the bear away, but it just moved closer to the sled until finally it was right on top of us. It was so close that I could touch its fur. I fell back in the snow, scrambling, trying to move as far away as possible, but there was no way that I could outrun a polar bear on the ice and snow. He was built for this environment—tough and strong, with claws for gripping the ice and lots of protection from the cold.

I closed my eyes. *Please be quick.* One swipe of the huge paw, with its sharp claws, and it would be all over. Dad had been right all along—expeditions were dangerous. The elements, the treacherous terrain, the wildlife can all harm a person who got in the way.

But nothing happened, and when I opened my eyes, I noticed a green bit of plastic dangling from one of the bear's ears. It looked like the same tag that was on Charlie's ear. But it couldn't be. I searched the horizon. Through my snow-crusted goggles, all I saw was the desolate landscape receding for miles.

"Charlie!" I yelled, my voice scratchy and foreign, sounding like a croak for help. But *Charlie* was gone. Only the bear remained.

I heard a rattle and clanking jingle. The bear had grabbed the reins of the sled and begun to pull it easily, as if it were a toy. It nudged my leg with its muzzle to move forward and then roared with a deep rumble. So I followed. What else could I do?

The polar bear pulled the sled, and I walked along, side by side with this huge majestic creature that could rip my head off in one second flat. And then I could have sworn I heard a word, a single word, drift on the air. Maybe it was my imagination. Or just in my head, but the word was *strong*.

I was snow-crazy, for sure. Hypothermia made people crazy with cold, made them see things like giant polar bears pulling a sled. But I wasn't about to argue with a bear. If it wanted to pull the sled, I was going to let it. I wasn't strong, but with a little help I was stronger than I had been.

We just had to keep walking. We had a long way to go. I was so cold. I leaned into the bear, which blocked the wind with its massive body. It never wavered. We were a strange team, plowing our way through the blinding, snow-crusted wind. The light grew darker and darker. I was so tired. I couldn't help pull the sled anymore, and I wondered if Dad's pockets were stuffed with gold and that was why he was so heavy, and just like a magical fairy tale, a spirit bear had ambled into my dreamscape to save me.

The bear made me climb up onto its back. I clung to its thick white fur. He was warm and strong and pulled the sled along behind us.

I don't know who or what Charlie was: an angel or an alien being. Was he the boy Icarus, fallen out of the myth, fallen from Mount Olympus, who never landed in the sea but in a frozen bed of snow, drowning in wind? White roared around me. The cold was a cocoon that clung to me. I was delirious. That's what dehydration and hypothermia do to a person. They make you see things like snow ghosts and polar bears. West was right. The cold was a monster, biting at me with its razor teeth.

White had a wide mouth. White had come alive.

My goggles were so crusted with ice that I could barely see. In the distance I saw my mother standing on the ice, wearing her stained T-shirt and mud-caked boots, her nose sunburned. I smelled the sweat on her neck. She had come to rescue me and take me home. She had dug me up like a frozen doll buried in the snow. She cradled me in her arms and rocked me like I was her precious daughter. Tears fell from her eyes in frozen droplets of ice like diamonds. I was going to be OK. I would be home soon. I wanted to close my eyes and go to sleep. I leaned into the soft fur of the bear.

Mom just stood there. She would die dressed like that; she would freeze to death. Her skin would shatter like glass. I waved to her. "Mom! I'm over here!"

She didn't move, not even a shiver. She was a mythical goddess, and so was I, riding my polar bear with a prince magically trapped inside. The cold was no match for us— let the angry white world eat us alive.

"Mom!" I yelled. "You came for me!"

Then I saw what she had in her hands. She raised a tranquilizer gun. "I've come for the bear."

But I knew what she really wanted. "You can't have him. He's mine. I freed him from the ice."

"One last chance," she said, and raised the gun.

"You're just jealous because everything you dig up is dead, and I found a living thing, a real boy with wings. He can fly, and he can mimic things, and change himself—he speaks through dreams, Mom. He's incredible."

I paused, my brain stalling out, screeching to a stop. That was it. Charlie was alive. That was what mattered.

I was not interested in the dead, their bones or tusks, fossils, old clothes, clay pots, or buried stuff—precious as they were to my parents—I was looking for the living, for breathing, talking, walking people. I wanted to make friends and meet interesting people, like Kyle and Charlie,

Justice and West. I might even make a few adversaries, too, like Katsu and Ivan, and a few in between like Randal and Jake. In that second, I understood what I was digging for, and it was all the colors bleeding into one—that's what the color white was—all the colors.

White wasn't alone.

I gasped, a smile cracking the ice on my face. I was thrilled to be awake and alive, and more than anything I wanted to go home. I waved my arm high in the air, but my mother just adjusted the sight on the tranq gun.

She fired. But I was too quick and dove in front of her prey. The dart pierced my snowsuit down to my skin and flooded my body with hot venom. I tumbled from the bear's back. Sinking into the snow, heavy as a feather. The sled was still there, but I couldn't move. I had to sleep, to rest, to close my eyes and dream.

The bear picked me up in its arms and carried me. The bear would save us. It would save Dad. The stars spun above me in their dark painted sky. Only humans would make a fake sky. That's what Zoey said. The little green aliens were laughing their butts off at us. I turned to the bear and said, "Look out for Pluto, will you? It needs all the friends it can get."

Then I closed my eyes.

22

Rescued

I felt myself sinking into a dark pool of calm. Snow buried me inch by inch, like the sand-swept deserts of Egypt swallowing up its kings. I felt the moist, earthy soil of the jungle pulling me under, snaking vines tying me down, like a doll played with by little girls a long time ago. But like Charlie, I was still alive, awake deep inside, a flame flickering in my chest. A rumbling sound penetrated my sleep, rousing me, pulling me back to the bright white surface.

Exhaustion had frozen me in place. The sound grew closer and closer, and I could see a spot of light moving toward me. Within seconds, I was lying in the center of the circle of light, the helicopter hovering above me like a giant metal bee, whipping the snow around my head. Justice's voice boomed over the loudspeaker. "Hold on, Maya. Help is on the way."

I tried to wave, so he would know I heard him. With a lurch in my stomach, I realized the bear was gone. The helicopter must have scared him off. But the sled was still behind me. Where had Charlie gone, and what had happened to the bear? Were they the same creature? I searched the small sphere of light, but there were no tracks in the snow.

As the rumbling motor of a snowmobile got closer, relief flooded through me, and I relaxed into the snow.

✦ ✦ ✦

When I woke up in the infirmary, I was warm, too warm. Buried under an electric blanket, I felt sweat drip down my neck. I kicked a feather comforter off my flannel-clad legs. That was when I noticed that I was surrounded. West, Kyle, and Justice were positioned around the room, trying to stay out of Dr. Kernel's way. When our eyes met, Kyle's face lit up with a goofy grin. Justice gave West a high five. And West said, "Rescue mission accomplished."

Dr. Kernel maneuvered around my bed to check my IV. The first thing she told me was that Dad was going to be fine. Randal had arranged to have him flown to the nearest hospital. The fall on the ice had left him with a mild concussion and a broken ankle. Dr. Kernel said that head wounds sometimes looked worse than they really were. He needed some stitches for the nasty gash, but that was all.

Relieved that Dad was going to be fine, I told my story about what had happened out at the skeleton site with Ivan, Charlie, and Dad. I also told them about the polar bear and Charlie. (Well, almost all of it. I left out the part about Mom and the tranquilizer gun. As fantastic as everything else was, I knew that part had to be a hallucination.)

"Honey, the cold does things to people's minds," Dr. Kernel said, clearly not buying my polar bear story.

"What do you mean? I was there. I think I would remember a bear." My throat was raw.

"When we found you, you were dehydrated and had hypothermia. You were barely conscious," Dr. Kernel said, her face tight with concern.

West stood in the doorway to the infirmary. "Happens to the best of us."

"No, I was fine. And the bear helped me. He saved my life." I realized this sounded made up, but it was the truth. A giant friendly polar bear with a tagged ear, just like Charlie's, had carried me through a snowstorm. Kyle sat at the foot of my bed. Justice listened intently.

When the doctor and West stepped out of the room, I squinted at Kyle. "You believe me, don't you?"

"Of course. But no one else does," he whispered. "What do you expect? They don't know Charlie like we know Charlie."

"You know what I think?" Justice said, lowering his voice. "I think you're telling the truth."

"Really?" I asked, relieved that another person—a grown-up person—believed me.

"I think you're special. One day, stories will be told about your adventure. The myth of Old Girl, who called to the gods and was so strong of heart and spirit that a bear was sent to aid her. You are a strong and wise girl. You asked for help, and help arrived."

"The myth of Old Girl. My mom would love that. I'll have to tell her."

"At least you're OK," Kyle said.

"What happened to Ivan?" I pushed my pillows up so I could sit up better.

Kyle answered. "After we realized that Ivan hadn't gone to town, we came back. We caught him trying to raid the supplies. With some convincing, he told us what had happened and where you two were."

"Where is he now?"

"Randal let him go." Justice stared at the floor. "I wouldn't have done it, but this is Randal's station."

"Let him go?" I couldn't believe it. "Why let him go?"

"Randal didn't want any trouble from Ivan's family. Technically, Ivan didn't hurt anyone. He just freaked out and stole a snowmobile. Randal thought it best to just get him off the station. He had West take him to the airport and put him on a plane home."

"That's not right. He kidnapped Charlie!" Kyle said.

"What happened to Charlie?" I asked.

No one would meet my eyes.

"Is he here? Did you find him?"

"The snow doesn't seem to have any effect on him," Kyle said.

A pang of guilt hit my stomach. "I had to leave him back there. He *disappeared* when the bear came, and then

I didn't see him again. Did you find him? Please tell me that he's OK." I would never forgive myself if he was hurt. Never. I still believed Charlie and the bear were one and the same, but neither of them was around when my rescue came.

Justice answered. "Yes, we found him. He returned to camp a few hours after we brought you back."

Charlie had to walk the whole way back to the station by himself. My throat tightened. I should have been there for him, but all I could think about was myself and Dad and getting back to safety.

"Where's he now?" I asked.

Just then Jake strolled into the infirmary and gave me a nod. Right behind him was Karen, who came over to my bedside. Stroking my hair, she said, "You don't need to worry about him now. Take care of yourself."

"Katsu has him locked up in the lab," Kyle said.

My pulse quickened. We were right back where we had started. "What's Randal going to do? He won't let Katsu take him away, will he? He'll do awful things to him. You all know that Katsu is going to experiment on him. He wants to clone Charlie. He told me."

"Don't get excited," Karen said.

"You didn't see Randal's Icarus Project," Jake said from the doorway. "Look, I'm no Benedict Arnold. I love my uncle. But he's in deep with these guys. He's going ahead with his plan. Katsu gets all the samples he needs, and then Randal goes public with Charlie and gets all the recognition for the discovery. No choice."

"What are we going to do?" I said.

"We can't do anything," Karen said. "We're dependent on Randal. This is his station and he controls what happens here. Remember, it's his helicopter and these are his employees."

"I'm sorry," Justice said. "But Doctor Gardner is right. I have to do what Randal wants. This is my job, and he's the boss." He stood to leave. "Get some sleep."

"I don't like it any more than you do, but we all knew coming into this project that whatever was found in the ice belonged to Randal," Karen said.

I felt tears well up, but I swallowed hard and brushed them away. "There has to be *something* we can do."

West had returned and was leaning in the doorway. "Get some rest and get better. You're lucky we found you. Today was a big win for us. A good day. We got our special girl back safe and sound, and that's enough for me. Justice and I need to make sure the chopper is ready. Katsu is leaving in the morning, and the rest of you will leave in the afternoon."

"The morning!" I blurted out. "So soon?" I couldn't believe it. Charlie was slipping away. It was all ending so fast.

Karen tucked in the comforter around me. "How about I go check on getting something to eat for all of us?"

Once everyone else had left, Jake, Kyle, and I stared at one another in silence for a few minutes. No one knew what to say. It was Jake who spoke up first. "Are we just going to sit around and do nothing, or are we going to plan a little jailbreak?" He smiled wide.

"I'm up for a jailbreak," Kyle said.

"Me too." We had to at least try to rescue Charlie. The others might work for Randal, but we didn't.

"Now we just need a plan," Jake said.

"How do we know we can trust you?" I asked. "No offense, but it's not like we're best friends. And you *are* Randal's nephew."

"Yeah, why do want to help us?" Kyle asked. "Your uncle is going to be pretty steamed at you."

Jake shoved his hands in his pockets. "Look, I'm not a PhD kind of guy. I don't claim to be a scientist. Heck, I don't know much of anything but filmmaking. I watch stuff. I'm like a witness to what goes on. And I don't like what I've been seeing around here."

"Really?" I wondered if he hadn't also taken a good look in the mirror. "You take after your uncle."

Jake glanced at the floor. "I don't like how I've acted, either."

"You can be kind of rude with that camera," Kyle said.

"I know it. I'm an opportunist. I step on toes to get what I want. Just like my uncle and now Katsu. And that's not right."

"This sounds good, but how do we know that you've really changed?" I asked.

"Yeah, what's the catch?" Kyle asked.

"I can't prove that I've changed." He shrugged. "I still want to get Charlie on film. Maybe I could get an interview before we help him escape?" He looked sheepishly at us, and both Kyle and I shook our heads. At least Jake was being honest. He wanted to document Charlie for his film. *That* I could believe.

"We have to figure out how to break Charlie out of the observation room and then what to do with him once he's free," Kyle said.

"I've been thinking about that. And something keeps going through my head," I said, then turned to Jake. "Remember the night I went outside and found your camera equipment set up under the tarp?"

"You mean when you heard voices and wandered out in the snow, thinking that the big tarp was Randal?" Kyle laughed.

"Yes, dork." I play-kicked him with my fuzzy slipper.

"How could I forget?" Jake asked. "I thought you had messed up a whole night of filming. But what does that have to do with anything?"

"It has everything to do with *what* you were filming."

Jake raised an eyebrow. "I'm listening."

"We all saw the Icarus Project. The creature had wings.

She was real," I said. "You and Randal have been tracking her."

"So what does this mean?" Kyle asked. "How will that help us rescue Charlie?"

"She's still out there," I said. "What if Charlie and the snow ghost are related? What if they're connected? Somehow the same species?"

Kyle's eyes lit up. "Charlie's a snow ghost . . . I see where this is going."

"What if the reason she appeared the same time that we brought Charlie to the station was that she was looking for him? That she came back for him?"

Kyle nodded. "Yeah, that makes sense."

"When Charlie and I were at the dome, I'm pretty sure he referred to himself as a snow ghost. He said he wanted to go home. I thought he was just mimicking me, but now I think he was talking about himself."

Both Jake and Kyle stared at me.

"Look, I'm up for anything," Jake said. "If you can get him out of the lab, I'll help you."

"We just have to figure out how to break Charlie out of the lab," Kyle said.

But I already had an idea.

23

Old Girl Versus Dr. Victory

After what happened with Ivan, Katsu convinced Randal that Charlie would be safe and secure only at his lab in Japan. Randal had no choice. He agreed to let Katsu take Charlie. That meant we only had one night to free Charlie. The next day, he would be leaving the station with Katsu to be ushered off to some lab in Japan. Randal had a debt to Katsu, and Charlie was the payment. A contract was a contract.

Well, I hadn't given my word to anyone, and I had a plan to break Charlie out of the lab and set him free. The plan was simple, as all good plans are. It was also crazy and probably not going to work, but I was pinched for time and had to move.

My hair flowed around my shoulders and billowed down my back like a silky white cape. Mom had read me fairy tales where the witch would grow her hair really long because it gave her power. I could use a little power.

I entered the lab to face my opponent, Dr. Victory. In my possession were a handful of weapons—a few tiny plastic mammoths, a stuffed polar bear, and a feather. I didn't believe in curses, but I did believe in dreams. Dad had a dream of unearthing a frozen mammoth, Katsu had a dream of duplicating DNA and making an exact replica, and Jake had a dream of telling stories with a lens. Dreams gave a person purpose and drive.

My goal was to get Charlie out of this cold, sterile lab. Get him back outside and set him free. I knew what I was digging for. I didn't care about the dead. I was looking for living people. Maybe that was why I knew that Charlie had been alive under the ice all along. My dream now was to save my friend.

Dr. Victory was in my way.

✦ ✦ ✦

"What are you doing here?" Katsu stood motionless behind his computer as I entered the lab. "This area is off limits." He glided toward me like a crocodile on the Nile.

"I want to see Charlie." I strode purposefully toward the door to the observation room where Charlie was being kept.

Katsu blocked my way. "No."

I clutched the stuffed polar bear to my chest. "I just want to say good-bye and give him a present." I motioned to the bear. I was hoping that the ploy would soften Katsu's clinical heart.

But Dr. Victory's cool demeanor never wavered. "No. No one goes in to see the specimen."

"Come on, Katsu." Jake, my unlikely ally, walked

behind me with his camera in hand. "Give the kid a break. She just wants to say good-bye to her friend. I don't think my uncle would object to that."

"She is tricky." Katsu pointed his finger at me. "No tricks," he warned as he grudgingly stepped aside.

"No tricks. Just good-bye," I said.

Hurdle number one had just been jumped.

Katsu unlocked the door, and I hurried into the cool observation room. He glided back to the computer but watched me from the corner of his eye. I plopped down on the bed next to Charlie.

"Here, I brought this for you. I thought you might like it." I passed the stuffed toy to him.

"Strength," he said, smiling. "Polar bears are stronger than people." He was wearing a pair of Kyle's pants and a sweatshirt, Karen's hat, and my scarf. The room was freezing. I was surprised that Katsu hadn't tried to freeze Charlie solid again in a block of ice.

Through the glass, I saw that the outside door to the lab was open, and, as I watched, Kyle wandered in. My reinforcement had arrived. He carried two huge plastic cups, each filled to the brim with root beer, and there was a bag of cheese puffs clenched in his teeth. Our eyes met, and he smiled, as much as a person with a plastic bag in his mouth could smile. Katsu moved to intercept Kyle and forgot about me. He did not shut and lock the door to the observation room. Hurdle number two, jumped.

"No, no, no." Katsu held his arms up, blocking Kyle from entering the lab. "You can't come in here with snacks. No snacks! I forbid sticky, cheesy snacks in the lab."

Kyle kept walking to a desk at the back of the lab, diverting Katsu's attention from me.

I took a deep breath and faced Charlie and hurdle number three. This was the crazy part of my plan. I reached into my pocket and pulled out a small herd of plastic mammoths. Kyle and I had confiscated them from Randal's mammoth park diorama. We didn't think the billionaire would need the plastic toys anymore. I lined the mammoths up in a row on the comforter.

"Mammoths," I said. I held up the first animal and showed it to Charlie. "This one is you."

"Me." Charlie looked startled. "No, I'm Charlie. I'm not a mammoth." Charlie's English skills were getting much better.

I continued. "Right—you are Charlie. This mammoth just *represents* you." I sighed. This was going to be harder to explain than I thought. "This one is you." Charlie opened his mouth to speak, and I held up my hand. "Just wait."

I put the mammoth back in line with the others. "See, this one is you. It is real. The real one. The real you." I held up the second mammoth. "This is another mammoth. It isn't real. It is a copy of the first one." I watched his expression, hoping he understood.

"Copy," he said. He leaned over and studied the row of tiny models. He fingered each one.

"A copy looks like the real one," I said. "Like in dreams. Remember the dream visions you made? My dad saw a snowy world filled with mammoths. Kyle flew with wings like the ones you once had. And I saw you alive in the ice. You made us see and feel all those things like they were real."

Charlie nodded. I wasn't sure what he could do—I wasn't sure if he knew his full potential—but the one thing I knew he could do was build dreamscapes. If I was right about his abilities, Charlie could make Katsu believe he was still in the lab, and make him believe he would get on a plane with Katsu.

"I need you to make a dreamscape of yourself sitting here in the lab."

"A vision." He said the word so clearly that I smiled. I knew it was a long shot. But if he could sprout wings and change into a polar bear at will, maybe he could create a dreamscape for Katsu.

"Yes! A vision of you here in the lab." My heart raced. Charlie understood. Maybe this would work out after all.

"A dream of me for pretend." He tilted his head.

"You get it. I need you to make a dreamscape of you to stay here in the lab, while the real you leaves with me.

Can you do that?" I searched his face, not sure if he was following. "We want to make Katsu believe you are in the lab and then traveling home with him."

"No," he said, shaking his head. "No more."

Great. My big plan was a wash. Stupid idea. "Are you sure?" I held up the stuffed polar bear. "Remember on the ice when you changed into the bear, so that you could be strong?" I just wanted to protect him. I wanted him to understand.

"You need me to be strong. Why?" Charlie asked.

Why? He needed a reason to be strong. So I answered, "Because Katsu wants to take you away, to Japan. Far away." *And experiment on you.* But I kept that part to myself, not wanting to complicate the matter further. "I want you to be free."

"Free?" He sat cross-legged on the bed and wove his fingers in the strands of my hair that stretched across a pillow.

"Yes. And the vision will help you to escape."

"No. I don't want to escape." He twisted my hair around the tiny stumps on his left hand, the one that looked like Kyle's hand.

I considered my options. Maybe Charlie needed a better reason.

"Don't you want to go home?" I asked. "Your home. Where you're from." He wasn't Kyle, but he was trying his hardest to fit in here. Didn't he want to be somewhere where he could be himself?

"Home."

"Please, Charlie. For home. Do it to go home." I held his hand.

"I don't know where home is. Where is my home? I don't remember." He looked at me like I had an answer, but I didn't know what to say. Because I didn't know. All I knew was that a freezing cold lab with a metal bed wasn't it.

"We will find out together, but I can't do it alone. Don't you see? Katsu is going to take you far away. And then I won't be able to help you."

"I can't. I don't want to go without you and Kyle. My new friends."

My heart ached. I didn't want to lose my friend, either.

"Katsu and Randal aren't your friends."

Charlie fingered the tag on his ear, but he said nothing. I had only one more idea left. I dug another mammoth out of my pocket and placed it on the bed. This one was larger than the other ones. "Mother," I said.

Charlie's eyes went wide.

"It's the mama mammoth. And these are her babies. Like you. You are the young mammoth. This one is the mother."

"Mother," Charlie said. His face went pale, sad. "Mother."

"We all have a mother, even if she is far away. She misses you."

"Miss me?" he asked.

"Look." I touched his sleeve. "I need you to create a vision of yourself right now to distract Katsu, and then I need you to follow me out of the room. Whatever happens, keep walking, so that the real you can escape."

Charlie stared at the mom mammoth. He didn't say anything, and I wasn't sure if he understood what I was trying to explain. I pulled the feather out of my pocket and handed it to him. "When we found you, you had wings. This was one of yours. You could fly once."

"Fly." He took the feather.

"I want to help you get your wings back."

Charlie smiled.

Suddenly, I heard yelling from the lab. Kyle had implemented the next phase of our plan. But when I turned and looked at Charlie, he was still sitting quietly on the bed, holding the feather. I didn't see any change in his appearance, any sign of a dreamscape. Our one chance was slipping away.

I looked through the observation window. Katsu was frantically unrolling paper towels, trying to contain pools of sticky liquid. Kyle had spilled both cups of root beer all over the table, his laptop, and the evil silver case. The bag of cheese puffs had exploded. Kyle was clearly a pro at orchestrated chaos.

Jake was staring into Charlie's room. "What?" he mouthed.

I shrugged and shook my head. "No go," I said. "He won't do it."

Jake's mouth hung open and he pointed at Charlie.

I glanced over at the bed . . . and sitting there were two Charlies. The Charlie closer to me pointed to the other one and said, "Vision."

It had worked! Charlie had done it! He had understood what I meant about creating a vision.

Jake was pressed against the window, trying to block Katsu's view, which for the moment wasn't hard since Katsu was kneeling on the floor, mopping up the root beer. Kyle had grabbed the roll of paper towels and unrolled practically a mile of paper.

Now we had to get out of the lab without Katsu turning around. I led the real Charlie from the observation room and guided him toward the door. On cue, Jake got down on the floor and started helping to mop up the spill, and distracting Katsu. Luckily, Kyle had covered the scientist with paper towels.

"Stop unrolling! Enough—we have enough!" shouted Katsu. He swatted Kyle away and got to his feet.

I made it across the room, pulling Charlie along. I shoved him out the door, just in time. Katsu looked up. "What's going on?" He glared at me. "What kind of trick is this? You are behind this mess!"

"I don't know what you're talking about," I said stiffly.

Dr. Victory walked over to me. "What have you done?"

"Nothing," I said. Guilt oozed over me. I was a terrible liar. My pulse raced.

"Where's the specimen?" he yelled.

I pointed to the observation room. Behind the glass, sitting on his bed, was Charlie. Or at least it *looked* like Charlie. Katsu glared at him. "What just happened in here? What were you two up to?"

I backed out of the lab. "We were just playing." I nodded toward Charlie's bed and the tiny herd of mammoths. "I just wanted to say good-bye," I said. Then I waved to the vision Charlie, turned, and hurried out of the lab. Kyle tossed a huge wad of soggy paper towels into the garbage can and followed me out.

We found Charlie sprawled on my bed, waiting for us. We had done the impossible. Now all we had to do was get Charlie home.

24

Flying Home

We waited until everyone had fallen asleep before sneaking out into the compound. Jake had created a mini fortress of crates, all hidden under the tarp. His camera had the prime spot. Kyle and Charlie were on one side, and Jake was wedged in next to me on the other. Jake and Kyle had created a nest made of neoprene ground cover and sleeping bags. A small solar-generated heater took the bite out of the icy temperature. I would have thought all the body warmth would have helped, but I was still freezing. Kyle wore his headlamp and had a string of glow sticks around his neck. It was Jake's idea to wait it out under the tarp, reenacting the other night when I saw the snow ghost, hoping that she would return and that we could reunite her with Charlie.

"What do we do now?" Kyle mumbled through his face mask.

"We're on a stakeout," Jake said. "We wait and we watch. Stay alert."

"Cool," Kyle said.

"Stay alert," Charlie said. "What are we looking for?"

"We're looking for someone," I said. "Someone I saw the other night who reminded me of you."

"The snow ghost?" Charlie asked. "Is she coming back for me?"

"Of course she is," I said. I hoped this wasn't all for nothing. I didn't want Charlie to get his heart broken. She *had* to come back.

A few minutes passed in silence.

"Stakeouts are boring," Kyle said.

I hated to admit it, but he was right. I shifted my weight. My legs were stiff from sitting in the cold, cramped den, and I was sick of waiting.

"OK, who's going to take first watch?" Jake asked. "We might as well get some shut-eye. It's going to be a long night."

"I'll do it," I volunteered.

"Good. Wake me up in an hour and I'll take the second shift. If you hear or see anything—anything at all—wake me up." He pulled a sleeping bag around his shoulders.

I rolled my eyes. "I get it. I'll wake you."

Kyle disappeared under his hood, while Charlie listened to an iPod Kyle let him borrow. Jake leaned his head back and pulled up his face mask.

"Do you think she'll come back?" I whispered.

"She'd better," Jake said through his mask.

"Or what?"

"Or not only have you adopted a dog, but you'll have

a new brother, too. Because he sure can't stay here." And with that, he rolled over.

Great. I hadn't thought of that. Dad would not be thrilled if I snuck Charlie home in the dog crate with Cinnamon. In fact, I wasn't sure I'd completely convinced him that we were taking Cinnamon home.

I focused my attention on the empty compound, willing the snow ghost to arrive. The wind blew thin drifts of snow across the hard-packed surface—it looked like a sheet being snapped. I could have sworn I saw the snow ghost a dozen times, but when I looked closer, the area was empty. The glow of the floodlight was hypnotic. My mind calmed. I waited. Time dragged.

+ + +

My body jerked. My mask had fallen down, pressing against my eyelids. My lashes were crusty with ice or sleep, I couldn't tell which. The tarp den was filled with heavy breathing. I yanked my mask up and looked around.

My heart jumped in my chest. I had fallen asleep, and I didn't know what had awakened me. How pathetic. I had to stay alert for only one hour and I couldn't do it. Jake and Kyle were in the middle of a snoring contest. The camera light blinked. The spot where Charlie had been sitting was empty. Panic crawled over my skin in a rush of goose bumps. I checked under the sleeping bags like a mad woman. Charlie was gone.

"Wake up! Wake up!" I shook Jake and Kyle.

"What's happening?" Kyle jerked up in his bag.

"I fell asleep, that's what," I said, totally disgusted in myself. How could I have let that happen? How could I have been so careless on the most important night of Charlie's life?

"Calm down," Jake said.

"Calm down? Charlie's gone!"

"No worries. We have the camera." Jake crawled over to his camera and checked the small screen.

I got to my knees. "That stupid camera is the only thing you care about. We need to find Charlie."

"We'll find him. All we have to do is watch the playback and see what happened." Jake focused on his camera.

"Dude! Look out there!" Kyle pointed out of the tarp enclosure to the middle of the compound. "He's back. Our boy is back!" He beamed.

Charlie stood in the snow about twenty feet away. He was wearing the old cloth that we had found him in, wrapped around his legs and torso. From his back sprouted two enormous wings. They were outstretched, huge, and glorious. They weren't harnessed on, glued on, or attached in any way. His wings grew right out of the skin of his shoulders. My immediate thought was, *Icarus, eat your heart out*. Charlie was the real deal.

His feet were bare and his hair had grown out and so had his fingers. He no longer looked like Kyle but like his old self. He looked amazing—even better than I remembered.

I don't know how Charlie did it. It didn't matter. Charlie wasn't from around here. He wasn't rescued from the past. He fell from the sky a long time ago, and now it was time for him to go home. He looked majestic, standing there in the snow.

My heart ached. He was going to leave—us, the station, everything—and as much as I wanted him to be safe, I knew that I would never see him again.

The wind blew across his face. The floodlight flickered. Static crackled around us under the tarp. The camera made a strange whining sound. A tingle rose up my spine.

The snow ghost was coming.

"Stay with me, girl." Jake was talking to his camera. He rattled the equipment, trying to coax it back to life. "Don't quit on me."

The snow ghost descended from the night sky like a streak of the northern lights. She was an electric pulse of winged energy. Charlie's chest was glowing gas blue, as if a flame had been lit inside him. She circled him, forming figure eights around his body. Her long hair floated behind her, making her look as if she were swimming. Her wings arched out, suspending her in midair. Her face was beautiful but strange. She watched Charlie, taking him in. A flicker of light pulsed at the center of her being, and Charlie's light pulsed in response. Were they communicating? Did they understand each other?

The expression on Charlie's face was foreign to me. It was a look of fear, a look I had not seen on his face before. He stretched his arms out and arched his back. His wings brushed at the black sky, and then he rose upward, higher and higher. I sucked in a mouthful of cold air and held it, for Charlie was a thrilling thing to watch.

But something went wrong, and his wings flapped madly, wrongly, and he plummeted back to the ground, landing on the icy crust with an excruciating thud.

"He can't fly," Kyle said.

"Come on, kid . . . Try again." Jake was watching through his camera lens.

The snow ghost flew away and returned again. She did this over and over. Charlie chased after her, lifting up and falling, and then running after her like a wounded bird, earthbound and heavy.

Finally, she stepped down from the sky, taking solid form. Ruffling her huge wings, she reached out a delicate hand to Charlie and then blurred back to light and took flight. This time I lost sight of her. She was gone.

Charlie fell to his knees.

I couldn't take it. "Where did she go?" I yelled, and grabbed Jake.

"I lost her," Jake said. He shook his head. "I got nothing here."

I couldn't stand to watch anymore. I jumped up and rushed out from under the tarp. The cold was a familiar slap. I was getting used to the harsh Arctic reality.

Kyle followed me, shouting at the sky. "Come back here! He's one of you. He's yours. Don't leave him!"

The sky was an empty pit of darkness expanding above us. The snow ghost was high beyond the floodlight. But she was there, waiting. And then something occurred to me: It wasn't her fault. She had done all she could do. Charlie had to follow. He had to *mimic* his own kind. Like a bird being pushed from the nest, Charlie had to learn to fly, not as a boy but as a creature of light.

I ran to him and grabbed his arm. "Charlie, you can't fly because you are too heavy."

He reached out and touched my cheek. "Heavy," he said.

"You need to change. You need to be like her." I pointed to the surge of light that zinged above the compound. "Mimic her. Be like her."

His eyes were dark black orbs staring into mine. "She's only here for me. If I go . . ." He paused. "Once I change, I can't come back."

"You can't?" Kyle asked. "Are you sure?"

Sadness filled his face and he nodded. "I will be gone from here. From my new friends Maya and Kyle and the camera boy." He nodded toward the tarp.

I swallowed the lump in my throat. The reality of saying good-bye was sudden and biting, but it was the only way. "You can't stay here. It's not right. Please, try."

Kyle stood beside me, hearing the entire exchange. "You gotta do it, Charlie. Friends never forget each other." He pulled his glove off and placed his left hand with the missing fingers on Charlie's chest. "It was cool that you wanted to be like me."

Charlie's chest glowed.

"Like you, friend. I won't forget." Charlie reached out and handed me the tag that had once hung on his ear. I gasped. I didn't want it. I didn't want to think of what Katsu had done. The plastic tag looked ugly in my gloved hand. "Keep it," he said. "You made me leave the lab when I was afraid."

"I'll miss you," I said. "But you don't belong here. Not in a lab or frozen in the ground. You deserve to go home." I was numb with cold and something else.

"Good-bye, Old Girl."

Charlie looked upward. Slowly his body was illuminated from the inside, and the glow spread from his core to his arms and legs. He lifted off the ground. His limbs blurred into a river of energy, just like the snow ghost. He rose up over the compound and flew through the air, circling us.

Kyle and I cheered.

Charlie made another pass. His form glowed and lifted higher and higher until he joined the snow ghost in the sky. He had made it! The snow ghost joined him in flight, and they both disappeared into the sky.

Kyle and I stood in the compound until Jake crawled out from under the tarp.

"Let's go inside," he said. "Get warmed up."

✦ ✦ ✦

"Where do you think he went?" Kyle asked as we sat in the mess hall, drinking hot chocolate.

"Far," Jake said. "Like over the Milky Way."

"He went home," I said, swallowing a gulp of the lovely warm drink.

Kyle walked me back to my room. His mom was asleep. Before he left, he handed me a tiny plastic mammoth. He must have grabbed it off Charlie's bed in the lab.

"Thanks," I whispered. "Though we never did find the mammoth."

"You don't find the mammoth—the mammoth finds you," Kyle whispered back.

✦ ✦ ✦

The next morning, it was time for all of us to pack up and head out. Katsu left the station with . . . *Charlie*. We all saw the dream vision of Charlie board the helicopter and leave. Once they were gone, Charlie was Katsu's responsibility, and if he happened to disappear suddenly, then Katsu would only have himself to blame. The contents of his silver case had been ruined. Root beer and tissue samples don't mix. But before he left, he assured Randal that no harm had been done, and he was satisfied that their deal was complete.

Kyle and I promised to stay connected. He gave me the stuffed polar bear as a memento of our time at the station. Karen did conferences in Washington, D.C., all the time and said that she would arrange a visit. I told them they could stay with Dad and me anytime. Jake gave us his blog address, so we could follow his filmmaking exploits. He never did show us what he had captured on film the previous night, but I couldn't wait to see his documentary when he was finished.

Randal personally took me to meet up with Dad at the hospital; from there we went on to the airport to fly home. Randal was in rare spirits. I climbed aboard the helicopter and got the center seat again, this time sharing it only with Cinnamon. My new pup curled up next to me, and I secured her harness. I hoped Dad wouldn't mind too much—Randal had insisted that I keep her.

Justice smiled at me with his bright white teeth. He had his aviator sunglasses on and looked like the charismatic pilot he was. "Let's get this bird in the air and get you home."

I couldn't agree more.

I looked out the window as the chopper lifted up, half expecting to see pages from the broken book fluttering by. Flying wasn't so bad, now that Charlie had showed me how. It could even be fun—freeing.

Kyle was right. It was better not to know how a book would end. That way, I got to decide and write my own ending.

25

Exploration Pluto

It felt good to be home. D.C. was filled with people lounging on blankets, soaking in the fresh air, finally free from winter's cold grasp. Spring had exploded all over the place, leaving a trail of fresh green grass and daffodils everywhere. The snow had melted and the temperature had warmed. White had disappeared.

Zoey and I were hanging out in my bedroom, dreaming of the future. My next expedition was going to be to Pluto. Zoey and I had it all figured out. Space tourism was not that far off. Well, OK, it was pretty far off, and then there was the whole money problem. But you never know when you might meet a billionaire with lots of time on his hands and an adventurous spirit.

I sat at my desk, staring at the computer screen. It flickered to life, and Mom's face appeared. She was at her apartment across town but wanted to see me right away. Her face beamed. We always had our window to each other's lives.

"How was it? Tell me everything!" Her tan had faded since the last time we'd talked.

"I'm seeing you tomorrow. Can't you wait?" I said, curling my legs up under me.

"No." She stuck her bottom lip out, pretending to pout. "This was your first expedition and I want to hear everything."

I pulled something from my bag and pretended to hide it from her. "Well, there is one thing I could show you."

"I knew it!" she said. "Show me."

"Tell me again what your first discovery was?" I smiled slyly at her. I loved this story.

"Oh, you don't want to hear about that," she said, waving the suggestion off.

"*I* do," Zoey said, and stuck her face in front of the computer. "Please tell."

Mom sighed. "Well, it was a very, very important discovery. Although I hate to brag."

"Really," I said. "Oh, go on. Please brag."

"Um, no. No, I can't. You go, tell me about the Arctic." Mom tried to stall.

"You first."

"Oh, all right. My first discovery was a bone."

"A bone . . ." Zoey glanced at me, expecting more the story.

"Well, I thought it was a bone, but it wasn't really a bone." Mom scrunched up her face.

"Tell Zoey what it really was." I loved this part.

"I thought I had made a huge discovery, so I created a

fuss and called together the lead professor on the dig and everyone over to see my fabulous find." Mom shrugged. "It turned out my groundbreaking discovery was a stick. A petrified stick."

"A stick?" Zoey laughed.

"I was thankful, really. A day later, another scientist discovered some petrified goat dung. I always said at least mine wasn't dung."

"Way to look on the bright side," I said.

"Now spill it," she said. "What do you have there on the desk?" She tried to peer down through the computer screen.

I held up a feather to the camera so she could see. It was one of Charlie's. I probably shouldn't have, but I didn't think anyone would mind. I turned it around to give her a good view.

"Guess what it is," I said.

Mom squinted, concentrating. "Um, a goose feather . . . No, no, it's from a swan."

"Nope. Try again."

"It's from an exotic bird. A magical bird. Um . . . a Vegas showgirl," Mom joked, and we all laughed.

Zoey leaned over my shoulder and stared into the camera. "You'll never guess."

"I give up. Tell me. Where did you get the feather from?"

A raised my chin and told her. "I got it from a boy."

"A boy." Both of her eyebrows rose. "A boy with feathers."

"Yep. He had wings."

"Really?"

"Really."

"And what did you do with the winged boy?" she asked me. "Did you keep him? Did you put him in a museum? Can I see this amazing boy?"

"No, you can't. I'm sorry." I shook my head.

"Why not? Where did he go?"

"We set him free, of course."

"Of course," Zoey said. "What else would you do with a winged boy? You can't keep him. Though I would have loved to have a winged boy to hang out with."

"His mom missed him," I said. "He wanted to go home."

"I bet she did," Mom said. "I'm glad you sent him home. And I'm even happier that you're home."

"Me too. The Arctic was fun, but a person can only take so much snow."

"It was tough not having you here when I got back," Mom said. "I had to wait for *you* this time."

"Well, the life of a scientist is a tough one," I said. "But you'll get used to it."

The smell of lasagna drifted in from the kitchen. "Time for dinner," Dad called.

A moment later, Cinnamon yapped at Dad's feet as he hobbled into my room, sporting a walking cast on his ankle. He was wearing two huge oven mitts and carrying a casserole dish. He tilted it forward so we could all see it.

"It's green!" Zoey yelled.

"Green lasagna?" Mom asked. "Is this a new delicacy?"

"Yes, a new invention. I call it Martian lasagna."

"I love it!" Zoey said.

"On that note, I'm signing off. I'll see you tomorrow." Mom smiled. "And save me a piece of lasagna."

Zoey and Dad took the dinner into the dining room. Alone, I stroked the feather a few times before putting it in a small box in my dresser drawer.

In fairy tales, the princess is always encased in a glass coffin, waiting for her prince to come and wake her up. When we found Charlie, we took the fairy tale into our own hands and breathed life into him, not with a kiss but with a push. Had Charlie been like the mythical boy Icarus, tumbling from the sky after his curiosity got the better of him and he flew too close to the sun? Charlie had fallen into a frozen world, stranding him in an icy tomb until we cracked open his prison and set him free.

Scientists always look for links to connect the steps that people have taken on their journey, moving from the past through the present to the future. But Charlie was more than a link. He was a bridge, but a bridge to where, none of us knew.

But maybe one day I would find out.

Acknowledgments

Special thanks to my critique group members Elizabeth Buck, Robin Galbraith, and Farrar Williams for all their help and support. And thanks to my editor, Maggie Lehrman.

About the Author

Laura Quimby is the author of *The Carnival of Lost Souls*, which *Booklist* called "a nicely paced, clever mix of ghost story and sideshow spectacle." She holds a degree in English literature from Towson University. She lives with her family in Maryland. Visit her online at www.lauraquimby.com.

This book was designed by Maria T. Middleton. The text is set in 12-point Apollo Regular, a typeface created by the reknowned type designer Adrian Frutiger in 1964. Apollo is a highly legible typeface designed specially for photosetting, a pre–desktop computer method of composing columns of type. The display font is Global Bold.

This book was printed and bound by R.R. Donnelley in Crawfordsville, Indiana. Its production was overseen by Alison Gervais.